HEART
of my
MONSTER

RINA KENT

To the beautiful, depraved corner of your soul

AUTHOR NOTE

Hello reader friend,

If you haven't read my books before, you might not know this, but I write darker stories that can be upsetting and disturbing. My books and main characters aren't for the faint of heart.

Heart of My Monster is the last book of a trilogy and is NOT standalone.

Monster Trilogy:
#1 *Blood of My Monster*
#2 *Lies of My Monster*
#3 *Heart of My Monster*

For more things Rina Kent, visit www.rinakent.com

ABOUT THIS BOOK

I'm a man with no morals or feelings.
The only reason I made it this far is to reign.
Nothing and no one will stop me.
Or that should've been the plan.
Now, my only goal is to get back the woman who belongs to me.
Sasha thinks it's all over, but we're only getting started.
She's my woman. My partner. My wife.
Mine.

PLAYLIST

Glasgow—You Me At Six
Just Pretend—Bad Omens
Nothing at All—Traceless
Redeemer—Palaye Royale
Crash—Mokita & Charlotte Sands
Best Excuse—Saint Chaos
Rain—grandson & Jessie Reyez
I'll Carry You—Tommee Profitt & Stephen Stanley
Maps—Maroon 5
The Grave—LOWBORN
Roads Untraveled—Linkin Park
New York—Snow Patrol
7 Minutes—Dean Lewis
Lose My Mind—Dean Lewis

You can find the complete playlist on Spotify.

HEART
of my
MONSTER

PROLOGUE

Sasha

Age Sixteen

"CATCH ME IF YOU CAN!"

My squeal echoes in the air as I jog through the snow. The twins, Erik and Eduard, follow right behind, their steps squishing in the wet slush.

They're wearing pants while I'm in a stupid dress that doesn't allow me to move as much as I want.

I'm screwed.

"You're so dead, Sasha!" Erik shouts, his voice reverberating in the silence.

I'm so tempted to check how far back he is, but that will only slow me down.

My shoes sink in the deep snow. Papa told the staff not to shovel it out of the garden, just the entryway. It's impossible to win the battle against snow in the northern part of the country.

And yet my family owns a few vacation houses in these areas due to the stunning, undisturbed nature.

As I sprint the length of the vast garden, my breath catches at the sight of the gigantic trees surrounding the property and the calming white that extends as far as the eye can see.

"Damn it, Sasha!" Eduard yells when I slip out of his reach.

I turn around and make a face while still running backward. "So slow, so slow. Can't believe you're supposed to be my age."

A few blond strands escape his beanie and get in his eyes. Eduard shoves them away with clear impatience. We're mostly blonds in this family, but our eyes differ. The identical twins have light blue eyes that can blend with the snow. They're also annoyingly taller than me. It's impossible to jump as high as they can, and they've been rubbing it in my face all through puberty.

However, I'm faster despite wearing a dress, girly shoes, and a soft pink coat to match.

"Cat got your tongue?" I mock. "What's the use of your height if you can't catch me…?"

I trail off when the back of my head bumps against a solid surface. I slowly turn around and wince as Anton, my older brother—and the eldest grandchild—stares down at me.

He's one of the exceptions to the blond genes running in the family. His hair is dark brown and often styled to perfection. While I'm always looking for trouble and riling up my cousins so they'll join in, Anton is the manifestation of collected and a bit boring.

What?

I really can't remember a time he's played something other than annoying board games with me. He says it's to teach me critical thinking, but I honestly don't see the point behind it.

"What are you doing, Malyshka?"

Did I mention that he loves scolding me? Because he does, and he does it all the time. He also tends to show love in the strangest ways, like buying me gifts but never giving them to me personally.

I kick the snow. "Just playing."

Erik and Eduard touch me on each shoulder, grin like Cheshire cats, and scream at the same time, "We won!"

"No, you didn't. This doesn't count!"

But they're already running back to the house, only turning around to make gloating faces at me.

I glare up at Anton. "It's all because of you. Why did you have to be here?"

Anton raises a perfect brow. "Shouldn't I be the one who asks that? Aren't you supposed to be waiting inside like Mama said?"

"Yeah, well. It's boring to stay inside all day. And Babushka would be like: *Sit properly, Sasha! Stop being a clown, Sasha! Don't make me repeat myself, Sasha!* And then she'd correct my posture with her cane." I huff. "I hate that thing."

My brother shakes his head more in resignation than anger. "You're never going to grow up, are you?"

I throw my hands in the air. "What's so fun about growing up anyway? Besides, you're grown up enough for the both of us."

His lips twitch in a smile as he grabs me by the nape and starts dragging me back to the house. "It's time for dinner."

"No!" I try to wiggle out of his hold to no avail. "It's still too early."

"Stop acting like a baby."

"But I don't want to. Leave me alone, Tosha."

He only tightens his grip and basically pushes me inside the house and deposits me like I'm a sack of potatoes.

A joyful atmosphere explodes all at once. Christmas vibes spill in front of us like a royal feast. A few trees decorate the circular entrance hall, and a huge one stands in the middle, nearly reaching the chandelier hanging from the ceiling at the end of the second floor.

It sparkles and glitters with dozens of golden ornaments and blinking lights. It's even surrounded by a ton of snow and there's a real snowman beside it that the twins and I insisted on bringing in.

Papa ordered for it to be preserved with some special freezing method since the house is warm.

Excitement, chatter, and endless footsteps echo around the house. The staff is busy carrying dishes, preparing the dining table, and making sure everything is as impeccable as Babushka instructed.

Yes, Papa and my uncles take care of business, but she's the absolute monarch of this house. My uncles' wives call her the queen dowager behind her back, but Mama never joins in the slandering my aunts enjoy.

She's just too nice and wouldn't participate in anything that hurts others—including my impossibly strict Babushka, who hardly likes anyone or anything.

Anton is the exception, probably because he's cut from the same authoritarian cloth as she is. He's never lived his life, never had any form of fun, and he's always concentrated on either his studies or whatever he does with Papa for 'work.'

"Malyshka!"

I wince at Mama's voice, and my bastard of a brother releases me with a small twitch of his lips.

Mama stands in front of me with a hand on her hip. She's a tall, absolutely stunning woman with dark hair, a round face, and big hazel eyes that she passed down to me.

Her dress for the night is a simple dark green one that stops above her knees, but it hugs her figure in all the right places and makes her look no different than a model. I've come to the realization that she might be a vampire, because she hasn't aged one bit since I was young.

"Hi, Mama." I play with the belt of my coat.

"Don't hi me, young lady." She reaches into her cross-body bag and retrieves a small brush. She always has these little kits and emergency stuff that can be used for everything. "You look like a rat who's out of the sewer. Didn't I tell you to be presentable, at least for today?"

"That's what I said," Anton adds needlessly. "Apparently, your daughter wants to act like she's ten forever."

I glare up at him, and he merely watches me with that stupid blank expression of his. I swear to God, he's growing up to be a second Babushka—minus the cane.

Maybe one day, he'll inherit our grandmother's cane and chase me out of the house with it.

Mama undoes the buttons of my coat and removes it in swift, firm movements. "I guess I should be glad that you didn't smudge or tear your dress yet. I don't even know what to do with you anymore, Malyshka."

She gives the light pink lace a little fluff and adjusts the ribbon at my waist, then brushes my hair.

"I'm okay, Mama. Look." I pull at my dress. "It's all good."

"Your shoes are ruined!" She rushes to the cabinet underneath the stairs and comes back with a second pair that looks exactly like what I'm wearing. Only Mama would buy duplicates of things because she knows I'll destroy them in no time.

She helps me change my shoes while Anton just shakes his head like a bastard. He could've left or something, but he's leaning against the wall, arms and ankles crossed, looking pristine in his suit and judging me six ways to Sunday.

He's also enjoying watching me being scolded until eternity by our mother.

All I get to do is lower my head and take it with a pout. If I attempt to defend myself, she'll really give me an earful. Not that I have too many arguments that could work in my favor.

The office door opens, and Papa steps out with Uncle Albert. My papa, Akim Ivanov, is the most handsome, compassionate, and charismatic man I know. I don't care that those who work for him think he's as authoritarian as Babushka. He's not that way with me or with the rest of the family, and that's all that matters.

Anton takes after him in almost everything except for the dark hair. I'm the opposite, yet I have Papa's golden hair.

Upon seeing me, he smiles. "Sasha!"

I release myself from Mama's merciless hold and run into his open arms. He embraces me and kisses the top of my head. "You look so good, my Sashenka."

"That's only because I salvaged the situation last minute," Mama says from behind me with a huff.

"And I prevented a disaster from happening," my brother supplies.

"Sasha will always be Sasha," Uncle Albert says with a heart-felt laugh.

"That's my charm." I smile coyly at my father. "Right, Papa?"

He caresses my head. "Correct. You'll be my little girl forever."

"Yes!"

"Don't encourage her, Akim," Mama scolds him as well. "You're the reason she's like this."

"I agree." Anton stands beside our mother. "You're spoiling her too much, Papa."

"I don't care. I want her to stay young for as long as possible." He hugs me again, and I nuzzle my nose in his chest.

Papa smells like winter. Harsh on the outside but with a warm core on the inside. He feels like an anchor that can never be snatched away.

Mama and Anton—who belong to the tough love club—shake their heads as Papa holds me by the shoulder and leads me to the dining room.

Everyone is already inside, chatting among themselves and starting to take their seats. The dining room is majestically decorated with a Christmas theme. The long table takes up most of the room, overflowing with countless dishes covered with golden cloches. Matching utensils are aesthetically placed in front of every seat.

Erik and Eduard both make a face, and I make one back as I grab onto Papa.

Uncle Anatoly intercepts Papa and Uncle Albert—and me. He's the youngest of my uncles, and the twins' father. He's leaner than Papa but is the same height and has similar features. His face is closed off, and he has dark circles beneath his eyes.

Papa is the most handsome, Uncle Albert is the least, so that puts Uncle Anatoly right in the middle. He's also funny and has made cracking jokes his entire personality.

Not lately, though.

In the past few months, it looks as if life has been sucked out of him and left a soulless skeleton in its wake.

I've noticed some changes in Uncle Albert, too. He usually has time to indulge us in playing or assembling something we buy, but not lately.

Only Papa is an unchanging anchor, short of some dark circles because he's been spending a lot of time in the office lately.

"What have you decided?" Uncle Anatoly asks in a low voice.

"This is not the time," Uncle Albert whispers back.

"You shut up!" Uncle Anatoly hisses. "We should've stopped this before it got to this stage, but no, we had to hold on to a sinking fucking ship—"

Without letting me go, Papa reaches out his free hand and squeezes his shoulder. "Not another word, Anatoly. This is neither the time nor the place. I need you to get yourself together. Go sit beside your wife and children and be an Ivanov. Control that turbulent energy of yours and calm the fuck down."

Shivers break on my skin even though the words aren't directed at me. This...is the first time I've heard Papa be so... insensitive.

It's clear that Uncle Anatoly is suffering with something, but instead of offering him any form of comfort, Papa all but humiliated him. No, maybe humiliating is a strong word. He *scolded* him.

In no time, a smile lifts Papa's lips, and it's like he's flipped a switch to return back to the father I know. "We'll talk after dinner."

Uncle Anatoly glares at both of them. "We're in immediate danger, and all you care about is a stupid fucking dinner?"

He shakes his head and, without waiting for an answer, walks to his wife, then flops down beside her while wearing a solemn expression.

"Never mind your uncle Anatoly, Sashenka. He's just tired." Papa kisses the top of my head. "Go take your seat."

I smooch his cheek and then trudge toward my chair. When a leg trips me and I nearly fall, Erik's and Eduard's shoulders shake with suppressed laughter.

Oh, you want to play?

I push Erik's chair and both of them almost tumble to the ground.

A cane taps on the ground, and I straighten. Babushka, who's at the head of the table, narrows her eyes on me and I smile and then sit beside the twins. These bastards want to see me die by our grandmother's cane.

After everyone is seated, Babushka nods at the head maid, who's as stoic as she is, and the lady motions to the rest of the staff to remove the cloches.

Sounds of appreciation fill the room as countless smells tickle our noses. There are different types of soup, a giant roasted lamb, and some of the vegetables are shaped like Christmas trees and stars.

We start eating, and chatter echoes around us. Erik and Eduard try to annoy me, but I kick and pinch them underneath the table until they whine out loud. This time, they're the ones who get Babushka's stare of disapproval.

Papa's chief of security rushes inside the hall, his face contorted with exertion. This is the first time I've seen him distressed and on edge.

Papa's harsh gaze turns to him. "Didn't I tell you not to bother us during family dinners?"

"This is an emergency, sir. The central security system was disabled, and I'm getting no updates from the guards stationed outside—"

His words cut off when a red laser dot appears on his forehead, and then it's blown to bits. Blood splashes on the Christmas decorations and the food in front of two of my cousins as the man drops with a thud.

A scream rips from somewhere in the room, but I can't look away from the man. When I finally lift my gaze, I find small red dots on Mama's forehead, chest, and stomach. Papa's, too.

Everyone has those laser dots.

Oh, no.

No.

Harsh footsteps echo outside, sounding as if they're coming from underground. No, maybe they're coming from a parallel universe.

My hopeful thoughts are slaughtered when countless men spill inside the dining room. They're dressed in black combat gear, heavy boots, and thick helmets, their faces hidden with balaclavas, and are carrying long rifles that are slung across their chests. The only time I've seen anything like this was in a movie about the Second World War. I hated that movie. It was all about the siege, young men dying, and rotting cadavers in the street.

It was about the worst time for humanity, where greed and power killed millions and millions of innocent people.

Why does this feel like I'm in that time?

"Everyone down!!" Papa yells and clutches Mama by the nape, but before he can push her to the floor, blood explodes on his chest, and he looks at me even as his eyes start to roll back.

Mama shrieks, but it's cut off when half of her head is blown away.

I scream and scream and scream, but my voice isn't heard in the middle of the shooting and other horrified shrieks. The soldiers are like robots, eliminating one person after the other.

Uncle Anatoly grabs his pregnant wife and starts to pull her toward him, but she's hit in her belly. He retrieves his gun and screams as he fires and empties it without any aim or sense of direction. Before he can finish, he's shot in the back and falls in his dead wife's pool of blood.

Pop.

Pop.

Pop.

All of a sudden, everything turns black.

The screams, wails, and raw shrieks don't disappear, though. Many things don't.

The gunshots.

The tangy stench of blood.

The wails and sobs.

The infants' cries.

The women's terrified yells.

I think it's a nightmare, which is why I'm not seeing anything, but then, I realize I've been pushed under the table, facedown, on the carpet. Slowly, I lift my head.

"Shh." Erik places a shaky hand over my mouth, tears clinging to his eyelashes. "Stop screaming…Sasha, please…"

I breathe against his palm. I'm not sure, but I think I've been screaming ever since I saw my parents being killed.

"It's okay," Erik whispers even as he trembles, his teary eyes filling with unprecedented terror.

Did he also witness his parents being murdered? Did he… where's Eduard? Anton?

I latch onto Erik's hand with both of mine, and he hugs me to his chest. Eduard is shielding us both, I realize, and so are Timur and Gavriil—Uncle Albert's sons. They're circling us as Erik and I curl on the ground together, crammed in the small space between the table and the wall.

My fingers tighten around Erik's back. We shake against each other, hiding our faces in one another's damp necks. Our hearts beat so loud, I feel like they'll explode any second. My eyes are shut so tightly that they hurt.

A weight falls on me, and I cry, jerking violently against Erik.

Something hot trickles down my head and face, and I open my eyes a little.

Blood drenches my soft pink dress and the top of Erik's head, his cheeks, and his neck. I stare up, and my mouth opens when I see Eduard's and Timur's lifeless eyes. Holes riddle their chests, and half of Timur's face is gone. Gavriil is also clutching his middle and screaming as blood pours out of him.

"No…" Erik sobs, reaching for his twin.

He releases me, his face ashen, and tears streak down the blood on his cheeks.

"Erik…no…don't…don't go…" I desperately hold onto his wrist with my unsteady hand. If he sits up, they'll know he's alive—

His body jerks back, and I'm about to scream, but he falls on top of me. The weight of his lifeless body suffocates me and I stop breathing.

For a moment, I think I was hit, too.

But if I were, would I still hear the gunshots? Would I feel the blood that's soaking me?

The shrieks and screams have died down, but the gunshots haven't. They keep going on and on and *on*.

All I can do is tremble and cry silently while covered by my dead cousins and a pool of blood.

At this moment, all I wish for is death.

I wish and wish…

But it never comes.

ONE

Kirill

TODAY IS MY WEDDING DAY.

Which happens to be the second in the span of a week.

And while I don't believe in wedding fever or the institution of marriage itself, certain circumstances have made this outcome inevitable.

This whole process is necessary for the survival of the house of cards. It won't be long before the chess pieces take their places on the board.

Truth is, they've been where they're supposed to be from the start.

Everything is going exactly according to plan.

The church brims with people. At the top of the food chain, there's the Pakhan, the leaders of the brotherhood, and the rest of the members from different organizations.

They're here to witness the birth of the new man all dealings will go through.

Aka me.

Considering the importance of this event, the church is mined with security detail from all factions. However, Viktor is the one who's leading the process. I don't trust anyone else to make this wedding a success.

Most of my men are stationed inside, while the others are guarding the external perimeter. I can leave it to Viktor to come up with the best security plans.

I check my watch and frown when I don't find an update from Maksim. He should've gotten in touch by now.

Unless…he was killed?

I internally shake my head. He couldn't be dead. Maksim is one of my best men, second best after Viktor in combat, so there's no one better than him to take care of this loose end.

"Sir?"

I lift my head to stare at the priest. Wrinkles of age surround his eyes as he carefully looks between me and my 'supposed' wife-to-be. Perhaps I spent too long staring at my watch and ignoring the robot of a woman who shouldn't be anyone's wife.

But she will be.

If everything goes according to plan.

"I apologize," I say, letting a charming smile tug at my lips. "I'm so eager to take my wife home that I'm counting the minutes."

Scattered laughter fills the hall. The priest smiles and mumbles that it's okay.

Kristina, however, is nowhere near amused. She looks too pale, as if she'll pass out any second now.

That's it, robot. Show emotions for once in your miserable life.

"You can proceed," I tell the priest and grab Kristina's gloved hands in mine. They're frigid cold, like her expression and corpse-like presence.

Her deep blue eyes look into mine, but they're lifeless, and the wrong fucking color.

The only color I approve of belongs to those eyes that flicker between green, brown, and yellow in a symphony of emotions.

Her hands were warm, too, when I held them, and she couldn't stop smiling. She even pinched her thigh when she thought I wasn't looking.

And when I said 'I do,' a sheen covered her eyes as they turned a bright glittery yellow and green. She was so overwhelmed with emotions, she looked to be choked by them.

This one, though? It's like she's having a fucking stroke. And not because of emotions, but more due to the lack thereof.

Should I make it worse?

To be completely honest, I don't believe this woman can ever be useful in my schemes, but if what I gathered about the situation is correct, then it might be worth a try.

I cast a glance at the first bench, where Yulia sits with my sister Karina, who's barely hanging in there. I told her she didn't have to attend the wedding, but she vehemently refused and had Anna accompany her. The old woman is holding my sister's hand—to Yulia's dismay. Needless to say, my dear mother didn't want either of them to attend since, according to her sociopathic thinking, they ruin the family's image.

In fact, she was against this entire wedding happening, and it shows in the lasers she keeps shooting from her rancid eyes.

But the star of this theatrical drama is notably absent.

Igor, his wife, and his son, on the other hand, are watching the show intently on the bride's side. Or more like, they're focused on Kristina and her frosty fucking demeanor.

She follows my line of vision, stares at Yulia—or who is supposed to be sitting beside Yulia—then she subtly turns to the priest.

"Do you, Kristina Petrova, take Kirill Morozov to be your husband, to live together in holy matrimony, to love him, to honor him, to comfort him, and to keep him in sickness and in health, forsaking all others, for as long as you both shall live?"

Her eyes focus on mine intently, but it's like she's not seeing me. Or perhaps she's seeing someone else in my lifeless gaze.

"I…" she chokes on the word, swallows, then closes her eyes for a brief second.

She sways on her feet, and a better man would reach out to steady her, but where's the drama in that?

From my peripheral vision, I catch Igor sitting taller and growing more agitated the longer his daughter remains silent.

"Kristina?" the priest asks as a low murmur breaks out in the crowd.

She opens her eyes, but when she looks at me, there are tears in them, even as her expression remains the same.

My, my. Who knew the robot was capable of feeling?

I didn't expect much from her today, so this is going way better than I anticipated.

"Is everything okay?" I say loud enough for the front row to hear. I need Igor to listen to me being an absolute gentleman to his daughter, who's fucking up his image as we speak.

Her lips tremble, and she whispers so low that I can barely hear her, "I can't…"

"It's just an 'I do,' Kristina. Say it."

She shakes her head.

"Everyone is watching, including your papa." My tone turns sinister, provocative. "Say. It."

"No! I can't!" she screams at the top of her lungs. This time, not only do *I* hear it, but the entire audience does, too.

This is really going above and beyond what I knew was coming.

Kristina screaming? In public? *At all*, for that matter? And with so many emotions?

Someone call the apathy police.

I didn't think she was capable of saying anything that didn't sound like a real-life imitation of a robot.

Without another word, she grabs the material of her wedding dress, hikes it up, and runs out of the church, leaving me stranded at the altar.

From the outside looking in, I should be either mad or humiliated. In reality, I'm barely stopping myself from breaking out in laughter.

Now, that's how it's done.

The crowd goes silent, but only for a beat before their voices rise and all heads turn toward a red-faced Igor and me.

Time to be a hero.

"Everyone," I speak to them in a calm, completely unfazed voice. "Seems that Kristina is a bit too emotional right now. Please remain seated. We will be back shortly."

I stride out of the church, tuning out the looks and the vain gossip. As soon as I'm out the door, Viktor falls in step at my side.

"Anything from Maksim?" I ask as I loosen my bow tie.

"Not yet, Boss."

Fuck.

"Keep trying to reach him." I stop outside the church and face him. "Where's Yuri?"

"He said he was feeling sick and had to go back to the house."

Hmm. Not like him to miss such an event, but I'll give him the benefit of the doubt. Both he and Maksim have been such assholes ever since I sent Sasha away, even though she said she wanted to leave.

Karina, too.

I caught her and Maksim having coffee together like when Sasha was with them. But instead of laughing and joking around, they were sighing like old ladies.

Then those insolent little shits confronted me about it and nearly got punched in the process. Yuri, on the other hand, stood there and glared at me. He schooled his expression when I looked at him, but I don't like it.

I'll have to look into that after I take care of this situation. One thing at a time.

"Block the exit," I tell Viktor. "No car leaves until I say so."

He nods and strides toward the entrance.

I take the route in the opposite direction, a hand in my pocket and a small smile on my face. Sure enough, Kristina has gone to the back entrance, where there's a parking lot that's usually used by the staff.

Although she was running, she wasn't fast, considering the heels and the impossibly long wedding dress. By the time I arrive, she's jogging all over the parking lot. Her tears come faster the more she frantically circles the cars and doesn't find what she's looking for.

I hide around the corner and check my watch. At this rate, I'll get back to my *actual* wife sooner than I previously calculated.

But for now, I'm only missing popcorn for the movie that I made sure would happen.

Kristina's headless-chicken phase comes to a halt and the ex-robot actually sobs. "Where are you? I came as you asked… Where are you—"

She cuts herself off and lets her dress drop to the ground as none other than my ex-baby brother—he's a fucking giant now— emerges from between the cars. He has a hand in his pocket and the other holds a gun as he breathes harshly.

"Konstantin…" she lets out in a murmur.

"You came," he whispers back, his face appearing boyish, like he's a decade younger.

A bit of a weird moment to witness.

Kristina takes a hesitant step toward him. "I…couldn't do it. Even if my parents disown me and my brother kills me, I couldn't… couldn't marry Kirill when all I can see is you in his face. I just… couldn't."

"Good, because if you didn't come, I was planning to kidnap you and hold you hostage before my fucker of a brother could marry you."

Fuck you, asshole. If it weren't for me, none of this would be happening.

"Oh, Konstantin." She palms his cheek. "I love you. I lived all my life for duty and accepted being my family's trump card. I didn't allow myself to feel or live or breathe for anything but duty, but that changed when *you* came along. I hate you for making me feel, but I wouldn't have it any other way."

He clutches her by the waist and hauls her toward him. "I love you, too, Meelaya. You're the only reason I manage to wake up every day."

And then he kisses her, open-mouthed while releasing repulsive noises.

I resist the urge to roll my eyes or cringe for eternity as I snap a few pictures.

Only my brother is cheesy enough to pick the most sickeningly sweet term to call his woman. *My darling.*

Though it surprisingly fits someone like Kristina.

When they break apart, she smiles and wipes the lipstick off his mouth. "What are we going to do now? If Papa sees you...I don't even want to think about it. And Kirill? What is he going to do to you?"

"Fuck that asshole."

Hey. Is this all the thanks I get for my services?

"Let's leave," he lets out in a determined tone. "No one will approve of us when you stranded my almighty bastard of a brother at the altar. The blame will fall on you more than me, and I don't want to see you suffer in this world."

"But...Papa and Alexei will hunt us down." She visibly shakes against him. "You don't know my brother. He's not as diplomatic as Papa and he'll kill you on sight. I can't...I can't do that to you."

"I'm willing to take the risk if it means being with you."

"But...what about your goals and aspirations?"

"I don't need those if I have to achieve them without you."

I finally get enough of my cheesy fucking brother and stroll out from my hideout clapping my hands. "Bravo! Love the concept of forbidden love. The execution, however, could use better dialogue."

Both of them stiffen and Konstantin actually hides Kristina behind him as if I'll snatch her away or something.

Now, I'm fully aware that my brother isn't as trigger happy as, say, Damien, but he still has his moments, and right now seems to be one of those as he tightens his hold around the gun that he never hid.

"Care to explain what you're doing with my future wife, Konstantin?"

His upper lip lifts in a snarl. "She's never going to be your wife. She's fucking mine."

I guard my nonchalant tone. "Is that so? Did you discuss this issue with Igor? Alexei? The Pakhan, for that matter? Because as I'm sure you know, this is highly frowned upon by the brother-hood. A bit taboo, too. Her neck is on the line, and, hey, so is yours."

"Let her go," he says almost pleadingly.

My brother has never begged me for anything since the day I enlisted. He hasn't asked me for anything, either, and has only talked to me to act as Yulia's obedient minion.

We haven't been on good terms since the day Karina was traumatized for life, but when I decided to leave, he looked at me with these same imploring eyes.

The ones a younger brother would have for his older brother.

Back then, he said, "Please don't leave us."

Now, he says, "You're powerful enough to break this mar-riage off."

"That I am, but I'm afraid I can't be the one who goes against the deal I had with Igor and the Pakhan. Otherwise, my interests will be in jeopardy."

"Kirill." He's struggling to remain calm when I'm sure all he wants is to punch me. "Can you, for one day, one *fucking* day, just stop being so selfish and do something for me?"

"Why would I? You said I was no longer your brother the day

I left for Russia, no? Am I suddenly back to being your brother now that you need me? Besides, I'm doing you a huge favor right now. Why do you think I got you riled up a few days ago?"

His eyes widen and recognition starts to show in his gaze.

So maybe I was being an asshole and told Konstantin that I look forward to having a wife that will serve me every night. I was thinking of a different wife, but he didn't know that and he would have punched me if I hadn't moved out of the way.

That's how I confirmed my suspicions. That, and I saw them together during the engagement party. I couldn't reveal anything back then, because I needed the wedding ceremony to happen.

Konstantin and Kristina look like ghosts, too caught up in their little romance to realize they're not the ones holding all the cards in this game.

I already built them a nice tidy house of cards, and if they play right, I might choose not to destroy it.

"You...did that on purpose?" my brother asks.

"Maybe."

"You knew?"

"Perhaps."

"Then why?" Konstantin breathes heavily. "Why the fuck did you make a deal that includes marrying *my* woman?"

"Because she wasn't your woman in public, and I had an opening to achieve greater purposes, so I took it."

"You fucking—"

"Calm your fucking tits." I stand toe to toe with him. "Igor, Alexei, and the Pakhan are on their way here. They might bring their guards or the entire wedding party, though I doubt it, because I sent Igor and Alexei this nice and tidy picture of you two kissing."

I unlock my phone and show them evidence of their cringey make-out session.

Kristina trembles and pushes Konstantin away. "Go! Leave! They won't kill me, but they will definitely kill you."

"No," my brother growls. "They might not kill you physically, but they'll still sell you to the highest bidder. If it's not Kirill, then it'll be someone else."

"Please go, Kosta." She desperately pushes him while crying, but he's not moving. "Please, I'm begging you."

"I'm not leaving without you." He clutches her waist and pulls her to his side.

"And lose everything you and Yulia have been building?" I ask in my patronizing tone.

"I don't give a fuck."

"I'm sure you do. Kristina is right. Her father and brother will hunt you down and kill you for sullying her honor. Besides, do you want her to live frightened for the rest of her life? And how about you? You're an ambitious man with lots of plans for the future. Will you be able to handle being cast aside with no option but running?"

"We don't have a choice since you refuse to help."

"Who says I refuse?" I raise a brow. "In fact, I'm going to give you the chance of your life. All you have to do is agree with what I say."

He narrows his eyes. "What are you planning now?"

"Something nice," I whisper. "Here we go."

As expected, only Igor, Alexei, and the Pakhan show up. Kristina partially hides behind Konstantin. The idiots have probably been seeing each other in secret for a long time, but only got their shit together and confessed their undying love when everything came tumbling down. But oh, well. It played in my favor.

"Kristina!" Igor snaps. "What is the meaning of this?"

She seals her lips shut then murmurs, "I… I love Konstantin. I always have."

Alexei raises a hand, probably to strike her or yank her away, but my brother catches it and glares at him. "Don't fucking touch her."

Alexei is a large man but around the same height as my brother, yet he still looks down his nose at him. "Step away from my sister before I kill you."

"Now, now." I effortlessly disengage them by standing between them. "There's no need for violence on a happy day."

"You'll marry Kirill this instant," Igor tells his daughter, to which she shakes her head and sinks her nails into Konstantin's jacket.

"I'm afraid I can't marry another man's woman, Igor. Especially if that man is my own brother."

Igor's face contorts. "We made a deal."

"Yes, and you didn't keep your part of it. I was promised your daughter, but I come here to find out that not only does she already have a man, but she's also pregnant."

Everyone falls silent, Konstantin and Kristina included.

Of course she's not pregnant, but it doesn't hurt to add more salt to Igor's wound. Besides, this plays an important role in the next part of my plan.

"You fucking bastard!" Alexei lunges at my brother again, and this time, I move out of the way so he can punch him.

He needed to get that one in to somehow lessen his anger. Kristina shrieks as blood explodes out of Konstantin's nose.

When Alexei lifts his fist again, I'm the one who blocks it and glares at him. "I let you punch him the first time out of courtesy, but if you hit my brother again, I'll break your legs."

I catch Konstantin's lips parting in my peripheral vision, and he looks like an absolute idiot.

So yes, I might have issues with him, but no one fucks with my brother.

"Alexei." Igor shakes his head at his son and he retreats back a step.

I look at the Pakhan, whose reign ends today. He's been watching the show with disapproving silence. Sergei isn't a fool and is probably working out exactly where this is going.

"Since Igor's side is the one that pulled out of the deal, as evidenced by Kristina abandoning me at the altar and the fact that she's carrying another man's child, I demand that my inauguration goes through."

"What the—" Alexei starts, but Igor shakes his head again.

"He's right. We're in the wrong on this, and there's nothing we can do about it."

"That is correct, but I'm a fair man, Igor. I won't throw you under the bus or announce your dishonor as per the contract we wrote. I would still like to offer you a partnership." I clutch Konstantin by the shoulder. "Kristina will marry into my family and we'll have the alliance we agreed upon."

Konstantin still has his mouth agape like a fucking clown, and I glare at him so he'll get his shit together. He clears his throat. "I will protect her with my life."

Igor remains silent, but then he releases a breath and nods at me. "Thank you."

"Pakhan?" I lift an eyebrow.

"You're one fucking manipulative bastard and you remind me so much of my brother, it's disturbing." Sergei exhales a long sigh. "But apparently, people like that make the best leaders, so you have your approval, Kirill. Let's see if you can keep the peace or you fuck it all up."

I smirk. "I guess time will tell."

"We're going home." Alexei seizes Kristina's arm, but she doesn't let Konstantin go, her eyes wild and scared.

"Our home is her home now," I say. "Since everyone is here for a wedding, let's give them a wedding."

Konstantin actually hugs me. The cheesy fucking asshole, I swear. I pat his back. Only for show. Nothing else.

Absolutely nothing.

I don't even remember the last time I hugged this little shit. Probably when we were kids. He still gives clingy hugs.

He hugs like a girl. Just saying.

Once this whole thing is over, I'll be Pakhan and I'll go to celebrate with my woman.

No, my *wife*.

TWO

Kirill

ATTENDING MY BROTHER'S WEDDING IS TEDIOUS AS fuck.

It was a hassle to convince the attendees that there was a slight change of the groom. Despite my spectacularly charming delivery of the news, I'm not sure everyone believes the tale.

Igor, the Pakhan, and I have to be present during the ceremony to show that we support this union and that Igor and I are still building a partnership.

Only one thing is worth this hassle—Yulia's contorting face. It looks as if she's constipated at best and having a stroke at worst.

She attempted to speak to Konstantin, probably to dissuade him. I heard her saying, "You could have someone much better than that devil's leftovers." The devil in this equation is me, by the way.

Konstantin actually got angry at her. No. He *yelled* at her for the first time in…well, forever. My brother might hate his mother's methods, but he usually tries to voice his disagreements diplomatically.

Not today. He looked that joke of a mother in the eye and pointed at the door. "Kristina is the only wife I will have. If you can't accept that, leave!"

Of course, she didn't. The sole purpose of her existence seems to be everything Konstantin. She'd rather be eaten by sharks than miss his wedding.

Now, I must point out that it was slightly comical to watch him get married with a bruised nose from when Alexei attempted to rearrange his features. Lucky for him, we share blood and I didn't allow for him to be hurt more than necessary.

The other person I share blood with—not Yulia, she doesn't count—teared up after Konstantin and Kristina were pronounced husband and wife.

Let's say Karina was actually the most giddy about this turn of events. Probably because she got to hold on to my arm during the entire ceremony and didn't experience any panic attacks. She seems to have forgotten her slight animosity toward me about Sasha's departure.

Since my sister has the attention span of a goldfish, she'll probably go back to her favorite hating game once we're home.

Once the wedding is over, she takes off like a bullet and hugs our brother. "Congrats, Kosta!"

He ruffles her hair. "Thanks, little Kara."

She grins and shakes Kristina's hand. "Welcome to the family. I'll show you all the things."

"Thank you," Kristina says quietly, shyly even. So many emotions from the robot in one day is starting to feel like an overdose.

"You're like the perfect couple!" Karina holds both their hands in hers, excitement emanating off her in waves.

I stroll to her side and adjust my glasses. "Is it just me or did you not sound this happy when I announced my marriage, Kara?"

She smiles awkwardly and links her arm with mine. "Of course I was!"

"Try again without the subpar acting skills."

"Well…I just didn't think Kristina was for you." She smiles at her new sister-in-law. "No offense. I do believe in you and Kosta."

Interesting. Karina and I happen to share the same sentiment.

I look at the newlyweds, who are wearing the rings I chose— or more like, Viktor did. I told him to get Konstantin's size, not mine, because I saw this scene long before it happened.

The only difference was that I was so close to pitying the sorry fuck for liking a robot. Turns out, she's not a robot around him. Which is all that matters, I suppose.

"Congratulations are in order," I say in my cool tone.

"Thank you," Kristina says. "I owe you."

"You sure as fuck do. I'll hold you accountable to that."

"Hold me accountable instead." Konstantin interlinks his fingers with hers, but he's not looking me in the eye.

"You'll both be. Make her pregnant as soon as possible or else I won't be able to defend you if Igor finds out the only reason he allowed this to happen is a sham."

Karina squeezes my arm. "Can you stop ordering people around, especially on their wedding day?"

"I decline," I say absentmindedly while checking my watch.

There's a text from Maksim.

Fucking finally.

There were some complications, Boss. I'm going to need to stay in hiding for a while. I'll speak to you when I have better capacity. I'm safe.

I know he said he's safe, but the fact that he has to stay in hiding and isn't returning immediately like I asked him to is derailing me from the initial plan.

He didn't even mention if the mission was a success.

Everyone heads out to the wedding reception that's been held at my house. I'd like to bail on this soul-sucking reception, but that's impossible, considering that the highlight of the day will happen during the event.

The afternoon weather is beautiful with a clear sky and a slight chill in the air. The reception is set up in the garden and around the pool with an enormous buffet section. Classical music echoes in the air, played by some famous quartet the wedding planner found somewhere. The guests chat and drink their hearts out, or more like gossip about the dramatic groom swap.

Brothers, no less.

As is customary, Kristina takes the heat since she's the 'whore' who got between brothers. I hear Rai putting anyone she hears saying such rubbish in their place.

"You should add Adrian to the list since she was engaged to him a long time ago," Rai tells someone. "It's not her fault she's popular and you can't have her."

God forbid anyone speak ill of any woman in front of Rai. She'll skin them alive and wear it as fur.

Konstantin and Kristina, who are the main topic of discussion, seem to have checked out. Over the past hour, they've been either dancing or kissing like some hormonal teenagers.

I expected Karina to hide in her room, but she appointed herself as Kristina's nonexistent bridesmaid. She's spent most of the time either adjusting the bride's hair, makeup, dress, or all of the above. She's taken a thousand pictures of them, too, and made me pose in a few of them—including some selfies of the four of us.

I'm just waiting for the day to be over already. Rai and Vladimir have been glaring at me nonstop, Adrian has shaken his head at me more than once, and Mikhail seems more confused than a virgin on her wedding night. Damien has misread the whole fucking atmosphere, and, I kid you not, he thinks the fact that I'm not married means we can fight.

How he came up with that correlation is a mystery, but I'm not going to ask. In fact, I'm ready to punch him to the next planet, except for the small fact that I need him today.

Finally, the Pakhan calls for a closed meeting in my office. No guards are allowed inside. It's just the leaders of the Bratva.

I linger in front of my office where all the senior guards are gathered and whisper to Viktor, "Keep trying to reach Maksim."

He nods. Apparently, Viktor got a similar text from Maksim—again, with no specifics as to whether or not the mission was a success or if he's really safe.

"And find Yuri. Tell him to pump himself with medication and get his ass here."

He nods again.

My expression is cool and collected as I walk into my office. The Pakhan sits behind my desk, and Mikhail and Igor are settled on the two chairs opposite him.

Vladimir stands to his right and Adrian to his left, leaning against the bookshelves, legs crossed at the ankles.

Rai and her husband Kyle sit on the sofa, both cradling her very pregnant belly.

Damien, on the other hand, is opening and closing, then throwing down books that his illiterate mind doesn't understand. I'm going to bet that he was looking for some images and is personally offended when he finds none.

The moment I close the door behind me, Damien chucks the book in his hand to the floor. "Fucking finally. Let's get this over with, Pakhan. I have shit to do."

Sergei stands with difficulty, his attention on me. I smile back so charmingly, I trigger a snarl on Vladimir's face.

I can tell Sergei isn't one hundred percent down for this option, but he, Igor, and even Adrian know that I'm the best choice for the leading position. Damien and Mikhail are too volatile. Adrian and Vladimir are anti-leadership. Igor works best when he's in a support position. Rai is a woman. Kyle is a new addition who has a long way to go to prove his loyalty.

I'm the most balanced and lucrative of the bunch, and that's a fact.

Sergei addresses everyone in the room, "As I announced at the beginning of this year, I'll be stepping down as Pakhan due to illness. It's time to bring new blood into the brotherhood, and while I planned to reserve this position for my son-in-law, my daughter went and married some lawyer who doesn't belong in our world. As a result, I nominate Kirill as the next Pakhan."

"You can't be serious!" Rai stands up with Kyle's help. "He's too manipulative to lead, Granduncle."

"Manipulative or not doesn't matter. Kirill brings in the most deals, money, and success to the Bratva, and he's managed to do that in only a few years since his return from the military. Not to mention his pure Russian ties who have been in the brotherhood for generations. I believe he's the organization's best option for survival, but I won't make a final decision on this until a vote is taken." He pauses for effect. "Those in favor of Kirill becoming the next Pakhan, raise your hand."

Sergei is the first one who does so, followed by Igor. Mikhail watches the other two, then focuses on me. He's always been a follower of Igor and Sergei, but at the same time, he's suspicious. However, I did promise him a hefty reward, so he puts his hand up.

It's still three to five, though.

I stare at Adrian. His poker face remains the same, and while he wasn't a fan of this idea, he's smart enough to slowly raise his hand.

Four to four.

"Damien?" I pin him down as he throws another one of my books aside.

This asshole has been promised more than anyone else, including any war he's in the mood for.

I didn't bother with Rai, because she'd never approve. Her husband is of the same opinion. Vladimir is a gray area that I would rather not count on.

So my only other option is this unpredictable motherfucker.

"I don't give a fuck that you're the Pakhan," he says as he raises his hand. "You'll fight me."

I think the vote is over, but then Vladimir raises his hand. I'd say that's a surprise, but it's not, not really. Vladimir might be this giant bearded mule, but he's logical enough to realize I'm the best choice.

Or, after Damien cast the deciding vote, he realized his side was losing and he jumped ship so as not to be cast aside by the new Pakhan.

Six to two. Seven, if we're counting mine.

Rai purses her lips and glares at me. I smile back, showing my teeth.

"Please join me in welcoming the new Pakhan," Sergei says. "Kirill."

It's all going according to plan.

By the time the meeting ends, I'm in the mood to kick everyone out, but I don't. One, I'll have to get used to them being in my space, considering that my house will be the base for all future meetings.

Sergei will go on a family trip with his daughter and son-in-law and is fully retiring. Adrian stays behind to fill me in on the special meetings he always has with the Pakhan, all while trying to convince me to step down before it's too late.

Damien is asking for a fight right after the inauguration.

Vladimir grunts but does fill me in on the security detail since he's the one in charge of that.

Rai wants to call me names but knows she can't. She no longer has her granduncle's support and, therefore, if I decide to prosecute her for the insolence, no one will stop me.

Me? I want to celebrate with my wife.

None of these people matter and their faces aren't the ones I want to look at while I'm sipping champagne.

I told Sasha she had to wait six months until I was more

comfortable in my position and then I could bring her back without anyone intervening, but maybe that's too long.

In the beginning, I had only a fifty percent chance of making this work, mainly because there were too many variables in the equation.

Now that the situation has changed, three months should be enough. At this point, I don't give a fuck if they find out Aleksandra is the Aleksander they've known for years. I'm just not sure she does.

Which is why I sent Maksim to Russia to take care of the last thread that's holding her back.

The fact that I still have no news of him is the only hitch in the plan.

After everyone leaves the office, Viktor barges inside, his face tight and his eyes dark.

"Anything from Maksim?" I ask.

"No, but I received unsettling news about one of our properties."

"I don't give a fuck about our properties. Get in touch with Maksim. And where the fuck is Yuri?"

"Kirill." He steps forward.

I pause.

Viktor rarely calls me by my name and only when shit is hitting the fan.

"What is it?"

"It's about the property you asked me for the keys to about a week ago."

My spine jerks upright and a buzzing rings in my ears.

I've always been the type who relies on his intuition to not only determine the next course of action, but to actually survive. Today was going perfectly well until Maksim's text, and I've had a horrible feeling since then.

I just didn't know how bad it was until now.

"What about it?" I don't recognize how calm my voice sounds despite the buzzing in my ears.

"I received a text showing the bombing of the cottage and then the remains being set on fire."

Every single win I had today comes tumbling to the ground at those words.

Fuck.

Fuck.

Fuck!

Only one thought fills my head—I need to find Sasha.

THREE

Kirill

THERE MUST BE SOME SORT OF A MIX-UP.

I refuse to believe that the cottage where Sasha is has been blown to shreds.

I just fucking *refuse*.

And yet, when we arrive at the scene, chaos unfolds.

It took us four hours more than I had to spare to arrive at the cottage, and we only got here in that time because Viktor drove at supersonic speed, narrowly avoiding a few accidents.

It was still not fast enough.

I spent the way here calling Sasha and getting her voicemail. I couldn't track her either since her phone is turned off.

I really should've inserted a fucking tracker in her flesh. I was fooled by the false sense of security of having her by my side for years, so I overlooked this angle.

If—when—I find her, I'll put that tracker in her skin. Personally, if I have to.

Bleak reality snaps my shoulder blades together as Viktor and I step out of the car. The view that greets us is that of emergency and police vehicles overcrowding the front of the cottage.

Or what remains of it.

The place has been destroyed to the point of unrecognition. Remnants of wood flooring, doors, and furniture are scattered in the aftermath—black, grimy, and barely recognizable. Some of the surrounding trees have also broken and fallen to their demise in the midst of the catastrophe.

I freeze, my legs barely holding me upright. The shouts and orders from the police and firefighters slowly fade away to a muffled noise, as if they're speaking from underwater.

A shrill ringing sound fills my ears, and I'm flung out of my physical body. We're separate entities now. While my outside remains calm, collected, and looking completely unfazed, my insides erupt in dangerous flames that threaten to eat me alive.

I catch a glimpse of the car I gave Sasha the day she left. Only the bones of the vehicle are visible and even those are barely discernible. The scene is straight out of some Middle Eastern war.

My feet move of their own accord to the ambulance. I expect to find Sasha standing in front of the destruction with a fucking rifle slung across her chest after she's managed to kill those who dared to attack her.

But maybe that's too optimistic. She's still one woman, and while she has balls bigger than most men, no one can predict a bombing.

She must've been injured in her attempts to escape—that's the only option I'll allow.

One of the medics has the audacity to try to stop me from opening the back of the ambulance.

He grabs my arm. "You can't do that, sir."

I twist it around and push him away so hard, he ends up on his ass on the ground.

When he tries to stand up again, Viktor is in his face.

I reach a hand toward the handle and stop when I feel a slight tremor in my limbs. A phenomenon that I've wholly purged out of my system. A phenomenon that only occurred after I was tortured for days on end by my father's band of sadists.

Calm the fuck down.

If I got through that dark period of my life, I can survive this.

Sasha is just clutching her injured arm or leg inside. There's no way in fuck—

My hand drops to my side the moment I open the door.

A body lies on the stretcher, covered by a white sheet. The smell of sickeningly burned flesh clogs my nostrils, but that's not the reason I find it hard to breathe.

It's the black skeleton-like hand peeking from beneath the sheet. I approach it slowly, my movements stiff and unnatural.

I take the roasted hand in my shaky one. Ash and burned flesh smudge my skin, but the only thing I'm focused on is the ring burned into the second to last finger.

I rub the top of it, and my heart fucking falls to my knees when the green is exposed.

No.

I remove it with some of the flesh, and *Kirill's* stares me right in the face.

Fucking no.

I frantically check her other wrist, and my hand shakes uncontrollably when I find the bracelet I gave her for her last birthday. I struggle to separate it from the burnt skin, but when I see *Sasha*, a scream builds at the back of my throat.

Fuck no.

I don't know how I remain standing as I remove the cover to reveal her face.

Or what used to be a face.

There's a black skeleton instead. Some flesh has melted off the bone, leaving a gory mess where her eyes, nose, and lips are supposed to be. Her hair is gone, and so are any other features I could identify her with.

I stand there for a long moment, studying every burn, every cut, every disfigured feature.

Maybe if I stare hard enough, this scene will disappear.

"Boss..."

My head slowly tilts in Viktor's direction. He looks at the burned body with a furrowed brow and pursed lips. It's the most seriously affected I've seen him since we lost Rulan and his brigade in that last Spetsnaz mission.

"Wipe that fucking look off your face, Viktor. This isn't Sasha." I don't know how the fuck I sound calm when I'm on the verge of losing my fucking mind.

The ring and bracelet burn in my fingers as if they're still on fire.

"I'm sorry, Kirill."

"What the fuck are you apologizing for? This isn't my fucking wife. Find her."

He doesn't move, not even an inch.

"What are you waiting for? I told you to fucking find her."

"You already did, Kirill."

I grip him by the collar and haul him against me to peer down his goddamn nonexistent soul. "Don't fuck with me, Viktor. I told you this isn't her, so your job is to nod your fucking head and go find her."

He clasps my hand, and instead of removing it, he squeezes. "My job is to tell you hard truths, and the current one is that we were too late. Lipovsky died in the aftermath of the bombing. I understand that you don't want to accept that—"

His words are cut off when I slam my fist in his face. He staggers back, barely catching himself before he falls.

"Shut the fuck up. She didn't die."

He says nothing, but his gaze falls on the ring and bracelet

I'm still clenching in my hand. He doesn't have to speak for me to hear "You're holding the evidence."

I lift my head and stare at the cloudy sky. It's gray, grim, and absolutely depressing, but it doesn't compare to the dark abyss that's currently replaced my heart.

The world has always been monotone to me—either black or gray. The only person who introduced me to a fucking rainbow of colors has now turned black.

She's now being ripped out of my heart and leaving a bottomless pit in her wake.

Everything has turned to ashes. All I can do is glare at the sky, feel moisture filling my eyes, and let out a raw scream.

⌁

I was ready to believe that Sasha wasn't dead.

Anyone could've put that bracelet and ring on the corpse to make me think it was my Sasha.

But then, the DNA test came out as a match, and now, I'm on edge, only a few moments away from pushing myself over.

But I can't join her yet.

It's been a week since I saw her skeleton. They had to search for her legs since they were scattered apart.

A week in which I haven't seen a wink of sleep, I've stumbled in and out of a drunken haze, and I've nearly started killing anyone I've seen walking down the street.

If the only light in my life was taken away, how dare they keep theirs?

If my world is flipped upside down, why the fuck is everyone else living as if nothing happened?

A week of Karina crying nonstop and trying to console me, only for me to shut the door in her face. Konstantin tried, too, but he was also given the cold shoulder.

Not even Anna has been allowed to touch me.

Apparently, Viktor told the family about Sasha's identity so they know she's a woman and my wife.

Was. Fuck. I still can't believe she became a *was*.

Still, I didn't accept anyone's condolences. I don't need fucking emotions. I murdered them a long time ago, and they're not coming back.

All this dizziness, disorientation, and pure fucking mania is a translation of my need for revenge.

We lost communication with Maksim after that text. Viktor sent men to look for him to no avail.

And with that, we lost our only lead to the Ivanovs.

As in, the founders of the Belsky Organization. I didn't make the connection at first, but after Sasha left for the cottage, Viktor revealed that, according to the KGB intelligence, the family behind the Belsky Organization is called Ivanov.

They're some form of aristocrats who, apparently, have always had deals with the governments in Russia and went as far as putting them in power. Until the current ruler of the Kremlin, who's been out to annihilate them ever since he got into office.

I doubted Sasha knew any of that. Her sole purpose seemed to be revenge for her family's murder.

However, no matter which angle I look at the tale from, there are still too many plot holes. One, I haven't dealt with any Ivanovs in my lifetime. The only incident involving them that comes to mind is when Konstantin was kidnapped and tortured by someone who I presume was one of them.

Their whole existence is still blurry.

Everything is.

Even Yuri disappeared off the face of the fucking earth. Which makes me paranoid as fuck.

Losing not only Sasha but also Maksim and Yuri is like walking around with gaping wounds.

It's been three days since I buried her in the family cemetery and ordered a tombstone with *Aleksandra Morozova* engraved on it.

It's been two days since we started searching for leads for whoever could've ordered that hit on her.

It's been one day since we located the most probable suspects—the Albanians.

I pull out my gun and stare at an old building on the outskirts of an ancient industrialized area in Boston.

The sun sets in the distance, casting an orange hue that will turn into red with the blood of those fuckers.

"We're ready," Viktor says from beside me.

Dark circles surround his eyes from how much I've overworked him this week. He's barely slept, and when he has, I've called him to my office to dig into any information I've gathered.

He doesn't complain, but he does bitch about how I need some rest and that I might drop dead.

Might as well.

I haven't been in my room since I saw that body. Every corner is full of her presence, natural scent, and soft smiles.

It's full of her care, her countless attempts to put me to sleep. It's full of her tangible concern about my well-being and safety.

Every inch of me revolts at the idea of being there when she isn't.

The thought of closing my eyes without her around terrifies the fuck out of me.

"We're taking a left, yeah?" Damien's eyes shine in the dark like a madman's. He's been my companion in my mission to wipe out everyone I suspect.

This time, we expanded our options to Boston because the leader of the Albanians here, Roel, is the cousin of the motherfucker we killed a few months ago in New York.

As the new Pakhan of the New York Bratva, the most reckless thing to do is starting wars or stepping on other factions' toes. There was an inauguration ceremony two days ago that the whole organized crime world attended, but I barely showed my face.

I don't give a fuck about the position.

I'm only using the power it gave me to figure out who's behind that bombing, and I need to know exactly why it happened.

"Do whatever the fuck you want. Just don't get in my way." I don't wait for Damien's reply as I walk toward the building.

Viktor advised me to cover my tracks, but fuck that. I want them to see me coming and scramble like rats. My guard curses low from behind me, then runs to cover me as the men inside filter out like ants.

All I see are people who need to be dead. Every last fucking one of them. I won't stop until they're all buried six feet under like she is.

I raise my gun and shoot anyone who comes into view. My movements appear collected, but they follow no rhyme or rhythm.

A bullet grazes my bicep, sending my arm flying sideways. I switch the gun to my other hand and continue firing away. My jacket saturates with blood before it drips on the concrete, but I don't feel the pain.

I feel nothing but fucking rage now.

If Sasha were here, she'd kill anyone who attempted to hurt me. If she were to see this wound, she'd fawn over me with affection and concern. For the first time in my life, I felt like my well-being mattered and that I meant the world to someone else.

And now, that someone who made me the center of her world has disappeared, turning mine into an abyss.

Damien laughs like a maniac as he kills everyone in his path, their blood soaking him in no time since he likes to do it up close and personal.

A car revs behind us, and I spin around and shoot all four tires. It swerves and hits the side of the building, and then it's a full-on shoot-out. My men cover me and manage to kill the ones in the car except for the one we're here for.

Viktor pushes a bulky man with a buzz cut to his knees in front of me. Damien's guards and my other ones are busy eliminating the rest of the Albanians, but I couldn't give a fuck about them now.

The only one who matters is this motherfucker right here. His name is Roel and he's a dead man, but not before he tells me what I need to know.

"What the fuck do you think you're doing?" he spits out in a heavy accent. "We have allies who will come after you and the whole fucking brotherhood, Morozov. You don't have any idea how much fucking chaos you're starting."

"Apparently, you don't either or you wouldn't have fucked with me." I retrieve my phone, then scroll to a picture that I've been staring at whenever I need something to ground me.

It's Sasha during my last birthday party. Maksim took countless photos that night and sent them to everyone. In this one, she's laughing with Yuri. I cut him out and only kept her.

I look at her carefree expression through a red haze. Literally. My glasses are splashed with blood, and I can't be bothered to clean them.

"Who ordered the hit on this person?" I ask calmly, apathetically even.

Roel stares at the picture, and there's no change in his expression. I'll give him that. But there is a flicker of recognition in his eyes.

He knows exactly why the fuck I'm here.

"I've never seen her in my life."

"I didn't say she was a she." I thrust the phone in his face. "Why was she killed?"

"I don't know," he mumbles against the screen.

"Very well." I pocket my phone. "Viktor. Bring me some motherfuckers."

I remove my jacket, throw it aside, and slowly roll my shirt sleeves to my elbows. The wound in my bicep has stopped bleeding, but not before it soaked my white shirt red.

Viktor and a few of my other guards push five Albanians in

front of me beside Roel. They look at their leader with both fear and pleading.

"What the fuck do you think you're doing?" he repeats from behind clenched teeth. "If you want something, torture me!"

"Where's the fun in that?" I fetch my knife. "Besides, you'll probably never talk, even if you're tortured to within an inch of your life, and I'd rather not waste any effort."

"You're supposed to be the fucking Pakhan! This is madness."

I grab one of his men, position him on his knees facing Roel, and hold the blade to his throat. "Who ordered the hit?"

"I don't fucking know!"

I slice his throat in one motion. Blood splashes from his neck, bathing Roel and me. I don't blink as I throw the sorry fuck aside while he gurgles and chokes on his own blood.

Roel curses while his other men look like they're going to be sick.

I clean my glasses with my shirt, then clutch the second one and jam my knife at his throat. "Who ordered it?"

"I said I don't fucking know!!" He's screaming now, so close to losing control as the one in my hold trembles.

I stab him in the back of the neck, then in his throat and heart and chest, over and over, and fucking over. I do it long after he's dead and mutilated, until someone actually throws up.

This time, I don't bother cleaning my glasses and throw them on the corpse.

"You're fucking crazy," Roel whispers, his whole body shaking.

I haul the third man to his feet, then kick him in the shin as he screams and fruitlessly tries to fight my grip. "Who ordered it?"

Roel shakes his head, hesitantly this time.

I snap the third's neck then shove him aside. "I can do this all night long. I'll bring your wife and children, too. I'll slaughter each and every one of them in front of your eyes. I'll stab them so many times that you won't recognize their fucking corpses. Just like I didn't recognize *her* corpse."

"Jesus fucking Christ!"

"Not the answer I need." I clutch the fourth by the hair. He smells of vomit, and he's pissed himself at watching his comrades being slaughtered.

He doesn't even fight me and mumbles what sounds like a prayer in Albanian.

No God answers him as I slice his throat open.

"Viktor." I wipe the blood from my face with the back of my hand. "Bring me Roel's family."

"Wait! Wait!" Roel breathes heavily, and the man beside him nearly faints with relief.

"After you murdered my cousin, I wanted to kill you with my bare hands, but that was impossible with my manpower." He pants as if he's coming down from running a marathon. "A few weeks ago, we met a man who said if I wanted to really hurt you, I should kill your girly guard. He told us to wait until he gives us the okay and an opening. That opening came a week ago when that guard was alone. He sent us the place's coordinates and told us to wipe it and everyone inside of it out."

My jaw tightens. "What does he look like?"

"When we met, he was on the other side of a wall and spoke using a voice altering device. Our subsequent communication was done through emails."

"Where are those emails?"

"In the car."

Viktor heads there and fetches a briefcase from the trunk. He opens it and retrieves a laptop, then brings it to Roel, who opens it with a thumbprint.

Viktor goes through it for a few minutes, then nods.

I lean down and stare at Roel's beady eyes. "You messed

with the wrong fucking person. I'll make sure none of you roam the streets ever again."

While looking at him, I throw the knife straight at his last man's throat. "I'm going to torture you until you wish for fucking death, Roel, and even then, I won't give it to you. I'll make your life as bleak as you made mine."

But I know—I just know—that nothing will ever fill the hole that's been growing bigger and deeper in my chest.

The only person who knew how is now gone.

FOUR

Kirill

IT'S NOT ENOUGH.

Not the killing spree.

Not the torture.

Not the lead that I'm following to lure out the person who gave that information to the Albanians.

Nothing is enough.

Especially not the fucking torture.

I'd planned to keep Roel alive for eternity as I tortured him to my heart's content, but I slipped, and he died on me only two weeks after I captured him.

My feet are heavy as I take the stairs to the house. A jacket is slung over my shoulder, and my glasses are blurry with remnants of the scum's blood.

A gasp reaches my ear before I look up to see Karina running down the stairs, a hand muffling her mouth.

Unlike her usual pink girly dresses, she's now in unflattering black pants and a hoodie. Her hair is gathered in a messy bun, and her face is makeup-free.

My sister stops in front of me looking like a shadow of her former self. Bloodshot eyes. Dark circles. Ghostly pale face.

"Are you okay? What's with all the blood?"

I mechanically look down at myself and realize my shirt is bloodied, and so are my hands. I must've forgotten to wash up. I'm forgetting many things lately. The world is starting to look like a black loop of nothingness that I couldn't put an end to even if I tried.

It could be the lack of sleep, or the fact that everything is empty and desolate. If I sleep properly, I might be tempted to never fucking wake up.

"It's not mine." I start to bypass Karina, but she blocks my path again. "What is it?"

Her lips tremble, and she chews on her dry bottom one. The flesh splits, and a strip of blood appears in the middle. "You're looking like you'll collapse. You should get some rest."

"Go to sleep, Kara."

"I can't." Her voice turns brittle. "All I think about is how Sasha felt before...before she was killed and...and I can't sleep or eat or bring myself to do anything. He...no, *she* was my only friend."

She.

Right. The name I wrote on her grave indicates that Sasha was a woman and my wife.

The wife I couldn't fucking protect.

Viktor took the time to explain the complicated situation to my family members.

Me? I don't give a fuck what any of them thinks.

I don't even give a fuck about the future anymore. I used to see patterns, paths, and courses of action. I used to be motivated by all the goals I had yet to crush.

Now, I only see fucking black.

I spent my whole life carefully building a house of cards, but Sasha's death has caused it to fall apart.

Karina throws her arms around my waist and squeezes the living fuck out of me. "If I feel this way, then it must be worse for you. She was always with you and…you married her so…so…"

I grab her by the shoulder and push her away. Nausea rises in my throat at the reminder of the last hug Sasha gave me.

And I refuse to let anyone else take that memory.

My wife loved this cheesy shit. She loved hugging me and trying to comfort me. She also loved singing and kissing. But then she left and took away her hugs, her smiles, and even her infuriating arguing.

The idea of being hugged makes me want to stab myself in the fucking gut and watch as my blood pours out.

Tears stream down Karina's cheeks. "I just…I just wanted to console you."

"Don't. I need no such thing."

"You…really don't?"

"I really don't. I'm perfectly fine."

"Fuck you, Kirill! How can you be *perfectly fine* after she died? She dedicated her whole life to you! The least you can do is fucking mourn her properly, you fucking asshole!" She punches, claws, and slaps my chest.

I don't stop her. I don't have the energy to do anything.

My sister cries and curses me all the way to the moon and back as she lets out her anger and frustration on me.

I feel nothing.

Absolutely fucking nada.

"Kara!" Konstantin rushes inside and pulls our sister away.

She thrashes and kicks the air, her tear-streaked eyes throwing lasers my way. "Let me go! This asshole is not even pretending to be affected. It's like six years ago when we begged him to stay, and he just gave us his back like a psychopath, Kosta! He doesn't care! He never cares! Even if the person who protected him with her life died because of him and all the shit he stirs up!"

My jaw clenches. Karina doesn't notice it, but Konstantin's eyes harden as he shakes her. "Shut it, Kara. You don't know what the fuck you're talking about."

"I know exactly what I'm talking about! Look at him being all nonchalant after coming from God knows where. He doesn't want to talk about her. But I will, every fucking day! I will remind you of the girl who protected and loved you but only got death in return!"

I reach an open-palmed hand to her face and nearly crush it in my hand. She finally shuts up, her eyes widening.

I don't recognize the calmness in my voice when I release her. "Get the fuck out of my face before I do something I will regret."

Her chin and lips tremble. A sob leaves her throat before she runs up the stairs, her sniffles lingering behind her.

My brother watches me with a furrowed brow.

"You have something on your mind, too? I can't guarantee your safety if you piss me the fuck off, so how about you disappear instead?"

"Never mind Kara." His voice is too fucking gentle for my liking. "She's too sheltered for her own good, and you know she's never been able to read the atmosphere."

"And you can?"

"Not when it comes to you, I'm afraid. But I'm starting to learn."

His eyes soften, and I'm so ready to punch him square in the face if he starts to pity me, but that expression doesn't come. Instead, I'm staring at a version of my brother I thought I'd lost.

A long time ago, when Yulia would decide to take him on a picnic or to some show, he'd hide in my room just to spend as much time with me as possible.

I'd ruffle his hair and tell him to enjoy whatever she was taking him to for the both of us. That's when he'd look at me with the same expression he has now.

I thought it was only sadness. Maybe discomfort, but now I realize it's a form of longing.

Konstantin always wanted to be with me, but Yulia happened, and that became impossible.

He releases a breath. "In case you didn't know, you're the hardest person to read, and that's saying something considering I've known you all of my life. No matter how much I try to analyze your actions, I can't find an explanation for the way your mind works. I can't tell whether you're truly a psychopath who doesn't feel or you just have no fucking clue what emotions are and, therefore, can't express them. I remember when we were young, you loved Kara and me more than anyone else, but that part of you disappeared, and you became…this. Whatever *this* is."

"If there's a point behind your tedious speech, you should've reached it by now."

"I know you still care about Kara, and possibly me."

"I didn't realize you were adding delusional to your repertoire of words."

"I know you do, or you wouldn't have made my marriage with Kristina happen." He grips my shoulder. "Which is also why I know Sasha's death is affecting you more than you show. You were always the type who looked eerily calm, even after you came back from Roman's torture sessions. You've been either on a violence spree or in this pretend calm mode, so I'm assuming you're suffering inside or bottling your pain or both."

"If you're done being an amateur therapist…" I rotate my shoulder, forcing him to release me, and sidestep him to head toward the stairs.

"You need to get your shit together, Kirill!" he shouts after me. "You're the Pakhan now, and your head is worth more than ever before."

"Save the concern for your wife." I don't look at him as I take the stairs up.

He's been subtly trying not to be all disgustingly lovey-dovey with her whenever I'm around. Even Kristina refrains from any form of PDA in my presence. They're both walking on eggshells around me as if I could be broken by seeing them acting like husband and wife.

To be fair, I did contemplate shooting them in the head whenever I saw them smiling at each other. It's not them. It's the sense of fucking doom I have whenever I witness others being happy when that feeling has been wiped out of my life for good.

I didn't know what happiness meant until I slept like a fucking baby in Sasha's arms. There were no nightmares, no thoughts about the future.

Just…silence.

For the first time in forever, I had a break from my brain and just *felt*.

Now that the feeling is fucking gone, I want to confiscate everyone's happiness, crush it to pieces, and bathe in its blood. I need to turn their worlds as black as mine.

Yulia crosses my path, lifts her chin, and pretends she doesn't see me. She's the only one who hasn't tried to talk to me, and I'm glad she hasn't or else we'd have a murder on our hands.

I might have some tolerance for Karina and Konstantin, but I'd strangle that woman to death if she ever brought up Sasha's name.

I've had the staff move my clothes to another room near the office. My old room is now locked with a key, and I told Anna to keep it and never give it to me.

My movements are mechanical as I remove my clothes and step into the shower. I watch the blood washing off me, mixing with the water, and disappearing down the drain.

Could *I* disappear as easily?

No. Not yet.

I still haven't found the motherfucker who ordered her death.

This isn't fucking over.

Torturing Roel didn't empty my thirst for violence. My rage

remains powerful, tucked under the surface, waiting for another outlet.

I close my eyes and rest my head on the tiles as the cold water beats down on me.

Soft arms wrap around my waist from behind, and warmth clashes with the freezing water. Her small hands stroke along my sides and pectoral muscles as she lays her head on my back. I feel her lips on my nape, kissing me gently.

I want to turn around and look at her, but if I open my eyes, she'll disappear.

She always does.

So I twist the wedding ring she slipped on my finger the day she said, 'I do.' I've been wearing it since I saw her body in the back of the ambulance. My hand feels heavy, though, like it weighs a ton now that hers doesn't wear her ring.

"You need to sleep, Kirill." Her soft voice carries in the air like a fucked-up melody. "Your body will eventually give out on you."

Sasha sounds so worried in my imagination. She always was. There were times when I thought she went over the top to protect me, but it wasn't until after she was gone that I realized it was her way of showing her affection toward me.

She proved in actions more than words how much she loved me.

I will remind you of the girl who protected and loved you but only got death in return!

Karina's words stab me in my bleeding heart.

"If I die, will I be able to join you?" I whisper in the silence of the bathroom.

"What are you talking about? You were born for greater things, not to die, Kirill. You're the Pakhan now. Isn't that amazing?"

"No. What's the point of being Pakhan if I couldn't protect you?"

"You always had your priorities straight, and I was never at the top."

"That's not fucking true!" I whirl around and curse under my breath when her warmth disappears.

Fuck.

Disgusted with my own skin, I step out of the shower and wrap a towel around my middle. It doesn't matter that I changed rooms. She's everywhere. Her soul clings to every corner and every fucking person in this house.

But maybe that's not a bad thing.

If her ghost fucking haunts me and blames me for her death, I'll still welcome it.

At least she'll be here.

I put on another suit and head to my office. The door opens as I snag a bottle of Macallan from the minibar. I don't bother with a glass and drink straight from the bottle.

My throat burns, but it does nothing to squash the constrictive weight on my chest.

Viktor stands across from me, and I motion at the minibar. "Have a drink."

He doesn't move a muscle. "Boss. You *really* need to sleep."

I lean against the cabinet, legs crossed. "Any news about the lead we got from Roel's computer?"

"No. It's a dead end. We suspect the sender to be from outside the country."

"Russia, for instance."

"I'm not sure."

"Well, I am." I swallow a long sip and wince slightly at the sharp taste. "I have a feeling that the Belsky Organization had something to do with her death. She admitted that she initially came to New York to spy on me—or, more accurately, on my father—but she eventually gave up on that and chose to stay with me. There's a huge possibility that they got rid of her once they figured out she'd switched camps."

"That's only speculation."

"Plausible speculation." I slam the bottle on the counter,

causing a few splashes to stain my hand. "I'm going to Russia to investigate this."

"You can't go to Russia with no evidence and no clue of their location, let alone their involvement. Besides, you're the fucking Pakhan now, Kirill. Your position is vulnerable, considering you haven't been in it for too long. Not to mention all the factions you've managed to offend in a small amount of time. The only thing you can do right now is stay and try to strengthen your authority."

"I don't give a fuck about that. I'm going to Russia. Make arrangements."

"No, I won't."

I stare into Viktor's dispassionate eyes. "Are you disobeying a direct order?"

"I am. I'm also telling you that if you go in blind, you're only heading to your death. You were a captain in the damn Spetsnaz, you know good and fucking well not to move without trusted intel."

"Get the fuck out of my way."

"If you insist." He pulls out his gun and tries to shove it in my hand. "Shoot me first. I'd rather die than see you spiral out of fucking control."

"Don't be ridiculous. I didn't know you'd learned how to be dramatic."

"I'm not joking, Kirill." He glares at me. "I've been with you all your life and have seen you being tortured and driven to within an inch of your life. I've watched you rise above any hurdle that stood in your path. You got this far because *you* made it happen. If *you* don't get yourself together and start acting like the Pakhan, you'll be killed. Do you think Aleksandra would like to see you being this fucking suicidal?"

"Shut up, Viktor."

"It's the truth. She must be rolling in her grave."

I grab hold of the gun and point it at his face. "I said. Shut the fuck up."

He stares me down, unblinking. "Kill me and then do whatever the fuck you want. Aleksandra is gone and so are Yuri and Maksim. I'm the only one who's able to keep you safe now, but you're making my job impossible by inviting all these threats into your life. If you don't kill me before you go to Russia, I'll shoot myself."

"Viktor," I growl.

"I'm doing what she would do if she were here," he says. "We didn't get along, but we had one thing in common. Keeping you safe. And I'll be fucking damned if I send you to your death."

I let the gun fall to my side and twist the wedding ring with my other hand.

As much as I want to strangle the motherfucker, he's right.

This isn't me. And she wouldn't want to see me throw myself into a dangerous situation.

She didn't die so I could follow her.

At least, not yet.

I need to find out who the fuck took her from me first.

Only when I rip their heart out with my bare hands will I be able to join her.

FIVE

Sasha

SOMETIMES, DEATH IS BETTER THAN STAYING ALIVE.
In death, you can feel no pain, no shattering of your
heart, and no need to cry every night before sleeping and
every morning after waking up.

In death, there's finally peace.

No more running, suffering, and having to witness your heart
being split open while hopelessly watching.

Like every morning, I jolt awake after the same mixture of
nightmares. My shirt clings to my back with sweat, and my hair
feels damp.

The small room I've been using for weeks appears smaller, as
if the walls are closing in on me and will crush me.

My heart that stupidly insists on beating goes overboard in
its attempts to remain alive.

I tap my chest as images of the nightmare overlap in my mind.
Some are filled with memories of my parents' deaths. The look

of despair on Uncle Anatoly's face when he realized everything would be over.

The pure terror in Erik's pale features when he begged me to stop screaming so the shooters wouldn't find us.

Eduard's blank eyes.

Timur's half-shot face.

Erik's raw shriek before he was silenced forever.

But most are filled with images of Kirill's wedding. I always dream about it in red as if I'm witnessing it through a blood haze. I see Kristina's throat slit open, her blood bathing him before he drops right beside her.

Till death do they fucking part.

I rub my hand against my face and slap my cheek. I need to focus.

It's been a month since Anton found me in that cottage. We nearly died in that initial explosion, but my brother pushed me underneath him and we took cover beneath a table. We managed to escape before the second bomb went off.

I still refused to believe it was Kirill's doing until I saw one of his guards speeding away from the site.

Makar.

He was Roman's senior guard. After his death, he became responsible for various independent tasks Kirill put him on, including, but not exclusive to, spying and carrying out hits on some of the enemies Kirill shared with Roman.

Makar never answered to me or even to Viktor. Since he had direct communication with Kirill, I barely saw him, if ever. Sometimes, I forgot he was there, considering he doesn't live in the house.

That moment, when I saw Makar, was when reality started to sink in. After I foolishly told Kirill my real name, he knew I was part of the family he and his father couldn't get rid of, so he sent Maksim to Russia to kill my remaining family members and tasked Makar with wiping me off the face of the earth.

When those facts hit, I wanted to die and honestly considered it until Anton shook me and reminded me of all our family members who died that day.

He reminded me of Papa and Mama and that it wasn't my time to go.

I still needed to exact revenge on the only man I've ever loved. The man who chose another woman over me.

And because he hurt me, I attempted to hurt him back.

That day, Anton was more concerned about getting out of that place.

But we weren't able to make a swift escape since it turned out there were also gunmen near the property who attacked us. After we killed a few, I picked someone who was about my build, put my ring and bracelet on him, then burned him and what remained of the cottage.

A part of me wanted to ruin Kirill's wedding day. But the other part knew he wouldn't care, considering he sent those people to kill me and all.

Besides, a DNA test would immediately prove it's not me.

I still wanted to ruin the ring and bracelet I once revered, just because he gave them to me.

"Sasha!!"

The door to my room hits the wall as my baby cousin Mike runs inside. He's grown so much since the last time I saw him over two years ago. His golden hair falls all over his forehead, nearly getting in his eyes as he crashes into me.

I pat his back. "Morning, Mishka."

"Morning! Morning!" He slides his hand in mine. "C'mon, we need to have breakfast."

I smile as he leads me down the hall of a small house located on the outskirts of Siberia. I never knew it existed, but apparently, it's one of several safe houses my family owns all over the country.

Since Siberia is relatively safer than Saint Petersburg or Moscow, it's the best place to be after the last attack.

We still don't know how many men were there, but I know for sure that Maksim was right outside one of our family warehouses. He and his men exchanged fire with my uncle and the mercenaries he employed before he left. But not before one of his men shot Babushka.

She's been recovering, but it's bad. She hasn't been able to leave her bed since. She hasn't spoken to me either, saying that I'm already dead to her.

"Papa! Antosha! Sasha is here," Mike announces the moment we arrive in the small kitchen downstairs. He then side hugs Anton, and my brother ruffles his hair.

Uncle Albert smiles at me and offers me a cup of coffee. His face has sunken, and he looks way older than I remember.

When Anton and I arrived here, my uncle hugged me, and I cried like a fucking baby while apologizing. He didn't say anything. He just consoled me like Papa would have.

"Morning, Uncle." I lower my head and sit down beside Mike. "Tosha."

My brother releases a sound from the back of his throat but says nothing as he cuts his eggs and eats in silence. It's weird to even look him in the face.

Apparently, Anton killed the real Yuri. One of Uncle Albert's close acquaintances in the KGB who's a plastic surgeon and a master of disguise gave my brother a nose job and altered his jaw's structure so it'd imitate the real Yuri's features. He also supplied him with some sort of pill to alter his voice. My brother cut and dyed his hair, bulked up, and wore brown contact lenses.

The result wasn't the perfect Yuri, but that was okay since Anton made everyone think Yuri had been in an accident and needed reparative surgery. Hence, his look was enough to resemble Yuri, but not identical. The reason he targeted Yuri out of all of Kirill's men was due to a couple of circumstances. Unfortunately, they shared the same body type, height, and eye shape. Two, he was a loner, an orphan, and didn't speak to anyone aside from Maksim.

It's like watching a psychopath in action. Anton didn't hesitate to end the life of what was the weakest link in Kirill's circle. He adapted some of his mannerisms and made sure to fit in within Kirill's elite men.

He'd served in the Spetsnaz and had high-speed driving training, but he managed to hide his superior combat skills effectively.

Hell, he managed to fool me, and I'm his own damn sister. When I asked him why he did that, he said he had to do it to avoid suspicion. Besides, we all had to make sacrifices for revenge and the family.

Now that I know it was all a façade, I can see some of my brother's old features in his face, but they're subtle. It helps that he removed the lenses and allowed his hair to grow back to its original color. No wonder I always felt a sense of closeness and familiarity with Yuri. Maybe a part of me already recognized him as my brother.

He's an older, more frightening version, though. While he was always silent and grumpy, now, he's like a wall.

His dark hair is messed up at the top, his jaw is set, and his movements are nearly robotic. There was never much light in my brother's eyes, but now, it's completely gone.

It makes me wonder if the laughs and smiles he sometimes offered back in the military or in New York were genuine or just another façade.

He surely hasn't smiled since we got back to Russia.

Not even once.

He stands up, and I snatch a piece of toast, then hastily drink my coffee, managing to burn my tongue. "Are we going on a run? Give me five."

My runs with him in the morning and the combat training that he's never stopped giving me since Kirill was shot are the only things that keep me sane. I've been channeling all my rage and feelings of betrayal and directing it at shooting targets and imagining Kirill's face on them.

He slips on his coat without paying me attention. "Not today."

"Why not?"

"I have an errand to run."

"Oh, okay."

He stares at me.

I shift beneath his gaze. "What?"

"Don't go out like that."

He means like a woman. I refuse to dress as a man again. I don't care if I have to die for it.

"I'm not doing that anymore. You stopped being Yuri, and I stopped being Aleksander. If we're going to do something, we'll do it while being ourselves."

He shakes his head but says nothing.

"Bring me candy, Antosha!" Mike asks. No, more like he demands.

My brother offers him a warm look and nods. "Okay."

"And cake!"

"What type?" Anton actually indulges our cousin.

It's weird to see him this patient with a kid, especially since he's stoic to a fault.

"Strawberry, chocolate." Mike counts on his fingers, his brows drawn with concentration. "Cheesecake and...and...all the cake!"

"I'll see what I can find." Anton pats his head and leaves.

Mike grins with triumph, goes to the adjoining room, and turns on the TV. Soon after, the sounds of cartoons fill the house. It's so tiny that you can hear everything from anywhere.

My uncle pats my shoulder. "Never mind Anton, Sasha. You know how close-minded he can get."

"There's something I still don't understand." I toy with the jam jar, even though I have no actual appetite. "He spent over six years in Kirill's company. How come he never took action? He could've easily killed him."

"It was only five. He spent the first year recovering from his injury and devising this plan."

Right. My brother was hurt badly in the shoot-out that I thought killed him. Anton has a gash on his back that's covered by some tattoos. Everyone back in New York believes it's from the accident he supposedly suffered. But it is, in fact, a souvenir from the massacre, after which Anton slipped into a coma for a few weeks, and Uncle hid it from us because he didn't want to give us false hope.

After he woke up, Anton told Uncle to keep his survival a secret and went on to infiltrate Kirill's men's ranks.

"At first," Uncle continues, "we had no concrete evidence that Kirill was the one who informed his father of the plan to annihilate our family. We only knew that Roman had something to do with the massacre."

"Are you going to tell me what he was talking about that day?"

He purses his lips.

"I deserve to know, Uncle."

"You know that our family is special, right?"

"Because of the noble blood, yeah."

"Not only the blood but also everything that comes with it. See, we don't just do business. We invent business. We've been the puppet masters of many politicians and have controlled the government. The president and his ministers needed to pay respects to us and ask our permission before they pass any law. We were— no, we *are*—Russia's secret royalty."

"What does that mean? We're a cult?"

"Not a cult. Royalty. We're what every government needs."

"But governments are supposed to be elected by the people."

"You really believe that nonsense? Every society has a secret order that controls politics and politicians. They might have different agendas, but the concept is the same."

"If we were that powerful, why did I have to see my own parents and the rest of my family butchered in front of my eyes?"

"Because we made a mistake and allowed outsiders into our family business." A distant look crosses his features. "We made a few investment errors, and the wrong person got into power, and that wrong person is now the president of Russia."

"Fyodor Petrov?"

"That's the one. He doesn't like the concept of anyone controlling him or his decisions. In fact, he dedicated his youth to the KGB, trying and failing to get any incriminating information about us. It was a disaster that he came into power, and we had to finish him before he finished us."

"And how did you plan to do that? Unless…you planned a coup?"

He nods. "We needed outside help for that. We had weapons and moles in higher positions, but not enough manpower to flip the Kremlin upside down."

"Let me guess, Roman was one of the outsiders?"

"Unfortunately, yes. He was acquainted with your uncle Anatoly, and he offered his mercenaries and logistic support. Until he stabbed us in the back. The government only needed to issue the order to the general, Abram Kuzmin. Slap 'elimination of a possible terrorist group' on the operation and come after us."

"So once Anton recovered, he decided to take things into his own hands?"

"Yes. However, like you, he believed Kirill had nothing to do with it until very recently."

"What…changed his mind?"

"The attack on us and you a month ago, maybe?"

I clear my throat. "Right."

"Just recuperate for now. There'll be a chance for us to finally get Kirill."

My heart aches, but I nod. Why the hell did I have to give my heart to the man who destroyed me? Not once, but twice.

I cram the toast in my mouth, then stand up and put on my coat. "I'm going to buy a few things."

"Like what?" Uncle asks. "We have everything."

"Woman…things," I lie through my teeth. "I'll be back soon."

Mike bounds into the kitchen, his arms open wide. "I wanna go!"

"Maybe next time, Mishka. I will bring you candy instead?"

"Okay!" He jumps up with excitement although he had Anton promise him the same.

I kiss his cheek and jog out the front door, then head to the garage, where we keep three snowmobiles. I check my watch and smile when a dot appears on the screen.

So Anton is up to something.

I know, because he tends to disappear for hours and doesn't tell me what he's doing.

I'm done being kept in the dark, so I planted one of the trackers Uncle keeps in the engine of every snowmobile. I grab my own, put on my gloves, and speed across the field.

It takes us one hour to get to the smallest town on a snowmobile, and it seems that's where Anton is heading.

I start to follow while keeping a safe distance. Before I can reach the town center, he's on the road again, this time seeming to head out of town and into…nothing. There are no buildings in the field he's entering. Only a forest.

Weird.

I follow him for another thirty minutes before he comes to a stop. Once I'm two minutes away from the target, I park the snowmobile beneath a low tree, mark the position on my watch, and then go on foot.

My movements are careful and silent, but I don't even need to put forth an ounce of effort. I'm a sniper, after all. Moving like shadows is what we do best.

Anton's snowmobile is parked outside a small cottage in the middle of the frozen forest. I hide behind a tree and take a closer look. The windows are busted, some of the wood is splintered, and the gaps are filled with ice.

What is he doing here?

As I get closer, I catch a glimpse of light from a window at ground level.

Of course.

Whatever this place is, it's located underground.

I lift up my coat's collar further, run to the entrance, then sneak inside and check my gun, just in case.

Sure enough, the interior of the cottage is shabby and fucking freezing at best. However, there's an ajar door at the far end. I carefully slip through it and am greeted by dark stairs that are illuminated by a faint orange bulb.

I go down one step at a time. Due to the heat, the feeling slowly returns to my limbs.

Voices reach me from below, and I pause at the bottom of the stairs before I peek from behind the wall. The basement is more secured than the room upstairs, but it's still shabby. The walls are made of concrete, but it has the same eyesore orange lighting as the stairway.

However, the basement isn't what makes me gulp.

It's my brother standing in front of a man hanging from the ceiling by his cuffed arms. I can only see Anton's tense back through the shirt he was wearing this morning as he shoves a container of food in his prisoner's face. "If you want to starve again, I can make that happen."

My spine jerks at his dark tone. This is a part of Anton that I never wished to see. In a way, it's similar to the version of Papa I was shielded from.

"Fuck you," the man whispers in barely audible Russian.

My heart lurches in my chest as Anton drives his fist into the man's face. "Try again and stop pissing me off."

I lean my head sideways and see that, sure enough, it's Maksim.

He's hanging half naked, his chest full of lacerations and

dry blood, his face bruised, and his lips bleeding from Anton's punch.

"What did Kirill send you to do here?"

"Maybe it's to see your true fucking face, asshole," Maksim mocks and then coughs, choking on his own blood.

Anton punches him again, causing the chains to rattle. "I told you not to piss me off."

My brother lifts his fist again, but I jump out of my hiding place. "Stop!"

SIX

Sasha

MY LEGS SHAKE AS I STARE AT THE GRUESOME SCENE in front of me.

I never expected there would be a day when Yuri—no, Anton—would be torturing Maksim.

He's his best friend.

Or, more accurately, *was* his best friend.

If I'm piecing things together correctly, then maybe everything with his friendship with Maksim was also a façade.

Like the whole Yuri persona Anton was immersed in for years.

My brother spins around, his muscles tensing beneath his shirt. A harsh look turns his eyes to a green that resembles a haunted mountain. "What the fuck are you doing here?"

"I should be the one to ask you that." I storm toward them, hiding my gun in the process.

Maksim's good eye widens as I approach them, even as he struggles to hold his body up by grabbing the chains. "Sasha…?"

His murmured question stabs me in the chest. I expected him to be shocked at my gender switch, especially since he was against my leaving the Morozov family. However, I didn't think it'd hit him to this extent.

He looks so betrayed, so…distraught.

Anton slides his attention between him and me before he zeroes in on who could safely be considered his ex-friend. His jaw clenches, and his eyes blaze in a way I haven't witnessed before.

No.

I actually have, when he inexplicably got angry whenever Maksim was acting familiar with me or others. But those were mere hints of his bottled feelings—this, however, is pure rage.

"You're a girl?" Maksim asks in a faint, uncharacteristic tone.

He was always the loud, untamed one, but now, he looks like a kicked puppy with wounds all over his body. Literally and figuratively.

"She is." My brother gets in his face. "She was a woman all along, but you believed she was a man like a fucking fool. Intelligence was never your strongest skill."

"You shut the fuck up!" Maksim lunges against his bindings. "This is none of your business—"

His words are cut off when Anton backhands him hard and fast. The slap of flesh against flesh echoes in the silent air worse than a whip. It's not a punch, but it feels so much worse, judging from the way Maksim freezes up.

"Anton!" I grab onto his arm. "What's wrong with you? Let him go!"

"Let him go?" he repeats slowly, menacingly even. "He led the men who attacked our family not too long ago."

"I'm sure there's more to it. Besides, he didn't know they were our family."

"This is why you never could've won against Kirill." He gets in my face. "You're naïve and always try to see the situation from an angle that doesn't exist."

My throat fills with nausea, and my limbs tremble, but I still stare at my brother in his damn unfeeling eyes. "The man you're torturing to within an inch of his life is my *friend*. He was also your best friend for years unless you have a split personality that made you forget everything that happened when you were Yuri."

"He's Kirill's guard."

"He's Maks." I extend my palm. "Give me the keys."

"You know, this is exactly why Papa sheltered you. He knew that you would let your emotions lead you in everything."

"I'd rather have those emotions than live like an empty shell. So unless you're going to chain me up to the ceiling, too, give me the damn keys."

We glare at each other for what seems like ages, neither of us willing to back down. Finally, Anton reaches into his pocket and produces the keys, but he doesn't hand them over. Instead, he jerkily undoes Maksim's bindings himself.

The moment my friend's feet touch the ground, he loses balance. My brother could catch him, but he moves out of the way, letting him fall.

Dickhead.

I rush to Maksim's side and try to help him. He pushes me away and agonizingly adjusts himself into a sitting position so that his back is against the wall.

Maksim might be easygoing, but he has a deep sense of pride. For instance, he's never liked imposing on people or being weak. He's always prided himself on managing to come out unscathed from all the operations we've had.

His combat skills are only rivaled by Kirill's and Viktor's, and he rubs it in everyone's faces—especially Yuri's/Anton's—all the time. So to find himself in this position must be humiliating.

My brother stands to the side, directly between Maksim and the door. If my friend attempts to escape, I'm sure this will end badly.

"Are you okay?" I ask slowly, maybe redundantly, because he

looks like shit. His lips are dry and bloody. One of his eyes is swollen shut, and his chest is a map of Anton's destruction.

"Who is he to you?" Maksim asks instead of answering my question and juts his chin to the side.

"He's…my brother."

"Brother," he repeats as if making sure he heard it right. "Does this mean you infiltrated the organization together?"

"No. I only found out he was my brother recently. I thought he was dead and…well, he looked different."

"He killed Yuri."

"And I'd do it all over again if I got a redo," Anton announces coolly, with enough apathy to piss *me* off.

Maksim snarls up at him although he's nearly collapsing.

I hastily grasp the container Anton placed on the table and settle back beside Maksim, then open it and give him a bottle of water. "You look dehydrated. You need to eat and drink."

Still glaring at my brother, Maksim snatches the bottle and drinks it all in one go. My chest aches at the view of the bruises and cuts the cuffs left on his wrists.

He must've been hanging from the ceiling for a long time.

I should've really followed Anton sooner.

Maksim snatches the container from my hands and pauses when he sees the medium-cooked steak and the vegetables—no carrots since he doesn't like them. His jaw clenches, but he empties the container in record time.

Once he's finished, he stares at me. "Are you in on this, too?"

"This?"

"Torturing me."

"No. Of course not. I just found out today, and only because I followed him."

"Does that mean you'll let me go?"

"In your dreams," Anton says. "You're not stepping a foot outside until you tell me what Kirill sent you to do. And even then, you won't leave my sight."

"Kill me, you motherfucker. If you don't, I'll be the one who kills you."

Anton reaches over, probably to slap or punch him again, but I jump up and stand between them. "Stop it, both of you, just stop. You were the best of friends. Can't you think of that?"

"He attacked our family!"

"He killed my real friend!" Maksim says at the same time.

I release a breath and sit between them. "This is going nowhere."

"Leave," my brother orders. "I'll deal with him in my own way."

"And let you torture, then possibly kill him? No." I face my friend. "I don't want to believe you attacked unarmed people, Maks. Those people are the only survivors of a family massacre, and they happen to be my elderly grandmother, my uncle, and my six-year-old cousin. But I recognized your face on the security footage. Unless you tell me what actually happened, Anton's version is logical."

"I wasn't here to attack anyone. I was on a mission to locate the last members of the Belsky Organization and try to start a line of communication with Kirill."

"Liar," Anton snarls. "If it were that simple, you would've told me that instead of withstanding torture."

"I prefer being tortured than talking to your ugly fucking face."

Anton's fist clenches, and I clear my throat before he moves into action. "Are you sure Kirill didn't want you to kill the last members of the Belsky Organization?"

"If he did, he would've sent an army and Viktor. I came with only four other men and they were killed by your side who opened fire first."

My heart that's been bleeding nonstop perks up at that. Isn't it sad that a mere sliver of hope—as minimal and speculative as it is—happens to be enough to revive my stupid heart?

I internally shake my head. "Do you know why he's attempting to start communications?"

Maksim shakes his head. "He's not the type who shows his hand."

Isn't that the damn truth?

He always kept his plans so close to his chest that even Viktor and I weren't privy to them until the final stages. That's how I was blindsided by his engagement, his marriage, and his damn betrayal.

Note to self: shoot more targets later.

"What are you going to do to me, Sasha?" Maksim speaks with obvious strain. "Fake asshole over there will be happy to put a bullet in my head like he did to Yuri, but I doubt that's your stance."

"I guess if I asked you to switch sides, you wouldn't, right?"

"Why ask something you already know the answer to?"

I get it. Kirill and his family are Maksim's benefactors. They gave him purpose and a privileged upbringing he wouldn't have dreamt of having anywhere else.

Not to mention that he genuinely respects Kirill and even Viktor. The latter personally trained him from a young age and was the reason he developed superior combat skills.

It was foolishly hopeful of me to wish he'd be on the side of two people who lied to him. One of them tortured him for damn weeks and killed his real friend.

"If you go back to Kirill…" My voice catches, as is the case every time I speak or think of him. "We'll meet again as enemies."

"Aren't we already?"

"I don't want to hurt you, Maks. You're the first friend I made after losing my family. You helped me integrate into the military and mafia life seamlessly. You always had my back and cheered me up whenever I was down without asking for anything in return. You easily became my best friend without even trying. I'll never forget those moments."

He gives Anton the side-eye. "That makes one of you."

"The fuck did you just say?" my brother snaps in a frightening tone.

"I said, one of you isn't an ungrateful motherfucker. Want to hear that again, dick?"

"You must be tired of living." Anton starts to grab him, but I push his hand away.

"Stop it, damn it. What's with all the testosterone between you two? It's exhausting to watch."

Maksim snarls, and Anton glares at him as if he wants to snap his neck. If I hadn't been here, I'm sure that's exactly what he would've done.

"But we can't be friends anymore," I say in a choked voice. "You're the guard of the man whose demise I'm planning. The man to whom I was loyal to, but he chose to betray me. We're on opposite sides of the board, Maks. If we meet as enemies, we might kill each other."

"We could've easily bypassed this if you'd been truthful about who you were from the beginning."

"If I had been, I wouldn't have been able to exact revenge."

"Both of you keep saying that. Look at your fucking faces! You're grown-up adults living in the past. So what if you get revenge? You think you'll be happier? Freer? Better? Well, here's a news flash for you—you'll just feel empty as fuck."

"We'll at least get closure," I say, deadpan.

"By killing the people who were once your comrades and protected you back? This isn't only about Boss. It's about all the other men's lives. Were they responsible for your family's death? No. But you'll kill them anyway because they'll be defending Boss with their lives. How are you any different from terrorists?"

"I swear to fuck, Maksim. If you don't shut your fucking mouth, I'm going to send you to your dear boss in a casket."

"Do it, damn it!" Maksim staggers to his feet using the wall for balance and clutches Anton by the collar of his shirt. "Kill me. Death is better than seeing your true fucking face."

My chest aches at the reminder of the feelings that ripped my chest open when I discovered Kirill's betrayal. Maksim must be experiencing feelings similar to that.

He genuinely liked Yuri, but he found out that it was Anton all along.

And while Yuri and Anton share the same silent personality, they're entirely different in everything else.

My brother was always the heir to the Ivanov empire, and that turned him into an emotionless person at a young age.

The massacre made his negative traits worse.

Even now, he looks at Maksim with cold eyes, as if he can't feel any of the rage that's targeted toward him. But he grabs Maksim by the hair, his fingers pulling back until it looks painful.

I stand up and carefully but firmly break them apart. Maksim sags against the wall, and my brother briefly closes his eyes and breathes deeply before opening them again.

"I think we could all use a break," I say softly.

"Are you going to let me go?" Maksim asks in a nonnegotiable tone.

"I told you, I don't want to fight you, Maks." I pat his shoulder. "I think it's better you stay here. At least for now."

"So the sadistic asshole can torture me some more?"

"I'm going to knock your fucking teeth out," Anton growls, slowly but surely losing his patience.

"There will be no torture," I announce.

"And how will you make sure of that? The moment you turn your back, your dear fucking brother will go back to his favorite hobby of marking my skin."

"I will stay here."

"You'll do no such thing," Anton says.

"Maks is right. I also can't trust you not to torture him just because you can."

"You're not staying alone with him," Anton enunciates each word.

Maksim grins with an edge. "What? Afraid Sasha likes me more than she likes you?"

"You fucking—"

"You can stay, too, Anton. But if we leave, we do it together. That way, neither of us is with him on our own at any given time."

I can tell Anton doesn't like this plan; however, he has no choice but to accept it. One, I'm not leaving. Two, he's also not leaving.

This is a complication I never considered, but for some reason, I'm happy for any event that manages to distract me from the bloody mess in my chest.

Even if temporarily.

SEVEN

Sasha

TO SAY THE ATMOSPHERE HAS BEEN STRAINED WOULD be an understatement.

It's been two weeks since I followed my brother and found him torturing Maksim after oddly buying his favorite food.

That was the detail that made me think that Anton's position on this might be skewed. I thought he was unfeeling and couldn't care less about what happened to Maksim. He certainly could win an Oscar for the performance he gave back in the military and in New York.

However, after the time the three of us have spent holed up in here, I'm starting to change my perspective.

One, Anton caught Maks when he was in hiding after Uncle Albert sent mercenaries after him, but he didn't tell my uncle.

He kept him here so that he's out of Uncle and Babushka's reach. He said it was because he wanted to extract the answers from him, but I think he wanted to protect him.

Two, he put him in a very well-heated place that's adequate to fight Siberia's freezing cold and snow in late October.

Still, I can't trust him since he actually tortured him.

The first few days, I stayed around most of the day, because Maksim was ill. He had a fever and needed constant attention.

However, whenever I attempted to wipe his body with a cold rag for the fever, Anton would push me aside and do it himself. He said I'm still his sister, and he doesn't like me touching men.

I tried to explain that Maks is my friend and I don't think of him that way, but Anton shut me up with, "No. I still don't want to think about whatever you were doing with Kirill every time he kicked us out."

If my heart wasn't already too broken to feel, I'd be embarrassed at the prospect that my brother knew about Kirill and me all along.

He probably didn't intervene because: A) he would've looked suspicious, and B) he thought all of that was part of my elaborate plan.

A plan whose result is to be broken to pieces, maybe. But I had no damn plan, and that's the saddest thing about this.

Despite my attempts, Anton didn't let me touch Maksim and was the one who singlehandedly took care of him while I started repairs upstairs.

But I did have to come back down to check that he wasn't killing him when I wasn't there.

Then he helped me with repairs, or more like, did whatever I told him to. Anton is surprisingly good with handiwork, a fact I didn't know before. Maybe it's because we grew up wealthy, so we never really had to work for ourselves.

But then again, Anton has had to enlist in the army and work in the mafia. Even though he did an excellent job at pretending he was a weakling combat-wise, in reality, he's not.

For two weeks, we come here in the morning and leave by

sunset. Uncle, Babushka, and Mike think we're doing special training, so they never suspect anything.

Maksim gave us the silent treatment at first, so I brought cards and board games and tried to get him to talk.

Considering he's a hopeless extrovert, it didn't take him long to talk to me. Anton, however, is a different story. The only time they speak to each other is when they're ready to rip each other's hearts out.

It's become worse ever since Maksim got better. We often find him pacing the basement like a caged animal.

He must really feel like one.

Maksim is a man who's been around violence since he was young. He enlisted in the army at the age of nineteen. Spent four years there living his best life and then went to the mafia world, where he was tasked with mostly on-ground operations.

So now that he's locked up, it's like we've cut off his wings. But I really don't see any other way to avoid conflict. If we let him go, he'll go back to Kirill, and it'll be a disaster.

Or maybe I'm merely trying to delay the inevitable.

Uncle Albert is already setting things in motion, and we'll eventually go to New York to kill Kirill.

We just have to wait for his spies in the criminal organizations to put everything in place. It has to happen during an event at his house, because Anton and I know that place like the back of our hands.

And because justice is poetic, he'll die in front of his family.

I'll be the one who kills him. Not Anton. Not Uncle Albert. *Me.*

I chose this. It's enough punishment for falling for the monster.

I probably won't survive after I kill him, but who fucking cares?

What's my future outside of revenge anyway? It's just a pipe dream. I don't remember what I wanted to be when I was a little girl. All I ever hoped for was to grow older with my cousins while escaping Mama's scolding and Babushka's cane.

Now, my sole purpose seems to have become revenge.

"Morning, Maks," I greet as I get inside.

He grumbles under his breath, his eyes hard, and his muscles tense beneath his shirt. I can tell he's on edge without him having to say a word.

"We need to do something," he says. "If I spend one more moment in this place, I'm going to punch the wall."

Judging by his bruised knuckles, I think he might have already done that.

"And no fucking board games," he snaps before I manage to speak.

"Watch your fucking mouth," Anton warns from beside me.

Maksim narrows his eyes on him. "*You.* Fight me."

I offer a placating smile. "I'm sure we can come up with something better…Anton!"

My brother is already removing his coat and stepping to the middle of the basement. Anton built him a new bed and we brought over a few weights and a TV, but apparently, those aren't enough to entertain Maksim.

"What are you guys doing?" I try to get between them.

"Stay out of this, Sasha." Maksim is talking to me, but his hawk-like attention is on my brother. "This is between me and the fake motherfucker."

"Yes. Stay out. I'm going to put this insolent fucker back in his place—"

His sentence isn't finished, and Maksim has already driven his fist into his face. "Not so fun when I'm not tied up and helpless, is it, asshole?"

Anton swings back with his own punch. Then they're downright throwing each other against the wall, on the sofa, and to the floor as they exchange blows.

I give up trying to break up the fight a few minutes after they start. This might well be what they need to get whatever animosity is lurking out of their systems.

With a sigh, I sit down and rearrange the cards.

So much for making the basement a bit homey. It's like a war zone now.

If we were in New York or even the army, Anton wouldn't have stood a chance against Maksim, but that was only because he was hiding his actual ability. Now, however, he doesn't hold back as he pummels Maksim into a corner.

My friend tackles him to the ground and slaps him across the face. No, he backhands him. Like Anton did to him before.

Anton growls and holds Maksim down, but it only lasts a second before they roll on the floor, hitting each other everywhere. Adrenaline must be stronger than whatever injuries they're giving one another, because they keep going. There isn't a sign that either of them will give up.

I go upstairs to grab a bottle of vodka and a couple of glasses. When I return, they're still as energetic as ever. I pour myself a cup and sit at the small table to watch their fight with keen interest. I expect it to end any moment, but it doesn't. It actually lasts for over half an hour before they finally collapse on the floor in the aftermath of the destruction they've wreaked.

Their harsh breaths, sweat, and the smell of blood lingers in the air, only interrupted by my casual sips.

"You guys get an A-plus for stamina."

Anton staggers to his feet and kicks Maksim in the ribs. "I won."

Maksim captures his ankle and brings him crashing back down—on top of him. "Like fuck you did."

Anton fists his shirt. "Admit that you're not a god, after all."

"I am to you, dick." Maksim throws him off and stands up, then walks in my direction and snatches the bottle of vodka and drinks right from it. "You watched, Sasha. I won, right?"

"Nonsense." Anton takes the bottle and drinks straight from it, even though a few glasses are lying about. "Anyone with eyes could see that I got more points on you."

"In your fucking dreams." Maksim steals the bottle back and pours more alcohol down his throat.

"I'm not sure, to be honest." I tilt my head to the side as they keep fighting over the vodka until they finish the whole bottle.

Both their faces are a map of bruises, cuts, and bleeding lips.

Maksim throws his weight on the seat beside me, dwarfing the wooden chair. "You obviously have nepotism issues."

Anton sits on the chair on my other side, causing it to creak under his weight. "Watch your fucking mouth when you talk to her."

"What are you going to do about it, motherfucker?"

"You—"

I slam my glass on the table. "Seriously, stop it. You're giving me a headache. You're like children."

"The only man-child in this equation is your brother, who has small dick energy."

"You speak as if your dick is all that impressive."

"You know it is."

"Okay." I lift my hand. "Too much dick talk for my taste, and seriously, Tosha is my brother, and I don't need these images."

The latter closes his eyes as if he's just realized he's been talking about dicks in front of his sister. Which is surprising, considering he's collected to a fault.

Maksim rattles him—or his rage toward him does.

Interesting.

Maksim hits my shoulder with his. "You lived with men for two years, and while you never participated in a dick measuring competition, you never flinched from it either."

"Well, that was before I knew Yuri was actually my brother."

"Guess I should feel like I'm in good company if he also managed to fool his own sister."

"Stop talking about me as if I'm not here," my brother says.

Maksim doesn't look at him and, instead, smiles at me. "What type of game are we playing?"

"Don't fucking ignore me." Anton speaks so low that goose-bumps erupt on my skin.

"Card game?" Maksim does a marvelous job of completely erasing him. "I prefer that over a board game."

"Are you an attention whore?" Anton's voice returns to normal.

Maksim raises his head slowly, the cards clenched in his fist. "The fuck you just say?"

My brother's lips tilt in a smirk. "Take a hint already. She's a woman and was never interested in you."

"Shut the fuck up."

"What? You're embarrassed that your crush turned out to be a woman?"

Maksim lunges up, and so does Anton. I lift myself in time to stop both of their punches. "Can you guys just chill for a minute?"

"You had no fucking right to reveal that," Maksim grinds through his teeth.

"I don't give a fuck." Anton stares down at me. "Maksim is gay, and since he thought you were a man, he had a crush on you. Now, all his hopes are destroyed. Just like that."

"You fucking—"

"Get out, Anton." I push him.

"No."

"I said get out." I soften my voice. "Please."

He grinds his teeth, but he heads to the exit.

My friend still wants to go after him, but I stand in his way. He walks into me, and since he's a damn bull, I can't keep him in place.

"Maks!" I push at his chest. "Ignore him. Anton was an ass-hole, but it's not worth it. Besides, I don't care whether you're gay or straight or an alien. You'll always be my friend."

He breathes deeply and stops pushing me, a bitter smile appearing on his lips. "Thanks for the thousandth kick into the friendzone."

"I'm a woman, so anything between us would be virtually impossible."

"You say that as if it would be possible if you were a man."

"I mean, you never know."

"Don't fuck with me, Sasha. You looked at Boss like he was your god."

"That's not…true."

"Yes, it is." He sighs. "I guess I wanted someone to look at me that way, too."

I pat his arm. "I'm sorry I lied to you. I didn't mean to hurt you."

"At least *you* didn't mean to hurt me."

"Anton is…" I pause, searching for the right word. "Not that bad. He's just too inflexible."

"If you continue to keep me locked up here, one of us will end up killing the other. You know it, he knows it, and I know it. Do the right thing, Sasha."

"I…will think about it."

"Think fast." He pauses. "Also, I don't believe Boss would ever orchestrate the death of children. He's not that type of monster."

"Save it, Maks."

"I mean it. He dedicated his whole youth to protecting his siblings, including making them believe he didn't give a fuck about them. A man like him wouldn't murder children."

A foolish part of me wants to believe his words, but Kirill killed that part in that cottage where I waited for him, not knowing what he had in store for me.

Maksim and I play a round of cards. But then Anton sends me an emergency text, and I have to leave a grumbling Maksim after giving him a hug.

I find Anton waiting by the snowmobile outside and hop on behind him. "Just so you know, that was an asshole move. You don't just expose someone's sexuality when he didn't come out himself."

"I don't give a fuck."

"You're really a bastard sometimes." I shake my head. "What's the emergency?"

"We might have to move up the attack date."

My heart jolts. "We have a lead?"

"Yeah. Uncle is working out the details." He pauses. "Babushka wants us to kill Kirill's family before his eyes."

I hop off the snowmobile and stare at him. "What are you talking about? We agreed we'd only kill Kirill."

"Babushka doesn't think the same."

"Babushka is an old woman who doesn't know what the fuck she's talking about most of the time."

"Watch it, Sasha. What the fuck is wrong with you?"

"Well, isn't it the truth? She's been in hiding all this time, and that's skewed her mind. You and I went to hell and back and agreed that only Kirill would pay. Karina and Konstantin have nothing to do with this. And, actually, neither does Yulia."

"We had nothing to do with the decision Papa and our uncles made, either, but we lost our whole family because of it."

"You...agree with this?"

"It wouldn't be poetic justice if he's the only one who dies."

"No, Anton! We're not going to kill them. Karina is my friend, and so is Konstantin, for that matter."

He narrows his eyes. "You left New York, but apparently, your heart is still there."

"We're not killing them, and that's final."

If I'm outvoted on this by both Babushka and Uncle, I'll take things into my own hands.

EIGHT

Kirill

MY KILLING SPREE NEVER STOPPED.

However, I've started to put on the brakes enough to protect my position as the Pakhan. It's not an easy or a fun place to be when everything else is…empty.

However, this is the throne I've worked hard to sit on. I might have lost Sasha, but she was by my side for years to help me get here.

More accurately, all she wanted was to help me. She didn't care whether I got here or anywhere else as long as she protected and supported me.

I'm the one who vied for this position and hurt her for it with that engagement. I didn't get the chance to celebrate our marriage properly before she was snatched away.

She's been gone from my life for fifty-three days, and I still can't go into my old room.

Avoiding my old room is pointless since I see her in every corner of my house, the garden, and even out in the streets.

She's fucking everywhere.

It's impossible to purge her out of my system or find closure. In fact, I refuse to.

"What do you think, Pakhan?" Vladimir asks from my right, bringing my attention back to the meeting.

It's one of those weekly ones where everyone in the organization bores me with their nonsense before we vote, and then they go on their way.

After I lost my shit and offended the leader of the Russian mafia in Boston by stepping on his toes with the Albanian issue, things were unsettled here.

Igor was highly displeased with my misconduct, but because his daughter is in my family, he reined it in. Rai asked for a re-election of the Pakhan and was a fucking bitch about it. In fact, she's been an absolute eyesore ever since she learned about Sasha's death.

If I die of poisoning, Rai did it.

Vladimir told me that he dislikes me, but I'm the Pakhan now, so I better act like it and keep the organization together.

Adrian threatened to withdraw his support and hang me out to dry if I put everything he'd built in jeopardy.

Mikhail and Damien are the only fans I have. Mikhail—because I gave him back some of the power he's been losing. Damien—because I've been fueling his sadism.

In fact, he goes as far as voting for anything I dish out as long as I keep him 'busy.'

After Viktor threatened me with his own life—which isn't something he's done before—I had to force myself into my current role.

The role I might have unknowingly chosen over Sasha.

It means nothing without her, but if I give it up, all I have left is death.

So I patched things back up with Juan's cartel and got us a better deal. On the bright side, some organizations asked to be allies after they witnessed how I annihilated the Albanians.

Therefore, Rai can bark but will never be able to bite.

Despite all the shit I stirred up, I'm still the best option the brotherhood has in order to survive.

"I think," I say in reply to Vladimir's question. "We should wait it out, take no action against the Irish and see how they'll react. If they choose violence…"

"I'll butcher them in their sleep," Damien finishes for me, rubbing his hands together.

"That." I jut my chin toward him, and he grins like an evil maniac.

"Can't we start the war first and see how it goes from there?"

"No," I say point-blank.

"Come on! Why does no one take my suggestions seriously?"

"Because there's little to no thought put behind them," Igor replies, then focuses on me. "I agree with that plan, but we should also try to insert spies."

"Already done," I say. "Adrian has his own network within."

The man in question nods. "We started that about a week ago. If there's anything suspicious, I'll report back to the Pakhan."

"Always one step ahead, eh?" Mikhail smirks.

"I wouldn't settle for anything else," I say and then wrap up the meeting.

Most days, I'm too numb to feel anything, but on other days, the cloud is too close. The gloominess suffocates my breathing, my being, and everything I've ever strived for.

Some days, I'm hit with the fact that I won't see her shadowing me and competing with Viktor over who can protect me better.

And then there are the days where I wonder why I'm still breathing when she isn't.

This is one of those days.

I need all these fucking people out of my face so that I can get drunk at her grave like I do every day. The few hours I sleep against the tree opposite her tombstone is the only sleep I ever get, and even that is riddled with nightmares of her corpse.

Nightmares of her crying, cursing, and hitting me because I chose to be engaged to Kristina—who's now actually pregnant.

Rai lingers behind, her eyes practically shooting lasers in my direction. Her husband stands beside her, mainly to stop her from getting herself shot. She has a loud mouth that needs to be reined in.

I lean my chin against my fist and conjure a nonchalance I don't feel. "Is there a reason behind your tedious presence?"

"Just so you know, I'll never forgive you."

"Very bold of you to assume I have any fucks to give about your views."

"How can you be this detached about her death, you fucking asshole!" She lunges at me, probably to punch or slap me, but Kyle holds her by the waist and flings her back.

"Let me go!" She struggles against him. "Someone needs to knock some sense into his thick head!"

"I would, but I'd rather not see you get shot, Princess."

"At least one of you is smart." I throw up a dismissive hand. "Get her out of my sight before I lose the little benevolence I have left."

"It's your fault Sasha died," she says calmly, her struggle gone. "She had no enemies, but you do. Hell, you collect them like badges of honor, not giving a shit how that could influence the people on your side. I already said that you weren't worthy of her and that you should have let her go, but of course, you didn't do that, and look how that turned out."

I stand up fast, but Kyle's reflexes are faster. He all but drags her out of the dining room. "We're leaving."

My hand balls into a fist at my side. If I'd touched her, I would've snapped her fucking neck. No doubt about it.

Kyle was quick enough to save her from my clutches. Even if temporarily.

I stand there for a second, two…

In one movement, I grab the edges of the table and send everything on top crashing down.

Dishes, glasses, and leftover food splinter and leave stains on the floor, but it does nothing to calm the raging fire inside.

Maybe I should be the one who poisons Rai to shut off her fucking annoying voice forever.

It's your fault Sasha died.

Those words repeat over and over again, clashing with the ticking sound of the old clock.

Tick.

I'm why she died.

Tock.

If she didn't know me, she'd be alive.

Tick.

If I'd chosen her, she wouldn't have been killed.

Tock…

My head seems to short-circuit. Either that, or I'm losing my fucking mind. My body can't keep up with my spiraling thoughts, and rage shakes through me.

The red type.

The type that needs to spill blood and would still be dissatisfied with it.

I roll the ring on my finger back and forth in a mad rhythm as I storm out of the dining room. I'm glad Viktor isn't here to nag me like my nonexistent mother. Or that Karina isn't waiting for me with a knife—she picked up that habit again after the last time she also accused me of being emotionless.

Cold.

Apathetic.

If I were as indifferent as she and Rai claim I am, would I be able to feel choked, no matter how much air I breathe?

Would I need alcohol and her fucking grave to have some semblance of vague rest?

Would I feel her with me? Even now? Walking by my fucking side silently, sadly maybe?

Maybe her ghost is haunting me because I failed to protect her. Though there's no particular haunting. Just a shake of the head here and a fucking hug there as if she's putting my pieces back together again so I can survive one more day.

I wish I were as unfeeling as Karina and Rai think. While I generally am, that's not the case when it comes to Sasha.

Living without her is similar to falling back into that weak, aimless, and absolutely pathetic version of myself.

No. I had a purpose then.

Now, I have fucking nothing.

I snatch a bottle of vodka on my way out. While I don't like the stuff, Sasha did.

It was her favorite drink on the rare occasion she consumed alcohol. She was a stereotypical Russian who loved her vodka.

Now, it's my poison of choice.

All the cars that crowded my driveway are now gone, letting my guards breathe a little. I don't want to seem biased—though I am—but I have the best men.

Adrian and some of his men served time there, too, but there were only a few of them. I was the only one with enough power to take all of my men with me when I left this house. I lost many of them, but the ones who remain are the most disciplined, loyal men any leader could have.

Despite their general depression at losing Sasha, Maksim, and Yuri all at the same time, they've been giving one thousand percent under Viktor's command.

They might be the only reason I'm still hanging on here and not buried six feet under with Sasha. She considered them friends, and I'll never forgive myself if I let anything happen to them.

If she learned about Maksim, she'd hate me forever.

And Yuri…I don't know what the fuck happened to him. It's like the earth split open and swallowed him without leaving a trace.

I thought maybe he went after Maksim, but it's not his style to disappear without informing me.

He could've defected or…I don't know.

I don't fucking care at this point.

"Boss!" Viktor comes running in my direction as I head to the car.

I ignore him and open the door. "Not now. I'm done for the day."

"This is an emergency."

"I still have no fucks to give."

He rips my hand from the handle and slams the door shut.

"What the fuck do you think you're doing?"

"You need to see this."

"I swear to fuck—" I halt in my tracks when a very familiar face walks toward us, wearing cargo pants and a disheveled T-shirt. "Maksim."

He offers a strained smile. "Long time no see, Boss."

I approach him slowly, as if I'm witnessing another ghost other than Sasha's persistent one. Short of some healing bruises on his face, he looks exactly like the Maksim I know.

"He got out of a cab in front of the mansion," Viktor offers. "The guards at the front called to tell me about his arrival."

"What the fuck happened?" I ask. "Why did you disappear?"

"I was captured after I sent you that initial text, and then they got rid of my communication outlet."

I narrow my eyes. "How did you get free?"

"One of them helped me."

"Who are *they* and *them*, Maksim?"

"Anton Ivanov and Sasha. Though you probably know Anton as Yuri. He was fucking lying all these years, Boss. Actually, he killed Yuri five years ago, faked that accident and took his place, then—"

"Wait. Go back." My throat grows dry with every word. "Did you just say Sasha?"

"Yeah. She said, and I quote, 'I'm alive. Though you probably know by now that the body was a ploy. Next time I see you, I'm going to kill you.'"

"She...is alive?" The words strangle me on their way out.

"Yeah. She managed to escape the bombing, but that's not the point right now. She helped me leave Russia because her family wants to kill everyone in this house, including your family. She said she wants to set up a meeting for just the two of you so no one else gets killed in this war. She's doing this behind their backs, so they can't find out..."

Maksim trails off when I drop the bottle of vodka. It crashes against the ground as I throw my head back and bark out a long, deep laugh.

Life rushes through my limbs all at once, washing away all emptiness and the hell that came with it.

I'm breathing. *No.*

I'm *alive.*

Fuck.

Fucking fuck.

She actually got me. She nearly drove me insane, but all this time, she was in Russia doing fuck knows what.

She wants to kill me the next time she sees me?

By all means.

Anything for my beautiful wife.

NINE

Sasha

"**S**ASHA!"

I straighten on the makeshift stool I made from some boxes as Anton barges into the garage. I let my rifle rest on my knees, my fingers strangling the cloth I've been using to clean it. I prefer to do it here so Mike doesn't see this side of me—or his family.

He's just a kid who loves his cartoons and candy, and I want to preserve that innocence for as long as possible.

Cold air penetrates my bones and the blizzard slips inside before my brother slams the door.

His coat is covered with snow and his face is so white, it could compete with the harsh natural elements. His eyes blaze worse than the storm outside, terrifying in their depths.

"What the fuck have you done?" he snarls, his voice and face tight with tension.

"I don't know what you're talking about."

"Maksim is gone."

"Really?" I rub the cloth across the back of my weapon. "And how do you know that? Unless you went to see him on your own?"

He's been sneaking out regularly, after he thinks we've all gone to sleep. I thought maybe he was going to exercise or meet with the men who still follow this fallen empire, but judging by his shit mood every morning, I'm sure he's been visiting that old cottage.

I considered following him, but since Maksim has gotten strong enough to defend himself, I thought it would be better not to interfere. Besides, they haven't been injured, at least not physically, so it was pointless for me to get between them.

Anton seems to take the asshole act up a notch whenever I try to break up their endless fights, so I chose the diplomatic route and let them fend for themselves.

Now, however, Anton looks close to ripping me to pieces. "So you did let him go."

"No, I didn't. But you didn't answer my question. Did you go behind my back to the cottage?"

"Sasha," he growls deep in his throat.

"Yes, Tosha?"

"Don't fuck with me." He storms in front of me, his shoulders, legs, and fists brimming with lethal tension. "When did he leave? How? What's his itinerary?"

"No clue." I lift a shoulder. "I might have dropped off a key there and smuggled in some ski equipment."

"You fucking idiot!" He reaches a hand out to grab me by the collar of my shirt, but I jump up and step away at the last second. The rifle drops from my lap and hits the ground with a clank.

"What?" I meet his cold gaze with my own. "Maks isn't your prisoner. He's no one's prisoner, for that matter. He was never supposed to stay in that basement forever."

"Yes, he was."

"What the hell is wrong with you?"

"What the fuck is wrong with *you*, damn it! You just sent him straight to New York. In no time, Kirill and his men will be crowding the front of our house to finish what they started."

"No, they won't, because Maks doesn't know the exact location of this house."

"You underestimate that fucker. He can pinpoint the area and they'd easily track us down."

"He won't do that."

"Oh yeah? And what makes you so sure?"

"He's my best friend and I trust him."

Anton barks out an obnoxious laugh that pierces my ears. "*Best friend? Trust?* You were and always will be a naïve fucking fool, Sasha. This is why Kirill managed to fool you and stomp all over you."

I get in his face, losing my cool as I push against him. "So what if I made a mistake? So what if I wanted love and stability in a fucked-up existence? Yes, I was an idiot. Yes, I trusted the wrong person, but that doesn't mean I'll lose my humanity because of it like you did! I'm not a robot, Tosha! I will never be a damn emotionless monster who's fine with imprisoning his friends and driving them insane. He's your friend, too. Or was, because you've definitely lost him now. I haven't, and I won't. Maks is one of the good ones. He has a pure, compassionate soul, which can't be said about you."

His nostrils flare and I can tell he's barely stopping himself from strangling me. "You're going to eat those words when the owner of that *pure, compassionate soul* betrays you. Just like Kirill."

"I refuse to have a black heart and believe everyone is out to get me."

"That black heart is the reason you're still alive."

"And I'm thankful for that, but I won't adopt your way of thinking. You believe we should've kept Maks forever, but you can't possibly be blind to how agitated he was becoming as the days went by. He had scratch marks on the back of his neck and blood beneath his nails from the aggressive way he was sinking his fingers into his skin. If he'd stayed, he might well have killed himself or you, just to end the cycle. You might not want to admit it, but I did the right thing by giving him his freedom."

Besides, Maks and I have a plan that ensures this whole tragedy ends with me and Kirill without involving anyone else.

Not my family.

Not his family.

Just him and me.

Over the past day, I've been wondering how Kirill received the message. I don't know if he really thought I was dead or if he had figured out the body wasn't mine.

The reason I left the bracelet and ring he gave me on that corpse before we burned what remained of the cottage was for the shock effect on him.

Or…that's what I hoped for.

Truth is, he might have welcomed it since he has a real wife now and would be glad to get rid of the fake one.

"Here's the thing you don't want to admit, Sasha. You fucked up big time." Anton steps away. "We need an urgent meeting with Uncle Albert and Babushka so that we can bring up the day of the attack. We're in a race against time now and have to get Kirill before he's able to get us."

⸙

Three days later, Anton, a dozen mercenaries, and I fly to New York.

My stomach has been upset since we landed. I'd like to blame it on cabin pressure, but I know that's far from the truth.

I'm back to the place I left in tears not two months ago, and the reminder that I'll probably also go home in tears squeezes my chest.

But that would mean I'd at least have closure.

At last.

Maybe the previous six—almost seven—years of my life will

finally have an ending. Maybe the nightmares about my family's death will finally vanish.

Though, that's wishful thinking.

The more realistic scenario is that I'll feel emptier than ever. I'll lose my sense of purpose and have…nothing.

I'll stand at the top of an abyss and long for the bottom.

All these years, I've resisted the urge to end it all, because I had to get revenge. Justice.

After this trip, I'll have nothing to stop me from giving in to the urge and embracing nothingness.

Right now, I'm standing at the top of a cliff—a literal one. Under the bright moonlight slipping in and out of trees, it appears steep, nearly bottomless.

If someone were to fall down there, they'd die.

Maybe this is my abyss.

"Sasha."

I slowly turn around to face my brother. We're wearing similar black combat clothes, the only difference being that he's putting on a balaclava.

As he checks his weapon, my lips part.

Seeing him in this outfit brings back memories of an incident we never found an explanation for.

"Were you the one who masterminded the attack before the shipment? The one who held the gun at Kirill's head at the top of that container?"

He doesn't lift his head. "And I would've killed him if you hadn't foolishly defended him and even shot me."

I wince. "You had a vest on."

"Is that a sorry?"

"Sorry," I murmur.

No one, not even Kirill, would've suspected that one of his most loyal men, Yuri, who he thought was searching for him, would hold him at gunpoint.

Now that I think about it, Yuri was uncharacteristically frowning during the entire trip back home.

He also wore his jacket closed, probably to hide a certain gunshot.

But there's something else I remember so vividly, even when I was stupidly emotional over the prospect of Kirill being hurt.

"You…hesitated."

My brother slowly lifts his head from his arm. "I did not."

"You did. He had no ammunition and you could've shot him in the head right then and there, and while you hit him, you didn't deliver the death blow. Is that maybe because…you also liked him? Or you didn't believe he could be behind the massacre?"

"Don't be fucking ridiculous. You're the one who interrupted me before I could kill him."

"You had other chances to get rid of him, but you took none."

"I'll definitely take this one if you don't shoot him between the eyes."

"But you didn't do it before."

"I didn't have evidence before. I got it after he set out to kill you and the rest of our family."

"That's fair enough."

Is it wrong that I take solace in the fact that Anton also fell for Kirill's charms? He probably also hesitated because he didn't want to hurt him.

And he thought that maybe Uncle Albert's evidence wasn't absolute.

My brother clutches me by the shoulder. "Can I count on you for this?"

I nod.

"There can't be any mistakes, Sasha."

"I know. We'll finally get revenge."

"Finally," he says with a level of conviction similar to my own. Barely there. Dismal. Filled with tension that neither of us will admit the reason behind. "We'll go back home after this."

"What's the point, though?"

"What?"

"Babushka and Uncle want us to keep fighting within Russia. Take up arms again and go against the government. We'll have to train men and spend the rest of our lives in a hopeless attempt to gain back control."

"We're getting revenge."

"I'm so sick and tired of that word. Aren't you?"

"It's my duty."

"Well, it's not mine anymore. This is the last thing I'll do for the family. I won't spend the rest of my life chasing a pipe dream or stand by and watch Mike being groomed into another version of you."

He sighs deeply. "You're awfully outspoken today."

"I learned from Maks."

His jaw clenches, but his mask soon slips back into place. "Let's get this over with first and then we'll talk."

The plan is fairly simple.

According to the intel Uncle Albert gathered, Kirill is having a meeting with one of the higher-ups in the Irish mafia here.

They've been at odds with the Bratva for all their lives, but the new leader is somehow fond of Kirill and is apparently ready to end the war. His beef was with the Sokolovs, as in, Sergei and his brother before him, but now that Kirill is Pakhan, the equation is changing.

Ironically, Kirill was the one who incited the war in the first place, just so he could keep his promise to Damien to give him something entertaining.

Now, he'll use this chance to engrave his position as the best leader the Bratva could ever have. The others won't have a reason to vote him out if he's bringing both peace and profits.

His dream of leadership is finally coming true. At least up until now.

Because I'll shatter everything he's worked for—including his life.

Anton and the other men will intercept Kirill's guards while I take care of him.

Just me.

After Anton and I separate, I climb a tree near the cliff and position my rifle in front of me. I'm not going to shoot him from a distance. No, I'll do it while looking into his cold eyes.

This is in case someone else intervenes.

Anton and the others have my back, but something could go wrong.

I sent a text to Maksim asking him not to come and to make sure as few men as possible attend this mission.

His reply was strange.

> **Maksim:** Can't you stop this and talk it out? Just fifteen minutes will do as long as you hear his side of the argument. Everything isn't as you thought, Sasha.

> **Sasha:** I'm done talking to him and there's no excuse he can offer that'll dissuade me from this.

> **Maksim:** In that case, I'll be there.

I'd really hoped he would change his mind. If he and Anton actually end up killing one another, the one who remains alive will be damaged for life.

And I'll have to hate them, too.

But I don't allow myself to think of that right now as I breathe in through my nose and out through my mouth. Gunshots sound in the distance and I tense.

Shit.

My heart beats loudly and I realize that I'm not terrified about the lives of the mercenaries who came with us. Aside from my brother, I couldn't give a fuck about them.

I'm actually shaking at the prospect that the men I knew and trained with for years are dying because of me.

What if Maksim is one of them? Or even Viktor?

Shit.

Shit.

Maybe this wasn't such a good idea, after all. Would I be able to live with myself if I knew I'd caused their deaths? They had nothing to do with my family's massacre and yet they're paying the price.

No.

It's not me.

It's Kirill who dragged them into this, knowing full well that he's leading them to their certain demise.

Something rustles to my right and I direct my rifle in that direction, my muscles tensing. It disappears, but then it appears again from the south, out of my range.

I hold on to my position, but I can't see the reason behind the commotion. Did some of Kirill's men manage to escape my brother?

The movement happens again, almost like a rustling of trees. If I shoot, I'll give away my position and that's a no-go if I don't have a definite target.

Carefully, I sling the rifle across my chest and slide down the tree.

The moment my feet touch the ground, a shiver rushes down my spine as warmth envelops my back and hot words penetrate my ears. "Miss me, wife?"

TEN

Sasha

I DON'T MEAN FOR IT TO, BUT MY WHOLE BODY GOES INTO A state of shock.

I know because breathing becomes a chore that I have to remind myself to do, and even then, it's chopped off and choked up.

I know because goosebumps erupt on my skin that ignites at the proximity of his warmth. It doesn't matter that it's been over two months since I last saw him.

One encounter.

A few words.

His presence.

And it's like we haven't spent a day apart.

My stupid dead heart pulses as if it's attempting to resurrect itself from the ashes.

I've dreaded this moment for weeks, the moment where I have to clash with the only man I've ever loved. The man I gave my heart to on a silver platter, only for him to crush it in the palm of his hand.

But I never thought I'd be shaking with emotions like I am right now.

Rage.

Betrayal.

Hate.

But more than anything—fucking disappointment clogs my throat.

I think there's something wrong with me lately, because I have all these strong feelings that don't allow me the peace of sleep anymore.

And it's all because of him.

The man who's casually standing behind me and has the fucking audacity to call me his wife.

His damn wife is Kristina, not me.

I swing around and simultaneously jump back while lifting my rifle and pointing it at him.

I expect him to point his gun back. After all, even if this is an ambush, Maksim already told him that I'm coming for his life.

Someone like Kirill doesn't think death applies to him. He's lived his entire life cheating it and manipulating it to his own advantage.

By feeding the Grim Reaper multiple lives, he's managed to escape his clutches over and over again.

So when I see him just stand there, one nonchalant hand in his pocket and the other hanging at his side, I'm taken aback.

There's no weapon or the hint that he'll use one.

Just like his voice invaded my ear just now, his presence does something a lot worse.

Now, it does feel like I haven't seen him in ages.

In the semi-darkness, his face looks harsher, and his jaw is more angular. A subtle gleam covers his usually emotionless eyes, shining from beneath the glasses, but his mouth is set in a neutral line.

Stubble covers his cheeks, and it adds a layer of mysterious danger to his already terrifying existence. The jacket stretches against his shoulders, but it looks like he lost some weight, and I hate that I notice that.

His gaze measures me from my feet up to my face, not bothering to pause at the weapon I'm pointing at him. I keep my glare even as a smile breaks on his lips.

Kirill isn't the type who smiles—at least, not genuinely—so to be a witness to this version of him makes bile rise to my throat.

"It's really you." His voice drips with what can only be described as...awe. Disbelief, maybe.

No. *Relief.*

"You thought you got rid of me?" I snap, unable to control the overwhelming rage flooding my veins.

How dare he look okay after he blew my world to smithereens?

How dare he look at me like when I married him after he stood at the altar with someone else?

I didn't expect him to be an emotional mess like I was every fucking night, but I'd at least hoped he'd be rattled a little.

Brought down a peg or two.

Something.

Anything.

I'm getting absolutely nothing.

"Too bad for you I didn't die that day you sent people to blow up the cottage."

His brow furrows. "What the fuck are you talking about? Why would I send someone to kill my wife?"

"So you could have a second wife."

He laughs, the sound vaguely amused at best. "Sasha... Sasha...your problem is that you always take things too seriously and at face value." He pulls his hand from his pocket and I tense, thinking it's a weapon, but he lifts it up so I can see.

Something glints in the air and my lips part when I make out the ring I put on his finger during our sham wedding.

Why does he have it?

No. This is another tactic of his to destabilize me. Drive me more insane than I thought would be possible.

"*You* are my wife."

I snort, feeling my expression close off until it's too tight to even speak, but I force the words out. "If you think I'll fall for that, then you've really overestimated your abilities, Kirill. What a shame. Seems your new position and life have taken away your critical thinking."

"Something did, all right, but it's neither my new position nor my new life." He pauses and glares at me as if *he* is the wronged one. "It was your fake death. You got me there, but it won't happen again."

"Nothing will happen again. As I said, I'm going to kill you today. For everything you've done not only to me, but also to my family, I'm taking revenge."

"Are you now?" His tone sounds light, amused, as he takes a step forward.

I lift my rifle, my hands steady. "Not another move or I'll shoot you."

"Do it." He taps his chest. "Right here so it's fatal this time."

My chin trembles. What the hell is he doing?

Is this another tactic? Will I be ambushed by Viktor or someone else who's hiding in the bushes?

Will he try to disarm me or shoot me with some gun he's hidden?

I tighten my hold on the rifle, finger hovering over the trigger. "I'm not falling for that."

"Falling for what? You said you'll shoot me and I'm telling you to do it."

"Is that all you have to say for yourself?"

"I didn't realize there was an open submission box for excuses."

"Don't fuck with me, Kirill!" I inhale and exhale heavily in a hopeless attempt to bring my breathing back to normal. "What do you have to say for your actions? I won't believe you, but let's hear it. Let's hear the reasons you thought it was fun to play with me all this time."

"You already said you won't believe anything I say, so why should I bother? Since you obviously came here with a sole mission in mind—killing me. Why don't you get on with it?"

"You asshole…" My voice breaks before I recover it. "You won't even try?"

"You're my only wife. I only wanted to reach an agreement with your family due to that fact. I went behind your back because I knew you'd never allow such a meeting to happen. I didn't try to kill you and never will. I've been going fucking crazy for the past couple of months until the moment Maksim said you were alive. I only half believed him until I saw you just now. There. I tried. Do you believe me?"

He says the words with an ease that's hard to take seriously, let alone believe.

He's telling me what I want to hear just so he can play with me again.

Fool me *again*.

This time, kill me for real.

He takes another step forward.

"I told you to stop!" I yell, my voice raw, as if I've been screaming for days.

"I won't. Not now, not ever. You're my wife and you belong by my side."

"Fuck you, Kirill. If you think I'll ever go back to you, or that I feel the slightest affection toward you, then you must've really lost your touch."

"If you don't feel any affection toward me, then shoot me. That's the only way to stop me from having you." He takes another

step, slowly, intentionally, as if he doesn't see the rifle in my hand
or my shaking finger on the trigger.

"Stop!"

"Make me stop."

"You were behind my family's death. I will kill you!"

"The real person behind your family's death could be a traitor,
but you're not ready for that conversation."

"If you take one more step, I'm going to kill you. I swear I will."

"Why? Because you're scared that if we touch, you'll remember that you only ever belonged to me? Not your family, not your
duty, fucking me."

"This is my last warning…" Sweat dampens my temples and
upper lip. I'm tasting bile on my tongue as my finger trembles.

"You're giving an awful lot of chances to someone you claim
you hold no affection toward." He reaches a hand to my face, ignoring the rifle that's now pressing against his chest.

Where his heart is.

The heart I never had a place in, no matter how much I tried.

The heart that never accepted me, even though mine is full
of him.

Before that stupid organ softens, before he can touch me, I
lift the rifle higher and pull the trigger.

My chest falls as he flies sideways and blood explodes on his
right arm from the gash in his skin. It trickles down to his limp
hand—the hand he tried to touch me with.

My heart that I thought was long dead bleeds at the view.

Fuck.

Shit.

Goddammit!

How am I supposed to kill him if I feel like I just shot myself
by merely hurting his arm?

Kirill groans, his face contorting, but he doesn't attempt to
stop the bleeding. I made sure not to hit a major artery, but I

must've shot a minor one because blood is still flowing from the wound.

Instead of getting help or even shooting me back, he gains back the few steps he lost and reaches his left hand toward my face.

"What the fuck is wrong with you?" I point my rifle at his left shoulder keeping him an arm's length away.

"You."

"Stay away from me!"

"I can't. You're my wife. Till death do us part, remember?"

"Have you lost your mind?"

"Probably."

"Kirill, stay away, I mean it."

"I won't. I mean it. You can shoot my other arm and I will walk to you. If you take my legs, I'll crawl to you."

"Are you crazy?"

"When it comes to you? Possibly." He pushes against the rifle with impossible strength, considering his right arm is fucked. "So unless you kill me, you won't be able to stop me."

I see it then.

In the depths of his arctic eyes that could freeze someone to death.

He means every word. If I don't put a bullet in his heart or head, he'll chase me relentlessly.

Until either I kill him or he possesses me.

And that's terrifying because at this point, I don't know which one is more likely to come true.

I'd hate myself in both cases.

I lift my rifle and shoot the sky, and just like that, a long, raw scream rips out of my lungs.

Until I nearly lose my voice.

Until my heart metaphorically spills out on the ground.

When I look back at Kirill, he's watching me with keen interest. His right arm is limp, dripping blood on the ground, but his complete, unwavering attention never leaves me.

I drop the rifle, letting it hang at my chest and glare at him.

"You can't kill me," he says it like a declaration.

No. An affirmation.

"You better think carefully about your next words, because they might be the last you say, asshole."

He offers me his left palm. "Let's go home and talk about it."

The audacity of this motherfucker.

Why can't I shoot him again?

"That's not thinking carefully, Kirill. Do you have a death wish?"

"Not particularly, but the only option on the table right now is for you to come with me."

"You're demented if you think I'll go anywhere with you."

"How else will you allow me to change your mind?"

"Nothing you do will make me change my mind."

"We'll agree to disagree."

"Can you stop being so calm about this? Why…just why are you like this when I'm going crazy?"

"If I don't force myself to be calm, I'm going to fuck you like a savage in the middle of the forest and punish you for all the time I've spent without you. But since I assume that's highly unlikely to happen, I have to be civil."

My teeth grind together. "You call this civil?"

"You know how I act when I don't get what I want, so yes, this is fucking civil. For now."

"What the hell is that supposed to mean?"

"Come home with me, Solnyshko."

"Don't fucking call me that!" I snap.

"Fine, are you coming?"

"No."

"You're my wife, Sasha. You belong with me."

"I belong anywhere but with you." Even if I don't know where the hell that is.

My family's patience has limits. If I go back after being unable to kill Kirill, Anton will do it and they'll kick me out.

I'll have nothing.

"Last attempt at being civil." He motions at his palm. "Take it."

"I said no."

"Very well. Don't say I didn't warn you." He slides his hand in his pocket, brings out his phone, and awkwardly types with one hand, then he shows me a picture of Anton, bound and gagged, blood trickling down his temple.

"No…" I point my rifle at him. "I'll kill you right now if you don't release him."

"Kill me and he's dead."

"You fucking monster!"

"I'm fine with being that." He pockets his phone. "I brought an army here, Sasha. Neither you nor your brother could've left."

"It was supposed to be only me and you."

"It is only me and you. Always was and always will be. I just made sure there would be no *complications*, for lack of a better term."

"As in, you trapped us."

"I prefer, I took you back. The only way to keep your brother alive is being with me."

"How dare you—"

"How fucking dare *you*?" His voice lowers to a frightening edge. "How dare you fake your death on me, leave me, plot against me, and show up to announce you'll kill me? Did you think I'd let that slide?"

"Don't talk like a victim when you stabbed me in the back!"

"I never did. You made up your own dramas based on your motherfucking insecurities." He releases a breath. "But that doesn't matter now. We're going home."

"Let Anton go."

"Not unless you come with me and stay with me."

"For how long?"

"There's no deadline for a marriage, Sasha."

"Yes, there is. It's called a divorce and I want one."

His jaw clenches and his eyes darken to a monstrous color. "No."

"Then I'm not going with you."

"I'll kill your brother."

"Then I will kill you and hate you forever."

"Don't fuck with me, Sasha."

"Three months."

"What?"

"In three months, you'll give me a divorce and we'll be out of each other's lives."

He starts to give his irritating knee-jerk response of 'No,' but I lift a hand. "It's either that or you give me a divorce right now. Your choice."

"Very well played." He says it with tension, even as he smiles and offers his hand again. "Take it, wife."

I slap it out of the way and say as I brush past him, "I'm not your wife, Kirill. I'm your future ex-wife."

ELEVEN

Kirill

SASHA IS ALIVE.

My wife isn't lying six feet under in a cold grave.

I buried her bones with my own hands and forced myself to look at her disfigured skeletal face because I thought that was the last time I'd see her.

Even if she didn't look like my Sasha anymore, I had to engrave the last image of her in my memory.

But it turns out that it was all an act to fool me.

She wanted to leave me so badly that she faked her own death and, consequently, drove a sharp spear into my chest.

The wound is gaping open and bleeding worse than the literal bullet she put in my arm.

Yes, she shot me, but it was less because she wanted to kill me and more because she was scared I'd touch her.

The mere thought of my skin on hers terrified her so much

that it triggered her defense mechanism. Her non-dominant leg was literally bent back in case she decided to run.

I wonder if she had the same reaction when she decided to leave me that fake corpse.

More accurately, she probably thought she'd left me for good.

That she can still leave me.

In her fucking dreams.

The only reason I agreed to her absurd three-month condition is because that was the only way to make her come with me.

Do I plan to keep my part of the deal? Fuck no.

But she doesn't need to know that.

I catch up to her forceful strides but linger a step behind to admire the way her combat clothes stretch over the dip in her waist and her hips.

For the first time—probably ever—she's wearing women's combat gear instead of the unflattering male ones.

She's dyed her hair back to blonde. It's now held in a low ponytail that stops at her shoulders. I knew her hair grew fast, but I didn't realize it was this fast.

I've often tried to imagine her with her natural hair color, but none of the pictures I've conjured in my brain have done her justice.

She's glowing as a blonde.

Also fierce.

Angry as fuck, too.

And that makes my dick twitch with the need to fuck that anger out of both of us.

Yes, I could've chosen not to make things worse and not taken Yuri—sorry, I mean Anton—but there was virtually no other method to force her to stay.

She might not have killed me, but she would've tortured me by another highly effective method—disappearing on me.

Forbidding me from seeing her ever again.

She would've vanished to where I couldn't find her and punished both of us for the rest of our lives.

And we can't have that, now, can we?

I take a step in front of her and lead her to where I parked the car. Sasha doesn't look at me, keeping her entire focus on the faraway horizon or the trees that are indistinguishable in the dark.

She's either escaping in her mind or giving me the silent treatment or both.

Not that I mind. I didn't expect her to come around this fast, but as long as she's here, I can come up with multiple methods to win her back.

When we arrive at the car, I open the driver's door with my good hand. However, my wound pulses with pain that travels all the way to my chest. I groan deep in my throat and close my eyes for a brief second to control the discomfort.

The bleeding isn't as severe as earlier, but there's still hemorrhaging, and I might have lost more blood than my body can afford to.

I'm still not interested in treating it until I get Sasha back home. What if she runs off on me again?

In the mansion, I have enough power to stop her from leaving.

She steps between me and the driver's door. Her face is still closed off, lips pursed, and brows pulled together in an adorable frown. "I'll drive."

I smile. "Worried about me?"

"More like I don't want to get into an accident if you drop dead against the steering wheel."

"You wound me in my little black heart, Solnyshko."

She grinds her teeth and glares up at me with her ethereal eyes. They look brown now, dark, and infested with an unhealthy dose of hate.

Her face is soft and delicate but a bit pale. She's lost weight and some of her natural glow. Dark circles line the contours of her tired eyes.

I hope she's suffered as badly as I have.

I hope she couldn't fucking sleep at night, and I infiltrated her nightmares as brutally as she invaded mine.

She sinks her fingers into my wound and then digs them inside with the intention of inflicting pain. "I told you to stop calling me that."

I groan as my arm catches fire and pulses. Yes, it hurts, but I don't give a fuck. "It feels good when you touch me."

Sasha releases me with a jerk, her hand all messed up with my blood. If we add my cum to the equation, it will look like a masterpiece.

But that's a thought for another occasion.

"You must really have some screws loose." She clicks her tongue. "How come you're not threatening me back with bodily harm?"

"You're the only one on the list of people I refrain from threatening."

"Funny because you're holding my brother's life for ransom."

"That's a different issue."

"How is it different? You know what? Forget it. You'll just twist the words around so that the situation plays in your favor, and it'll just piss me off more. Let's get this over with."

I smile.

She really is able to read me better than anyone else. Not even Viktor and his shadowing skills could measure up to her.

Sasha is trying to have a clean break, but she's failing miserably. The more I hear her talk, the deeper she gets herself into the exact situation she's running away from.

I will never—and I mean *ever*—let her go.

Not even if I have to suffocate her in the process.

She puts her rifle in the back and settles into the driver's seat as I struggle to get in.

Sasha reaches into the glove compartment, her hand touching my thigh, and that slight movement twitches my dick against its confinement.

It's been too long since I got a taste of her and let's just say my cock has been having a strained affair with my hand that he's ready to end.

My wife retrieves a first aid kit and then turns me around so that I'm facing her. She doesn't look at me as she wraps a bandage around my bicep and over the gash she gave me as a reunion gift. The first few wraps soak with blood immediately, but she keeps going while applying pressure.

Her brow is furrowed, but I can't help the smile that lifts my lips.

It doesn't matter how long we've been apart; she'll always worry about me and make sure I'm not hurt.

"Your care is touching."

"Get over yourself. If you die, Viktor will kill Anton. This is only for my brother."

"Hmm. We'll have to agree to have different definitions for this gesture—fuck."

Sasha smiles sweetly after she ties the bandage against my injury and then practically throws my arm aside.

She wants to prove that she could and would hurt me? Fine. I'll let her do that to her heart's content.

"Oh, I'm sorry." She feigns innocence. "Did that *hurt?*"

"Anything for my beautiful wife." I smile even as pain throbs in my arm and extends to the rest of my body.

Her humor disappears, and she hits the engine button and then speeds down the dirt road.

She's caught off-balance.

Good.

As long as I still affect her, I'll get to her. Whether it's today, tomorrow, or next month. I don't give a fuck.

One day, she'll get tired of this silent treatment kink and go back to other entertaining kinks.

I lean on the headrest and stare at her as she drives with pursed lips and hawk-like concentration.

The more I watch, the tighter she grips the steering wheel. It's subtle at first, but in no time, her knuckles turn white.

"Stop looking at me like that," she grinds out without looking at me.

"Like what?"

She casts a fleeting glance my way and waves her hand in a vague gesture. "Like whatever that is."

"This is me getting my fill of you after two months of believing you were dead."

Her attention remains on the road, but her lips part before she clamps them shut again. "How did you fall for that? Just because I left the ring and the bracelet?"

"The DNA test was a perfect match. I suppose you falsified it so your careful plot would drive me up the fucking wall." The fact that I didn't double-check the DNA results makes me want to strangle the me from two months ago.

"I...didn't falsify anything."

"Maybe your damn brother did." I can't believe I didn't see the Yuri angle coming.

According to Maksim, Anton Ivanov switched places with my guard after his 'accident.' Yuri didn't want to join me and the others when I decided to go to the army, so I found it weird that he caught up to us later. However, it wasn't weird enough to suspect him since a few other men did the same.

I'd barely noticed him before. He was incompetent and slow. But after he followed us post-accident, it was like a different person had come along.

Turns out, that's exactly what happened.

He fooled me in the sense of his loyalty, but for some reason, I always kept him at arm's length, compared to, say, Viktor or Maksim. I liked his plans, but I always made my own tweaks before I employed them.

I also never sent him on solo missions or let him in on the Belsky Organization investigation I assigned Viktor with.

Maybe I didn't suspect him, but something inside me was wary of him. For all the right reasons.

He's good, though. Not only did he manage to fool me, but his own sister and best friend didn't know either.

Now, I need to decide how to deal with the motherfucker.

The trickiest part is that he's related to Sasha, and I can't exactly kill him and still have her.

"No, he didn't," she says to my earlier statement. "We barely had time to plant the corpse. How could we falsify the DNA when we were in Russia?"

Hmm.

Interesting.

Since she has no reason to lie, that means someone else did it.

Namely, the one who got in bed with the Albanians to plot her death. If the person who did this could plant the DNA test so effectively, that means they might be a lot closer than I thought.

Now, I have to rip their hearts out and watch as life leaves their miserable eyes.

The nerve of making me believe she'd died.

The fucking audacity.

By the time we arrive at the house, I'm boiling with a flood of rage.

At Sasha for daring to leave.

At the fucker who must've been watching from the shadows as I slowly decimated into the abyss of nothingness.

They must've been laughing as their plan came to fruition.

I hope they're also watching now as I bring Sasha back. I won't look for them. Sooner or later, they'll let their true colors shine through.

Sasha opens the door with more force than needed and jumps out as if she can't stand being with me in the same space for another second.

Fuck that.

I refuse to believe that she forgot us in the span of two months.

Unless she never really loved you, and she really did have a lover that she went back to.

I shut down that sadistic voice and step out of the car. The moment I stand, dizziness takes hold of me, and I slam against the side of the vehicle.

Did I overestimate my ability to not bleed out? Probably.

Sasha rushes in my direction, then stops at the last second and clenches her fists as if recalling that she shouldn't be caring about my well-being anymore.

"Can't keep it together?" She inserts as much venom as possible in her words, but it sounds strained, fake.

"I might die," I say with a fake groan.

"Good. Less evil in the world."

"Will you cry for me if I do?"

"No." She lifts her chin. "In fact, I might celebrate."

"You look adorable when you say things you don't mean." I touch her cheek with the backs of two of my fingers, and she freezes. I freeze, too, as a rush of chaotic emotions stabs me in the chest.

It's a mere touch, but it's enough to kill all the dark thoughts I had after I saw her fake corpse.

For the first time in months, I breathe fresh air.

For the first time in months, I feel everything.

She's here.

She's mine again—even if she'd argue otherwise.

Her wide eyes fill with fire, and she slaps my hand away. The gesture stings more than the hit itself.

If it were any other time, I'd grab her by the throat, tie her up, and fuck her for the insolence.

But considering the circumstances, I let it go.

For now.

"Don't touch me." Her voice drips with tension.

"You're awfully terrified of my touching you. Have you noticed that?"

She shoots me another glare, which seems to be her modus operandi today, then storms to the house.

I'm about to follow when my phone vibrates. It's Viktor.

It takes me more effort than needed to answer. "Status."

"All cleaned out. We're keeping Anton—aka the fake Yuri—under surveillance. Should we torture him for answers?"

"No. He probably won't talk." And I don't want to lose points with Sasha if she finds out I've been beating her brother up.

"Maksim wants to guard him personally."

Hmm.

There's been something different about him ever since he came back from Russia. It's like his soul was crushed, and he struggled to put himself back together again.

He hasn't joked around with the others and has spent more time alone or with me and Viktor—which is out of character for him. And most importantly, he's thrown himself into his work again as if nothing had happened. In the beginning, I thought it was because of the torture, but I've come to the conclusion that it could be more.

Like being betrayed by who he thought was his best friend.

And who am I if I don't deliver poetic justice? This way, I'm not torturing Anton or giving the order for him to be tortured.

Maksim will have complete responsibility for it.

"Let Maksim have full custody of him," I tell Viktor.

After I hang up, I walk to the mansion's entrance, my steps heavy as fuck.

By the time I catch up to Sasha, a loud gasp echoes in the air, and then Karina is running down the stairs. The little shit trips on her nightgown and falls a few steps, but she catches herself and continues to run the rest of the way.

"Sasha! Oh my God, Sasha!" She throws herself in my wife's arms. "Please tell me it's you and that I didn't actually summon you with the voodoo I performed to call your spirit."

She did *what?*

"It's me." Sasha pats her head with her clean hand.

My sister doesn't seem to notice me or my near-unconscious state as she pulls back. Tears cling to her eyes as she smiles wide even as her voice shakes. "It's really you."

"How have you been, Kara?"

"Don't give me that!" She hits her shoulder. "How could you make us believe you'd died? Don't you know how much you mean to me?"

Little by little, emotions slip into Sasha's gaze. An acute sense of guilt turns her eyes a deep shade of yellow that wars with the brown.

This isn't me. This is Karina.

She did nothing to her, but Sasha hurt her and others by faking her death. My wife is slowly but surely realizing her mistake.

"I'm sorry," she whispers. "I didn't do it on purpose, and I really thought you'd find out the body wasn't me."

"Just don't do it again, okay?" Karina hugs her once more, and while Sasha tries to remain unaffected, her shoulders droop.

Now, I know it's inappropriate, but I still want to throw my sister against the wall so that I can take her place.

On the other hand, Karina might be one of the methods I'll use to keep Sasha here.

You get a pass, Kara. For now.

"Kara?" Kristina appears up the stairs. She's actually been getting along with my sister, especially after Karina learned she'd be an aunt soon.

Sasha turns into stone as she stares up at Kristina, who's slowly taking the stairs down.

Huh.

I was about to collapse a minute ago, but I think I'll stick around and watch this show unfold in real time.

Sasha pretends she doesn't want me, but the look in her eyes says she wants to strangle Kristina to death.

My wife can lie all she wants, but I'll bring her back.

TWELVE

Sasha

MY BODY TENSES. The back of my throat feels dry and sandpaper-like.

Everything heightens.

My nostrils flood with Karina's lavender perfume and the metallic stench of blood.

My ears fill with a shrill sound, as if I'm standing in the aftermath of a bomb.

It dawns on me then.

This is my fight-or-flight response.

I should go for the latter, but why are my fingers twitching to reach for my gun and put a bullet in her head?

It's not her you should shoot, it's the stupid asshole you couldn't kill.

It's not her fault that he chose her over you.

Both of those are legitimate arguments, but does my bleeding heart listen? *Absolutely not.*

In fact, I find myself illogically comparing myself to her. Where she's wearing an elegant dark red dress and has her hair styled to perfection, I'm in a stupid combat uniform, and my hair is held so tight, my scalp hurts.

Where she's wearing natural-looking makeup and soft pink lipstick, I'm makeup-free, and my lips are chapped and dry.

We might both be women, but we're in different leagues.

I bet she can't shoot a gun to save her life, though. So there's that.

Kristina watches me peculiarly as she reaches the bottom of the stairs. She must be wondering why Kirill's guard is now a woman.

Or maybe she's heard about me. Did she feel any of the fire that's been eating me from the inside out when she saw that ring on his finger?

Though that unfeeling asshole Kirill could've gotten identical rings, and the one he's wearing could have her name engraved within.

Karina pulls away from me, and I don't know if it's because Kristina called her name or because she felt me tense against her.

Is it wrong that I feel a bit vindictive that Kristina is on a diminutive form level with Karina? I thought she didn't make friends easily and I was her only one. But like her damn brother, she didn't seem to have any trouble quickly replacing me.

Karina grabs her by the arm and grins at me. "Sasha, this is my new sister-in-law, Kris!"

My stomach falls, and I try to swallow, but it's blocked by the ball stuck in my throat. I side-eye the fucking liar Kirill, who's casually leaning against a pillar, ankles crossed and a knowing smirk painting his lips.

Only wife, my ass.

I can't believe the level he was willing to drop to just to get what he wanted.

"Also, also!" Karina pats Kristina's stomach. "She's carrying my baby niece."

A blush covers Kristina's cheeks. "We still don't know the gender, Kara."

"Don't care. I only accept baby girls. I already started shopping for pink."

Did…I hear that correctly?

Is Kristina pregnant? Already?

Nausea explodes at the back of my throat, and I physically shudder.

I think I'm going to throw up.

"Oh, Kirill." Kristina walks up to him. "You look pale, and your bandage is all soaked with blood. Shouldn't you see the doctor?"

She places her hand on his arm, and I think I'm losing the battle, because I'm already reaching for my gun.

Stop touching him.

Or I'm really going to kill him now.

I'll make your damn child fatherless before it's born.

"Don't worry about him." Karina scoffs. "He's like a cat with nine lives who refuses to die already."

"Kara!" Kristina scoffs softly.

She still has her hand on his arm.

Stop touching him.

Stop fucking touching him—

My thoughts come to a halt when Kirill's lips slowly tug in a smirk. He slides his gaze to my hand that's on my waistband. I hate that he knows exactly what I'm going to do.

I hate that he can read me this easily, and there's nothing I can do to stop that from happening.

"At least you have the courtesy to worry about me, dear sister-in-law." His brows draw together. "My actual wife is heartless and couldn't care less whether I live or die."

What…?

Sister-in-law?

"What the fuck happened to you?" Konstantin walks in from the entrance and stops at the view of Kirill bleeding and barely standing.

He holds Kristina by the waist and kisses the top of her head.

"A little dispute," Kirill says in his usual provocative yet amused voice.

My mouth is open, and my hand drops from the back of my pants.

It's safe to say I don't have the slightest clue about what the hell is going on here.

"Sasha." Konstantin grins with contagious happiness. "You're alive."

"Sort of," I whisper.

"And I was wondering why Kirill didn't have demons whirling around him by the dozens." He walks toward me and pats my shoulder. "Welcome back."

"Thanks." I stare between him and Kristina. "Are you guys… married?"

"Yeah." They look at each other with a deep sense of affection that slices my heart open. Probably because I used to give Kirill that naïve look before he stabbed me in the back.

"Wasn't Kristina…supposed to marry Kirill?"

"He plotted that whole thing to bring us together," Kristina says softly and looks at Kirill with deep gratitude.

Someone is actually grateful to the monster.

I must've landed in an alternative reality.

And yet I can't help the sense of relief that washes through me at the knowledge that he never married her. She's not pregnant with his child, and she loves his brother.

The asshole knew this all along, but he still enjoyed playing with my emotions. It's probably a test of sorts for him.

It's always a test with Kirill.

Everyone and everything is.

"Congratulations." My low voice carries in the entrance, and it actually sounds as if I'm being honest.

And I am.

I just don't know what to make of the situation anymore. All this time, I've held on to the sense of his betrayal as fuel for my hatred.

Every night, I've dreamed about him at that altar with Kristina. I've had nightmares about their happy lives together after I was out of the picture.

But now that I'm seeing for myself that they were never a couple, I have no clue how to keep my hatred and rage at the same level.

A significant amount has been purged from my system, and I'm not sure I'll be able to restore it in the foreseeable future.

"Kirill!" Konstantin leaves his wife's side and catches his brother just before he falls to the ground.

I lunge forward but only manage to stop myself a few steps in. Yes, old habits die hard, but why the hell do I still view myself as his protector?

Even after I put a bullet in his arm?

Konstantin holds his unconscious body upright with difficulty. Karina jogs to them, her expression morphing from contempt to worry in no time.

Kirill's face is pale, and his lips are changing color. Not only that, but the blood has also soaked the bandage and is dripping on the floor.

An illogical part of me is uncomfortable, and I'm not sure if it's due to Kirill losing consciousness or the fact that I'm the reason behind the scene in front of me.

I release a long breath.

No. I'm not doing this anymore. I'm just *not*.

The only reason I'm here is to save my brother.

Once that's done, I'll leave Kirill in a heartbeat.

While Kirill is getting treated in the clinic, I go to search for my brother in the basement where Kirill usually keeps the prisoners.

My hands shake when I pass by the room in which we got married.

The room was both my nightmare during that captivity period but also the place for the happiest time of my life.

I keep searching, but the entire basement is empty. There's no trace of Anton, or anyone else, for that matter.

If Viktor isn't here, then my brother isn't here either.

I know there's a warehouse where Kirill prefers to torture people for answers, but since I'm aware of its location, I doubt he took him there, either.

God forbid the control freak miss any detail. When I go back upstairs, I expect to find Karina since she refused to go to the clinic with Konstantin and Kristina despite having a trembling chin.

However, the person who greets me is none other than Anna. She's carrying a stack of clothes and standing near the stairs as if she was waiting for me.

It hasn't been that long since I last saw her, but she's gained a few wrinkles, and her eyes have lost some of the sharp gleam that was a massive part of her personality.

"Hi, Anna," I say slowly.

"Don't hi me, young lady." She pushes the clothes into my hand. "Here are some of Mrs. Kristina's clothes that she asked me to give you. She figured you're closer to her in height and body type than Miss Karina."

My fingers tighten around the clothes. "Thanks."

I guess that means Kristina is the one who alerted her about my arrival.

Anna reaches into her apron pocket and retrieves a key. "This is for Kirill's master bedroom. He's kept it locked for two months and only gave me the key so I could oversee the cleaning."

He…kept his room closed for two months?

She places the key on top of the clothes. "I don't know what's going on between you two, but he better not turn back into whatever bloodthirsty demon he was after you left."

"What…do you mean?"

"For the first month, he came home soaked with blood. Every single night. Viktor said he was looking for the one responsible for your death and that he was even killing anyone who proved to be useless in his search. Every night, he'd stop in front of his room, touch the door, and then go to his new room. Every night, I had to throw away bloodied clothes because there was no way of salvaging them."

My fingers tighten around the clothes. On one hand, Anna has no reason to lie. In fact, she's honest to the point of being blunt and doesn't stoop to lying.

But on the other hand, I can't possibly trust Kirill again. Maybe he did those things for an entirely different reason than the obvious.

Anna hikes a hand on her hip. "Today better be the last day I get a new batch of bloodied clothes."

"I don't think I can control Kirill's mood and decisions."

"You're the only one who can, you naïve child."

I try not to be affected by that and fail miserably. So I rush to change the subject. "Are you going to ask why I was pretended to be a man?"

"I assumed it had something to do with your security. Which is also why Kirill kept it a secret as well."

"You…knew?"

"I suspected it after seeing you in his bed multiple times. I suspected maybe he swung in the other direction, but…well, there was no other evidence to back that theory."

"Oh." So all that time, Anna was turning a blind eye and pretending not to notice.

"Go take a shower and clean up all that blood. I'll send you some food in a bit."

"Oh, okay. Thanks."

"Welcome back, Sasha." She pats my shoulder. "Both the house and Kirill were unbearably grim without you."

My chest swells, and I resist the urge to blurt something stupid like, 'Really?'

I head to the room with heavy steps. I stop in front of the door, and I have to take a few shaky breaths before I turn the key in the lock.

When I go inside, I'm hit by multiple emotions. Everything is exactly as I left it, only there isn't one of Kirill's jackets scattered around or my chest bandages thrown on some surface.

The smell is weird, though. It doesn't smell of us anymore.

I curse to myself. Why the hell would I want it to smell like us?

I storm to the bathroom, take off my clothes, and go into the shower. As I stand beneath the stream of water, images of other activities I did in this same shower slip into my mind, and I have to close my eyes.

But that doesn't stop the erotic pictures from playing again and again, as if taunting my sexually frustrated body.

With a groan, I turn off the handle, hastily dry myself, and put on the new underwear Kristina gave me, moaning out loud when I accidentally rub my nails on a hard nipple.

Shit. What's with them being so sensitive? Is it because I'm back here when I thought I never would be?

After regaining my breathing, I put on the soft checkered nightshirt. It's tight on the hips, but it's good enough.

I go back into the bedroom and find a tray of food on the coffee table. My stomach growls, and I drink some soup and then eat some fish as I send my uncle a text.

Mission failed. Anton has been captured. I'm staying here until I can bring him home safely. Please don't interfere while I get this resolved.

I don't know if he, and especially Babushka, will agree to that. She looks at Anton as if he's the answer to all her prayers.

But they need to understand that I'm the only one who can save Anton. Knowing Kirill, he'll make sure of that.

After I finish eating, I yawn.

Today was such a long day. Probably one of the worst I've ever had.

My brother is being held captive God knows where.

I can't leave for three months.

And most importantly, I've realized with bitter irony that I can't kill Kirill. In fact, a part of me is revolting at the fact that I shot him in the first place.

It's the stupid, loyal, naïve part that completely lost it when I saw him at the bottom of that hill with a gash in his chest.

I guess I'll never forget that scene, no matter how much I try or how long it's been.

With another yawn, I lie on the bed and close my eyes. I'll just rest for a minute, and then I'll look for my brother.

Only a minute…

A strong arm wraps around me, and warmth spoons me from behind. It's a nightmare, I realize.

No, a dream.

The presence behind me doesn't feel threatening in the least. In fact, I lean into his touch, a soft moan leaving my lips.

I like the Kirill from my dreams. He doesn't talk and only allows me to use him as comfort against the haunting nightmares.

They don't come when he's cuddling me like this.

They don't interfere with this small fantasy I've been pretending I don't like.

But then the supposedly dream-like Kirill slips what feels like a ring on my finger and whispers in my ear, "Welcome home, Solnyshko."

THIRTEEN

Sasha

A HEAVY WEIGHT RESTS ON MY MIDDLE.

Instead of being a burden, it's actually comforting. I nuzzle my nose against the pillow, and my nostrils flood with the forbidden scent of deep forest and cedar.

Could it be that I'm imagining things?

That's the only explanation for this sensory overload or why I'm leaning closer to the source.

Warmth engulfs my body and spreads to my chest and core, so I inch over farther, needing more.

My movements pause when something hard nudges my stomach, poking me through my clothes.

"Mmm."

The rumble of a very familiar deep voice causes my eyes to pop open.

Please tell me this is my imagination—

No.

Nope.

It's definitely real. I'm actually trapped in Kirill's embrace, my face resting on his neck until I can almost taste his shower gel on my tongue. I realize with horror that this is what I've been smelling since I woke up.

Our fronts are glued together, and the thing that's poking my stomach? It's his erection.

Oh, and one more thing.

He's naked.

What gives him the right to touch me? Hold me as if he owns me?

How dare he?

I jerk away, forcing his hand to fall from around my waist.

Kirill grunts since that happens to be his injured arm. My eyes meet his arctic ones, and judging by the focused look in them, he probably woke up much earlier than I did. Or maybe he didn't sleep at all.

I scoot to the other side of the bed, trying not to ogle his hard inked chest and arms. Under the morning light that's slipping in from the windows and balcony, his tattoos appear darker. Menacing, too. Like everything about him.

I can't help staring at the two bullet scars on his chest. They're covered up with a new intricate tattoo and would be invisible to someone who doesn't look hard enough. I, however, could find them even if I were blind.

After everything, the thought that he nearly died in Russia because of me still turns my stomach.

You're playing a dangerous game, Sasha. You're having empathy for the monster who wouldn't hesitate to destroy you.

He sits up, and the covers drop to below his navel, revealing the defined V-line that leads to—

I snap my attention back to his face and purse my lips when I find him smirking.

"Morning, wife. Did you sleep well?"

"No, I didn't."

Oh, wait. I actually did.

My lips part. I didn't have any nightmares last night. Or dreams.

I had nothing. For the first time in a very long time, I just did something normal and slept.

"Is it the mattress?" He presses down on it, then on the covers. "The pillow? The bed itself?"

"More like the one in the bed," I mutter under my breath.

"That's your defense mechanism speaking, but that's fine. I can wait."

"Wait for what?"

"For the day you become my wife again."

"I was never your wife, Kirill."

"Yes, you are. You said 'I do' and took my cock like a very good wife that same night. Besides, I have a marriage certificate to prove it."

"That doesn't count since we're getting a divorce."

His permanent smirk disappears, but his expression remains light, playful even, but it doesn't appear natural. "Until then, you're still my wife."

"Reluctantly."

"Legally."

I lift my chin. "Temporarily."

"Currently."

The bastard gets off on any war I attempt to start. If I want to get anywhere in this situation, I need to stop feeding his perversion.

I cross my arms over my chest, and his gaze falls to my breasts, catching fire and causing my body to heat. I clear my throat. "When are you going to release Anton?"

"Once I make sure you're keeping your word."

"I'm here, aren't I?"

His ethereal eyes slowly slide to my face. "Not fully."

"What is that supposed to mean?"

"Nothing worth explaining."

"You can't just keep holding him hostage against me."

"That's exactly what I plan to do."

"And you think that will make me accept you?"

"I don't believe anything I do will make you accept me at this point, so I might as well create some leverage in the form of your brother."

"You're a damn asshole."

His lips twitch. "You know I love it when you compliment me."

"That was the exact opposite of a compliment."

"Not from you."

I release an exasperated sigh. "At least take me to see him."

"Not yet."

"Why not?"

"He enjoyed your company for two months after having the audacity to take you away from me." His voice deepens with every word until my skin crawls.

"He's my brother."

"Doesn't excuse his actions. The only reason I'm stopping myself from chopping him into pieces is you, so don't test my already limited patience."

"Your patience is limited? *Yours?* Are you kidding me right now? *My* patience should be the one that's drained. Not yours!"

He watches me for a beat, his eyebrows dipping. "Is this your attempt at channeling Karina's over-the-top emotional state?"

I punch him in the chest. *Damn. That felt good.* "Call me emotional again, and I'll fuck up your face."

He grunts and massages his chest with his good hand. "Are you sure? I thought you loved my face, and you find it, I quote, *gorgeous.*"

"That was before I realized how manipulative you are. None of my previous feelings count."

"We'll see about that. Besides, you learned last night that I didn't marry Kristina and actually reunited her with her lover, who happens to be Konstantin. So your reasons for hating me are null and void."

"You still went behind my back and stood with her at the altar."

"The marriage was never going to happen. It was all for show."

"Then why didn't you tell me that?"

"Would you have accepted it if I had?"

I purse my lips.

"There." He throws a hand in my general direction. "Your answer."

"It doesn't matter now. Also, this isn't only about the marriage. It's about sending someone to eliminate my family and me after realizing we were the last living members of the organization whose annihilation you plotted."

"I told you that wasn't true, but it's clear that you're not ready to be open-minded and consider that angle."

"Then…tell me. You mentioned the possibility of a traitor in my family last night. Who is it? Do you have the evidence?"

"Who knows? I need to wait until I make sure you're not planning to use me for information and then discard me."

"You already have Anton as leverage."

"Doesn't hurt to acquire more." He reaches over, palms my face, and kisses the top of my head.

The motion is so fast and sudden that I only realize it after he's done it.

I push at his chest with enough force to nearly send us both tumbling down.

He hits his injured bicep on the headboard and groans.

Shit.

Did he open his stitches?

I cross my arms, my voice dripping with guilt. "I told you not to touch me."

"I'll touch my wife whenever I fucking want." He stands up,

and I'm slammed head-first by the glorious view of his naked body. He doesn't even try to hide his half-erect cock.

But something other than his shameless nudity steals my attention. He's a lot leaner than the last time I saw him. It's more drastic than after he was shot in Russia.

I look the other way, refusing to get caught in that web. "Can't you put some clothes on?"

"Why should I wear them when I'm in front of my wife? Speaking of which, care to relieve the hard-on caused by your constant rubbing against me?"

"I…didn't do that."

"My cock would like to respectfully disagree. His state is physical proof of the harassment, as unintentional as it was."

"It's not my fault you're a pervert."

A low chuckle leaves his lips, the sound flowing around my head, and then he ruffles my hair. "That's where you're wrong, Solnyshko. It's entirely *your* fault."

I push his hand away and glare up at him, trying to ignore his dick that's a tad too close to my face.

He lets his hand drop to his side, his humor dwindling away. "Go get changed. I got you clothes last night and put them in the closet."

Before I can reply, he heads to the bathroom.

My gaze lingers on his muscular back, his tight ass, and the strong tendons of his thighs that flex with every movement. The tattoos covering them seem like they're animated.

Kirill stops at the threshold and peeks back with a smirk as if he knew I'd be staring.

I spring up from the bed and throw the covers down. It's too hot in here.

On my way to the closet, I catch a glimpse of the ring on my finger. The green jewel sparkles under the morning light. Kirill also clasped the bracelet on my wrist. I can't help the mix of emotions that run through me. A part of me always mourned losing these two items, but now, I'm apprehensive about being back to square one.

Shaking my head internally, I text Maksim.

Do you know where Kirill is keeping Anton?

When no reply comes, I send another one.

Please tell me Viktor isn't personally responsible for his confinement. That bull would kill him for daring to betray Kirill.

Another more grim thought comes to mind.

Don't tell me…it's you? Maks, I know Anton can be an asshole, and he had no right to imprison and torture you all that time, but you're better than him, okay? Please don't do something you'll regret. Text me back when you get this.

My chest constricts as I stare at the screen and still get no reply or evidence that he read it.

Please be the better man, Maks. Please.

I leave my phone on the table and head into the closet. Sure enough, there are countless dresses, pants, shirts, and even jeans. All new and in my size.

Kirill put them with my old clothes that are still there. He must've unpacked the duffel bag I took to the basement and also placed the suits and men's clothes here.

My throat closes when I find my wedding dress hanging at the far end of my old clothes. The veil is draped around it, and the amateur crown of flowers I made sits on the box with my shoes in it.

An influx of emotions hits me, and I fetch the first item and then slide the door shut.

It turns out to be a dress with fashionable, long sleeves. But I'd probably look weird in it.

So I put it back and opt for jeans and a white T-shirt.

After Kirill finishes showering, he walks to the closet and abandons his towel in the doorway. I have to run out so he can change his clothes. He doesn't seem to be apprehensive about getting naked any chance he gets, as if he's enjoying playing with me.

After I leave the closet, he merely smiles and shakes his head.

A few minutes later, he emerges dressed in one of his usual charismatic black suits that's tailored to his body.

I force myself to focus on his face. "Have you assigned Maksim to watch over Anton?"

"Who knows?"

"Stop messing with me. How could you do that?"

"How could your precious brother torture Maksim? He's lost so much weight and all of his spark, I almost didn't recognize him when he came back. Don't you think he deserves closure?"

"You're just inflaming the situation and making it much worse than it already is."

"I'm only playing the role of a dark horse of justice. Nothing more. Nothing less. Besides, I told Viktor no torture. So rest assured."

I'm not confident. He's relaxed, which is never good news for whoever is against him.

"Now, let's go. We're late for a very important announcement."

"What type of announcement?"

"You'll find out shortly."

He starts to grab me, but I step out of his reach. "You need to seriously stop trying to touch me."

"Why would I stop touching my wife?"

"Your touch disgusts me, for starters."

"Is that so?" He tilts his head to the side. "Isn't it, perhaps, the exact opposite?"

I jam my forefinger into his chest. "You mean nothing to me anymore."

He clutches my hand and is about to kiss the back when I pull it away. "Stop touching me. I mean it."

Kirill raises his hands as if in surrender, but the gesture is mocking at best.

Is it just me, or did he become tenfold more infuriating in the span of two months?

The moment we get to the main living area, I pause. Everyone, and I mean every single member of the guards, stands near the door, led by the mountain Viktor himself.

Well, everyone except for Maksim.

Did Kirill really assign him as Anton's guard?

I don't have the capacity to think about that as I also see the members of the staff standing opposite them with Anna at the front.

Konstantin, Kristina, and Karina are sitting on the sofa, and even Yulia is there, crossing her arms and appearing displeased with the world as always.

As soon as she sees us, her expression changes to that of utter loathing. "What is the meaning of this—"

"Sit down, Mother," he cuts her off.

"I will not have you tell me what to do, you devil. How dare you have your brute man bring me out here by force? Do you know who you're dealing with?"

"I have an idea. But you'll know exactly who you're dealing with if you don't sit down this instant. I won't repeat myself another time."

Karina shakes and inches closer to Konstantin as droplets splash from her cup of coffee. She's always been this unfortunate mess of nerves around her mother.

I really hate that woman.

She's vile, heartless, and has caused her own daughter irreparable damage. Hell, she did the same to Kirill, but probably worse. It would've been much better if they'd never had a mother.

Stop it. You're feeling bad for him when that should be the last thing on your mind.

Konstantin grips Yulia's hand, and that's when she reluctantly sits back down.

I try and fail not to look at the guards' expressions. They must be shocked about the transformation, even though I'm technically the same 'Sasha' they've known for years.

"I gathered you all here to announce something of utmost

importance." Kirill's commanding voice confiscates the attention of the whole room.

Even my own back snaps upright before I catch myself.

Stupid old habits.

Kirill slides an arm around the small of my back and clutches my hip. Shivers break out on my skin although layers of clothes separate us.

I'm about to push him away, but then he says, "Sasha is my wife. From today on, you'll respect and protect her as you do me."

FOURTEEN

Kirill

SASHA HAS BEEN ACTIVELY AVOIDING MY PRESENCE, TOUCH, and company.

In fact, she could bag an award for being irritatingly consistent in her no-touch rule.

It's been a week since she returned to the place where she belongs—by my side.

However, there's no sense of closeness whatsoever. Yes, she's here in body, but her soul is either scattered somewhere or she's suppressing it until it's almost invisible.

She goes to sleep before I do with her back facing me. If I try to touch her, she slaps, hits, or pushes me away as if I'm the most disgusting thing to ever exist.

It doesn't matter how many methods I use or how far I go to reignite any form of connection.

The more I try, the harder she works to demolish those plans.

I know she's forcing it. I can feel it in the subtle tremor of her skin whenever I touch her. I see it in her parted lips and chameleon eyes. I hear it in the hitch in her breathing whenever my body is near hers.

But she's determined to not give in to those emotions.

Sooner or later, she will.

I won't give up until she becomes my wife again.

Lately, she's been spending time with the guards, catching up and what-the-fuck-ever. I don't like that she smiles with them, Konstantin, Karina, and even damn Kristina, but those smiles are never directed at me.

Have I considered punishing my guards for that very irrational reason? Absolutely. The only problem is that no matter how much I subject them to my wrath, it won't change Sasha's position toward me.

The day I announced to everyone that she's my wife, she stiffened in my hold as if I were announcing a death sentence.

The others had all sorts of questions, to which she answered that she had no choice but to be a man. But now, she's snatched back her power and is choosing to be herself again. She also apologized for 'lying' to them all this time.

Admittedly, they took it a lot better than I expected, probably because they already knew she was a woman after I buried her fake body. Their acceptance, however, brings up the issue that she's too close to them for my liking.

The same applies to the damn members of my organization. We just finished our general meeting and I brought her into the dining room, held her by the waist, and introduced her as my wife.

Most of them have their mouths open, except for Rai, who has the audacity to pull my wife from my grip and hug her.

"I knew your time wasn't up!"

Says the woman who's been threatening me with bodily harm every time she's seen me because she thought I'd killed my wife.

Even I started to believe that damn theory deep in my deranged heart.

I thought I'd taken things too far and I was paying the price for my failure.

Sasha hugs her back, though tentatively and with enough awkwardness to show in every line of her delicate face.

My wife has never been the best with social interactions—at least, not when it comes to touch.

A few months ago, I was the only one whose touch she craved. Anytime, anywhere.

Now I'm the only one she desperately wants to escape.

Do I want to punch Rai to the next planet because of that? Yes. But I'm always plagued with thoughts of violence when it comes to that shit Rai.

Mikhail and Igor pretend they've never seen Sasha before. Vladimir narrows his eyes, but keeps his unnecessary opinion to himself.

Damien, who was either asleep or stuffing his face with cookies during the meeting, watches the scene with a furrowed expression. It's weird that he doesn't call Sasha out on it, but no one actually knows what goes on in that crazy man's head.

Adrian raises a brow, but it's more out of amusement than anything else.

Kyle is standing behind Rai, probably to protect her from me if I decide today will be the last one she's allowed to breathe.

If she didn't have him, her corpse would be in the concrete of some upcoming shopping center as we speak.

Rai finally breaks away from Sasha. "We have a lot of catching up to do."

"No." I yank Sasha to my side, my hand tightening on her hip. "I refuse to share her time."

My wife subtly pushes my hand away while smiling at Rai. "I'd love that."

My jaw tightens and I glare at Kyle with the clear message, "Take your wife away."

He lifts a shoulder and fails to hide a smirk that I'm going to shoot right off his face.

Everyone starts to filter out of the room, Sasha and Rai preceding them, chattering happily about fuck knows what.

Adrian lingers behind. He approaches me and taps his index finger on his thigh with his stupid eyebrow still raised.

My attention remains on the exit through which Sasha just left and I say absentmindedly, "You have something to say, say it and stop standing there like a clown."

"I'd argue that someone else in this room is a better fit for the clown's position."

My attention slides to him. "Is that the point you wanted to make?"

"Hey, don't be irritable toward me. I'm not the one who took away your wife." He pauses. "Does this mean you'll stop being a crazy motherfucker now that she's back?"

"Too early to tell."

"I can relate." He squeezes my shoulder. "Want her to stay?"

I narrow my eyes. "What makes you think she won't?"

"A hunch. Besides, why do you think I can relate?"

I face him. "I can't believe I'm taking relationship advice from you."

"At least my wife is with me, unlike yours, who seems to already have one foot out the door."

"That's not funny."

"It wasn't supposed to be. At any rate, if you want her to stay, don't give her a way out."

"If I don't, she will leave."

"She'll leave anyway, but if you use the method I mentioned, there's a higher success rate." He releases me. "All I care about is your head being in the game."

And then he strides out of the dining room.

I take a few moments to compose myself and stop the constant creative murderous thoughts I have toward Rai, then go outside.

In the living room, a few voices reach me, namely that of Damien, who thinks it's a wonderful idea to test my hospitality and join my wife and Rai.

"I must say." He pokes her cheek as if she's a lifeless doll. "You look like this pretty boy Sasha who was Kirill's guard. You even share the same name."

"Are you serious?" Rai rolls her eyes. "She *is* Sasha."

"Oh." He studies her closely again, and I'm tempted to poke his eyes out and break that finger he's touching her with.

"You became a woman?" he asks like a fucking idiot.

"I was always a woman, Damien."

"Oooh. That's why you were a pretty boy. Makes sense." He pokes her cheek again. "You look much better as a woman."

That's it.

I stride to them and seize his finger, then twist it back and away from Sasha.

She stiffens, her lips resting in a line. Although she's wearing jeans and a simple T-shirt, she's glowing and looks enticing.

Or that could be my cock speaking in an attempt to finally get a taste.

"What the fuck?" Damien releases himself from my grip and inspects his finger.

"If you don't want the rest of them broken, don't touch my wife again."

Rai rolls her eyes. "Let's get away from all this revolting testosterone, Sasha."

"No," I say.

My wife glares at me, then gives me a sweet smile, which looks forced at best and evil at worst. She's probably going to spend the rest of the day with Rai just to fuck with me.

Like she spent the last few days either with the guards or Anna and Karina.

In the beginning, I thought I needed to give her space and

she'd eventually come back to me, but she's been using that opening to drive an even bigger wedge between us.

Since that method is obviously not working, I'm going to have to up my game.

I capture her elbow and tug her close. In Sasha's book of *How to Avoid Your Husband*, any form of touch is completely prohibited, so she tries to wiggle free.

She does it more subtly in public, though, which means it's less efficient.

I lower my mouth to her ear and whisper, "If you're in the mood to see your brother today, stay fucking still."

She freezes and all her attempts to struggle stop.

I smile at both Rai and Damien. "My wife and I have business to attend to. You can leave now."

Rai tries to protest, but she reluctantly gets her unwelcome presence off my property when Sasha says they'll meet up some other time.

Not on my watch.

Damien says he'll be back, too, and I really wish he was being an asshole just to get on my nerves and not for some other reason.

Once they leave, Sasha steps away from me. "You're taking me to see Anton?"

"Only if you're a good girl."

Her lips purse, but there's a pink hue that covers her cheeks. I bet she doesn't even know it's there, but then again, she can't really control her body's reactions.

One more reason why I'm sure she's just suppressing at this point.

Looks like I need to take matters into my own hands.

⤜⤏

Contrary to what Sasha prefers, her hand is in mine.

It's for an entirely necessary reason other than touch or se-duction, and she doesn't have any choice but to hold on to me for dear life.

"Can't I remove the blindfold? I was wearing it during the whole car ride and you made sure I had no clue where this place is."

"You could still pinpoint this location, so the short answer is no."

Her nails dig into the flesh of my hand with the sole purpose of inflicting pain, but that's okay. Her being angry and frustrated with me is still better than the bitter pill of indifference.

"Careful, we're walking on an unsteady bridge and there's a strong current underneath us," I say as I lead her down a slippery dirt path with the water far enough not to reach us but close enough for her to hear the sounds.

What? I have to keep her close as much as possible.

"I know how to walk—" I start to remove my hand and she slips, then grabs onto my bicep with both hands, her nails clench-ing my jacket.

The late afternoon sun casts orange shadows on her pale face and parted lips. Her blonde strands fly in the wind and get in her mouth and blow over the blindfold.

She looks so beautiful with her hair down, especially since it's grown to reach her shoulders.

I wrap an arm around her waist and whisper in her ear, "I told you to be careful."

She purses her lips and starts to push me away.

I tighten my grip. "If you don't want to fall to your death, stay still."

She gives up, but only slightly. "I'm just doing this out of necessity."

"If you say so." I lean down and catch a whiff of her scent. It's…like her old self, but she started wearing some perfume Karina bought for her. Its floral fragrance has a subtle note of mystery.

Note to self: Thank my sister for her immaculate taste.

This is what I would've imagined Sasha to smell like if I'd first met her as a woman. Soft but shrouded in mystery.

"Have we left the bridge?" she asks.

"Not yet."

She wraps her arm around my back to get better balance. Am I enjoying this? Definitely. Maybe more than should be allowed.

This is the first time she's willingly touched me since she came back. Some would argue I gave her no choice, but I don't give a fuck.

I still enjoy every minute of having her warmth mixed with mine. Yes, I could've had Viktor drop us off in front of the safe house, but how else would I get Sasha clinging to me like this?

Too soon, we arrive at the safe house that's about a two-hour drive from home, plus the twenty minutes in which I thoroughly enjoyed Sasha's touch.

Also, I'm obviously sexually frustrated, because my cock won't be on speaking terms with me until I get him in my wife's cunt. However, he likes to twitch to life at the merest touch, so his current state is that of complete irritation.

"Are we here?" she asks tentatively.

"Almost." I open the main door with my thumbprint. Only Viktor's, Maksim's, and mine can open this door, or any other door on the property.

After we're inside, we cut through the garden and head to the annexed garage, where Anton is. I open it with my thumbprint again then remove Sasha's blindfold.

She squints even though the sky is getting darker.

I motion ahead with my chin and she eyes me suspiciously before she carefully goes in and takes a few steps down the stairs.

The walls of the underground bunker that's hidden beneath a garage are both soundproof and shockproof. It was built by my father to withstand bombs if need be. Not sure who he thought would bomb him, but he was always paranoid to a fault.

Other than that, the space is large, so the metal bed in the corner and the few shelves scattered around look like a toddler's attempt at decorating.

Sasha stops when she spots her brother sitting cross-legged on the bed, eyes closed and hands resting nonchalantly on his knees as if he's in a meditating position.

The cuffs that should be around his wrists are hanging from the wall.

Maksim is doing one-handed push-ups on the other side of the room, but he stands upon seeing us.

Sasha runs to Yuri—sorry, *Anton*. Don't expect me to keep track of his multiple personalities.

"Tosha." She stops beside him.

He opens his eyes, stares at Maksim and me, then focuses back on his sister with a cold expression. "What are you doing here?"

"What do you mean? I came to check on you."

"Leave," he orders. "And I don't mean here, but the country."

I'm going to kill the bastard.

Maksim stiffens beside me, his arms crossed.

"What the hell are you talking about? I'm not abandoning you," she argues.

"I'm ordering you to."

"No." She lifts her chin. "I'm done taking orders from you, Uncle, and Babushka. From now on, I'll only execute my own decisions."

That's my woman.

"Sasha…" he warns.

"I'm not going, Tosha. Not without you."

He closes his eyes briefly and releases a frustrated breath. "Can't you see that he's using you against me?"

The *he* is me, in case no one noticed.

"I don't care." She squeezes his hand. "I'll be fine."

I approach them and wrap an arm around her shoulder. "I'll take good care of my wife."

"You motherfucking—" He lunges up to punch me, but Maksim gets to him in no time and pins him against the mattress with an elbow on his throat.

"Stop, stop it!" Sasha fruitlessly pulls on Maksim's shoulder.

Anton's face reddens as he hits Maksim's arm, but the more my guard crushes his trachea, the weaker his struggle gets.

"Maks!" she shrieks, but he's not hearing her. "Please, let him go."

Finally, she realizes who she should be talking to and turns to me. "Tell him to stop."

I stare down at her. "Say you're sorry first."

"Sorry for what?"

"For leaving me. For making me believe you were dead. I want you to say you're fucking sorry."

"Fuck you," she grinds out.

I lift a shoulder as Anton's thrashes mixed with his raw struggles for breath echo in the air.

"Maks, please," she begs him, but he's still not hearing her. Judging by the reddening of her brother's face, he probably has about a minute left before he crosses to the other side. If not less.

Sasha looks at me with tears clinging to her eyes. "I'm sorry."

"For what?"

"For ever loving a monster like you."

My jaw clenches and I'm tempted to suffocate the fuck out of her, but I'm not sure I won't kill her if I do that.

"Let him go, Maksim."

My guard doesn't seem to be listening, so I push him, destabilizing his elbow from Anton's neck.

"I said to let him go."

He stares at me as if he just came out of a trance, which might as well be the case.

Anton coughs, the sound raw in the giant space. Sasha sits beside him and pats his back. Her expression is that of pure horror.

Not the one I was hoping for.

I glare at Maksim. He slowly lowers his head because he knows exactly how much he fucked up.

Maybe I fucked up, too, because I'm not sure my next plan will work as I'd hoped.

FIFTEEN

Sasha

I'M SO CLOSE TO THE POINT OF ERUPTION.

Chaotic emotions swirl through me and I want to burst into a spree of violence or release a long scream.

As long as I inflict pain on the asshole who's gripping me by the arm and leading me through fuck knows what.

Again, I had to wear the blindfold so I don't find out the location of where he's keeping my brother.

My mind buzzes with the reminder that Maks could kill him at any second. Hell, if Kirill hadn't used force earlier, I might be mourning my brother's death as we speak.

My friend didn't say a word to me, let alone try to explain why he's been ignoring all of the texts I've been sending over the past week.

Maybe Anton was right and Maksim is blindly loyal to Kirill, and, therefore, he won't hesitate to kill my brother if my monster of a husband gives the order.

My muscles are tense to the point of pain and I have to put up with touching the bastard despite wanting to throw him down and kick him in the nuts.

All I see is black and it's a true translation of my current mood. The worst part about having my eyesight taken away is the heightening of my other senses.

I can hear the distant howls of the night creatures and the rustle of the leaves beneath our shoes. Even Kirill's steady breathing sweeps through me like an irritating highlight of the sounds.

My arms erupt in goosebumps, and I want to blame that on the night chill, but if that were the case, why am I hotter than normal?

In fact, they feel like they're disconnected from the rest of my body and living in a strange in-between. One that's filled with Kirill's overwhelming presence.

His scent clashes with that of the forest—woodsy, deep, and most importantly, bottomless. Like his emotions.

"Aren't we there yet?" I ask with a brusque tone.

We've been going for what I'm sure is longer than half an hour—though it feels like ages.

The walk to Anton's prison was twenty minutes. I was able to tell by calculating the time between when he put on the blindfold and after he removed it.

"So you do have a voice. And here I thought you'd lost it."

I glare at him even through the blindfold. "You think I'm in the mood to talk to you after you made me watch my brother's attempted murder?"

"You know very well that wasn't my intention."

"Know very well?" I repeat in an incredulous tone and force him to a halt, then yank away the blindfold. I'm greeted by shadowy trees and Kirill's stoic face. "You're the type who gives people a safety net just to pull the rug from beneath their feet, so no, there's no way of knowing your true intentions."

He steps forward, invading my space and trapping me with

his arctic wolf eyes. "That might apply to everyone else, but never to you."

I punch him in the shoulder. "Stop saying things like that!"

"Why?" He cradles my fist in his hand and keeps it caged against his chest. "Are you by any chance afraid that if you listen to me without projecting your self-induced hatred, you'll actually believe me and eventually forgive me?"

"*Forgive* you? For what, exactly? For keeping me a secret while plotting to marry someone else? For sending your people to get rid of my family and me because you couldn't finish the job six years ago?"

"If you were my secret, I wouldn't have introduced you to my family and my organization as my fucking wife. I didn't send anyone to kill you or your family. Not now, not six years ago."

"But I saw Makar that day! He was there near the cottage to make sure I was blown up inside it."

He pauses, eyes narrowing. "Makar?"

"Your father's senior guard who's been loyal to you since his death, or are you also going to pretend you don't know him or didn't give him the order?"

"I do know him, but he was under no such fucking order. In fact, he's supposed to be working closely with the Bratva branch in Chicago and has been for months now."

"So you're telling me you're not the one who called him back to eliminate me?"

He grabs my shoulder with his free hand, and shakes me, nearly knocking all my senses out of their confinements. "This is the last fucking time I'll say this, I'd never hurt you."

"But you did!" I punch my chest. "You took the stupid feelings I had for you and used them against me in the cruelest way. But it doesn't matter now. I'm over it and *you*."

"Liar." His huskily spoken word sends a jolt of electricity through my stupid heart that refuses to die already. "If you were over it, you wouldn't go out of your way to avoid me. You wouldn't be shaking in my arms like you are now."

I try to jerk away, but he wraps an arm around my lower back and slams my front against his.

In the dark, our harsh breaths echo in the air, intertwining with the sounds of the night creatures.

"Let me go." I push at his chest.

"I made that mistake once. I believed you were dead and buried what I thought were your fucking bones with my own hands. I'll never do that again."

"You're only delaying the inevitable."

"We'll see about that."

"What is that supposed to mean? You agreed to divorce me in three months."

He lowers his head so that his face is nearly level with mine. I almost forgot how beautiful he is up close. His straight nose complements his sharp jawline and his defined lips. He's one of those people who has model-like features but with the charm of a shrewd businessman.

No matter what happens, he stands there like an unmoving mountain, forever in control and unperturbed. It's almost inhuman. I wish I could see the version of him where, according to Karina, Anna, and even Rai, he was a ghost of himself after I was gone.

I wish I could stop trembling when he touches me.

I wish I could...just make him disappear and not miss him.

"Why didn't you tell me about Makar?" he asks instead of answering my earlier question.

"Why is it important?"

"Let me think. Because of the fact that I have a fucking traitor in my ranks? Thanks to you, he might've already fled."

"So it's *my* fault now?"

"Just stop it. Stop trying to invent a fight and drive a deeper wedge between us. For once, stop fucking running."

Easier said than done when my flight trigger is awakened. In fact, all I want to do is run into the middle of an unfamiliar, far-away place, as long as I'm not in his immediate vicinity.

His merciless grip is the only thing keeping me in place, and he seems to recognize that, too, because he tightens his arm around my waist.

I don't know if it's the added pressure of his touch or the fact that a foolish part of me is starting to believe him, but my fight slowly wanes until I can barely sense it.

Tension lingers in the air even as my fist tries to push at him. It's my last desperate attempt to keep some distance between us.

He squeezes my hand, but it's not meant to crush my fingers as I would expect. It's more like he's demanding my attention. "Work with me, not against me."

"Or else what?"

"Why do you need the or else, Sasha? You think I don't see your feeble attempts at provoking me? You're wishing for me to give you an ultimatum again so you can convince yourself that hating me is the right thing. I'm sorry to burst your delusional bubble, but that won't be happening."

The asshole.

Can't he be less perceptive?

"You've already given me an ultimatum by imprisoning Anton."

"That's because if I gave you the choice, you'd run away again, and I can't bear to be separated from my wife."

"Stop saying things like that."

"Like what? That you're my wife, Mrs. Morozova?"

I feel heat rising within me and the unconscious loosening of my muscles. I'm losing the battle again.

You can't, Sasha.

If you trust him again, you'll end up being hurt. This time, you won't be able to pick yourself back up.

But even as I tell myself those words, I'm not confident I can hate him forever either. Hell, I haven't been able to hate him ever since I found out Kristina married Konstantin and he was the one who plotted it.

A rustle comes from off to the side, but I could barely hear it over the heartbeat that pounds in my ears.

Kirill, however, is more alert. He subtly releases my hand that's on his chest and reaches beneath his jacket for his weapon.

I finally snap out of it and do the same, then whisper, "Is it Viktor?"

"No. I sent him home."

"What? Who's going to drive us back?"

"We were never supposed to return tonight." He studies our surroundings. "We have unwelcome company. Three of them. One is in the tree behind you, another is behind me, and the third is northwest of the first. There could be more."

I swallow. Please tell me these aren't men my uncle sent. I told him not to interfere, but he and especially Babushka have never listened to me.

Besides, this has to do with their precious heir, Anton, after all.

"Go north." Kirill's voice interrupts my thoughts, and then he taps a few times on his watch. "I just sent you the coordinates of the cabin we're spending the night in. I think they followed us, so they don't know about the cabin's location, but if by any chance it appears they do, run as fast as you can."

"What about you?"

"I'll stop them and join you at the cabin."

"You think I'll let you do that on your own?"

"I mean it, Sasha, go."

"And I mean it, Kirill. I don't need your protection."

"You—"

"Let's lose them by going separate ways," I say, and without waiting for his reply, I head east.

I can hear him curse before he runs in the opposite direction.

Before I can find a safe location, I sense light footsteps closing in on me. I swing to the side, then shoot and miss.

Shit.

I need to only take calculative hits. Otherwise, I'll run out of ammunition and put myself in a deadly position.

They shoot at me, but I manage to duck and hide behind a tree.

If they're shooting to kill, they couldn't have been sent by my family, right? At least, I hope they're not trying to eliminate me.

Though that's a huge possibility if they think I went back to Kirill.

Damn it.

I catch my breath, hold my gun with both hands, and slowly peek around the tree.

That's weird. While I was fast, they probably are, too, so where are they?

All of a sudden, a doomsday-like feeling ticks in my head and I look back just in time to see a black-clad figure staring at me. I shoot him right before he kills me.

Blood splatters on my face as he hits the ground in front of me.

I don't have time to check his identity since other footsteps are approaching me. So I take note of his weapon and run deeper into the forest.

In the meantime, I manage to exchange bullets with one of my pursuers.

It isn't until I'm far into the thick trees that I manage to kill the second.

But I keep running, suspecting a third to be close behind.

If that's the case, what about Kirill?

Once I make sure no one is hot on my trail, I check the location he sent me. I'm twenty minutes away from the cabin, which I can get to without going back through the forest.

I spent approximately thirty minutes in the cat-and-mouse

chase with the second one. It'd be easier to meet Kirill at the cabin rather than go back to the forest and risk being shot.

Especially since I have only one bullet left.

I reach the cabin in record time. It's located in the mountains, surrounded by trees for as far as the eye can see.

Instead of heading inside, I do a tour of the entire property, my finger on the trigger.

Fortunately, Kirill was right and they don't seem to know about the place.

One problem, though. I don't have the key. I try under the mat and beneath the porch, but I end up finding it in one of the flowerpots lining the steps.

After I'm inside, I release a breath, but I still track the cozy-looking area in case there's an uninvited guest. Once I'm sure I'm the only one here, I lean against the back of the sofa and call Kirill. It goes straight to voicemail.

Fuck.

I pace the length of the cottage. He's okay. It's Kirill, after all. Those guys couldn't get him.

Unless he was ambushed.

Maybe the two who followed me were a red herring and the actual army is out for Kirill's life.

Shit.

Shit.

The longer I call him and he doesn't pick up, the harder my heart beats.

I completely forget why I want him out of the picture or that if he's gone, I'll finally be free of him.

But that's the thing. I don't think I ever will be.

The bitter truth slaps me in the face: I prefer being in this fucked-up coexistence with him than being happy without him.

I'm so damn sick.

But apparently I don't give a damn, because I sprint out of the house and run the length of the garden.

He should've been here by now.

He should've—

My feet come to a halt when I catch sight of him walking onto the property, a gun in his hand and blood covering his neck and chest.

"Kirill!" I run toward him. "What's wrong? Have you been shot—"

The words die in my throat when he meets me halfway and slams his lips to mine.

SIXTEEN

Sasha

I'M STUNNED.

No, I'm paralyzed.

A part of me is completely aware that I'm supposed to fight this. I'm supposed to kick him in the nuts and run as far away as I can because I know of his nature. A few months ago, he manipulated the situation to have me *and* his ambition. I'm not confident that he won't do it again. That, one day, he'll strike a deal in which he has to sacrifice me.

But the other part is so tired of my flight mode. It's impossible to remember why I should be resisting, leaving, and disappearing.

My lips tremble beneath his hard, demanding ones.

Being kissed by Kirill has always been an experience, but this kiss? It's as if I'm facing a hurricane and my only choice is to let myself be whisked away.

He captures my chin, his fingers pressing on the skin with

nonnegotiable power. Everything about him brims with control and command.

His touch.

His chest that's pressing against mine.

His hand that's glued to my back.

My lips are pried open—or maybe I willingly let them part. Emotions cloud my head until I can't tell which is which anymore.

That slight hesitation is what Kirill needs to invade my mouth. His teeth nibble on my tongue, the pressure rising in increments, holding me hostage in its intensity. Just when I think he'll cut the skin, he sucks on the assaulted part.

I bite him back just as hard, maybe even harder. I have to inflict pain for all the confusion, the betrayal, the disappointment.

I want to hurt him.

No, I *need* to hurt him for everything he made me go through just because I stupidly loved him.

This time, a metallic taste explodes in my mouth. He has to taste it, too, but he doesn't stop or pause in his mission to conquer me.

I hold his jaw with my shaky fingers and throw my hand that's holding the gun on his shoulder.

Kirill isn't deterred by how I drew his blood. In fact, he lowers his hand to my throat and squeezes as he kisses me deeper, nearly sucking my soul out of my mouth.

And you know what? I'm doing the same.

I went months without touching him, and now that I'm finally doing that, I can't stop.

I *won't* stop.

This is all because of whatever foolish emotions are running through me and the damning thoughts I had earlier. I believed he was dead or hurt or had been taken, and only by touching him again am I finally convinced that he's alive.

I could put an end to this now.

I *should.*

That's what I tell myself as I meet him stroke for stroke. Our heartbeats thunder against one another's, and I revel in that.

I memorize it in the deepest part of my soul so that I can revisit it when he isn't by my side. Kirill's heartbeat has always been mild, unperturbed, and completely controlled. Like the man himself.

This is the first time he's ever let his emotions explode.

I feel the bursts through his bites, the controlling way he squeezes my throat, and how his lips invade mine in a war of dominance.

A yelp rips out of me when he releases my neck, slips both hands beneath my thighs, and lifts me up. I have no choice but to wrap my legs around his sculpted waist and let my arms rest on top of his shoulders.

He walks toward the cabin without cutting off the kiss. In fact, it's deeper, more animalistic in nature, as if he's trying to engrave himself into me.

Brand me.

Completely own me.

He kicks the door open and slams me against the nearest wall. The thud sends a shock wave through my back, but I can't focus on that when he throws down his gun and wrenches his lips from mine.

He doesn't pull away.

Doesn't look away either.

Our foreheads meet, and he releases a long, charged breath that mixes with my shaky one.

"I thought I'd lost you again." He lifts a hand from my thigh and strokes my hair, my cheek, and my swollen lips. He touches me everywhere as if wanting—no, *needing*—to make sure I'm actually here.

I don't mean to, but my hand loses its grip on the gun, and I unload it before I let it hit the ground.

My hands hesitate before I grasp the strands at the back of his head.

"I thought you were hurt." My whisper sounds convoluted in the tense air.

Kirill slowly opens his eyes, and I stop breathing at their intensity. "So you came out to save me?"

"That's not—"

"Don't lie to me, Sasha. Not now."

I remain silent, scared of voicing the thoughts I had earlier out loud. Hell, I'm terrified to admit them to myself.

"Very well. We'll do it your way then."

His lips devour mine again, this time hungrier, angrier, and brimming with a decadent rage I've never felt before.

He clutches my hand and drags me up the flight of stairs, then stops in the middle and glues my back against the wooden railing that creaks at the impact. When he puts me down, I can barely stand on my unsteady legs.

"What are you doing—" My question is cut off when he bites my lower lip. One of his hands squeezes my breast through my shirt while the other unzips my pants and yanks them down.

My legs clench together, but that only manages to heighten the throbbing pressure between my thighs.

"You seem to have this strange idea that you could leave me, Sasha." He slides his fingers over my panties, and they're wet. They've been like that since he started kissing me senseless.

Despite myself, I find my heart and body reacting to Kirill's presence and touch in the most wanton way.

My hips jerk when he slowly but firmly circles his fingers around my clit, stimulating, but not really giving it enough attention.

I tilt my head back, held hostage by the torturous bursts of pleasure.

Kirill wraps his hand around my throat and flings my attention back to him. "Eyes on me."

My gaze clashes with his icy one. Only, there's fire there now. A dangerous flame that could and would engulf everything in its path—me included.

"Answer me. Do you truly believe you'll leave me?"

"We had a deal." My voice is throaty, low, and definitely not what I want to sound like in this screwed-up fight for power.

"A deal." He slides my panties to the side and thrusts two fingers in my opening. "You want to abide by the deal? Very well, wife."

He adds a third finger, and I sink my nails in the railing to stop myself from tumbling over or actually holding on to him.

His thumb glides back and forth on my clit as he fucks me with his fingers. It's enough pressure to make me want to come, but not enough to get me there.

I release a frustrated sound, but that doesn't seem to deter him. If anything, he slows his pace whenever I'm jerking my hips faster.

"Did anyone else touch this cunt, wife?"

I glare at him. "That's none of your business."

"Wrong answer." His rhythm dulls to a mere caress and I hate it. I want the rough touch, the violent orgasm.

I need it.

Maybe he truly corrupted me, after all.

"We'll try again." He thrusts with a heightening pace and applies the perfect pressure on my clit. "Did any other fucker touch my cunt?"

"Oh, shit."

"It's a yes or no question. Which one is it?"

His hand starts to ease off my pussy, and I jerk, grabbing his wrist to keep it there. "No."

"No, what?"

"No one's touched me since you."

Flaming possessiveness shines in his eyes, and he goes all the way, pounding into me in an animalistic frenzy.

I come with a violent shake, my clit and pussy throbbing in synch with his touch.

"And no one will," he whispers against my throat. "I'm the only one who's allowed to touch my fucking wife."

I'm still riding the shock waves of the orgasm and can't exactly speak, let alone think.

All I can do is give in to the carnal temptation and the unforgiving pleasure Kirill wrenches out of me.

He removes his hand from my pussy, and a sense of emptiness rattles me to the bone. I want to be filled again and fucked savagely like only he knows how.

To my horror, he also releases my throat, leaving me entirely empty. His harsh eyes remain on me as he unbuckles his belt and wraps it around his palm.

Arousal floods my inner thighs at the image. That belt has always been associated with my most depraved tendencies.

He frees his cock with the other hand. It's veiny, hard, and has a hint of precum glistening at the crown.

I'm unable to stop staring as he jerks himself in a few violent strokes, making it even harder.

I wrap a hand around his and slowly push it out of the way so that I'm the one touching him.

It's been such a long time that I nearly forgot how much I love his cock and the way it twitches to life beneath my fingers.

"That's it," he groans back in his throat and throws his head back. "Do it faster. You won't hurt me."

I up my pace, and when I feel him tensing, I squeeze as hard as I can. "Did you fuck anyone else after I was gone?"

His eyes focus back on mine, and he bites his lower lip like some sort of a sex god. Then he wraps his belt around my throat and tugs me against his strong chest. His cock is trapped between us, and I'm still squeezing.

The more I picture another woman having him, the harder I tighten my fist.

In my mind, he was never supposed to be anyone else's. I honestly don't know what I would've done if he'd actually married Kristina.

I like to think of myself as a good person, but I would've definitely become a fucking devil if she was his wife.

"You think I had the time to look at other women when I was fucking mourning you?" His deep voice drips with unveiled anger, and I don't think it's due to the pain I'm causing.

It sounds more raw and intrusive. More…hurt.

That's when it hits me.

Earlier, when he demanded that I apologize for leaving him, I thought it was some sort of a power play, and I hated him for it. But now that I get a clear look beneath his mask, I'm tempted to believe that he was actually hurt.

The mighty Kirill Morozov was in pain because of me.

I have to stop myself from blurting the apology that's trying to burst through. Instead, I jerk him up and down in an attempt to reawaken his pleasure.

Kirill forces me to release him and I kick my jeans and panties away to give him a better angle. He lifts one of my legs so that it's lined up with his waist and his mythical eyes meet mine.

I'm momentarily distracted.

No, the correct word would be *trapped*.

I'm completely caught in a trance by the depth in them. The mystic emotions swirling through them. It's almost as if…he's releasing a beast that's been lurking inside him all this time.

Or maybe it's the man that he's finally letting loose this time.

Kirill holds the belt in one fist and tightens his grip. My breath constricts, and that causes my pussy to throb harder.

"You're never allowed to leave my sight again." And then he thrusts inside me.

My body jerks, and my hip hits the wooden railing behind me. It's been a long time, and Kirill is fucking huge. A tinge of pain mixes with the overwhelming pleasure, and I have to grab onto the railing so I don't collapse.

The first few weeks after I left for Russia were physical and emotional hell. I told myself I hated him, and I did, but that didn't mean I stopped missing him or the animalistic touch that only he could give me.

The bastard ruined me for all other men. I can't look at anyone else and feel this overwhelming pleasure and these damned emotions.

No.

I roll my hips, taking him as he goes deeper. There are no emotions involved here. There shouldn't be any emotions.

This is only about physical attraction and taking care of each other's bodily needs.

"My wife." He tightens the belt further, and I clench around his cock. "My woman." *Thrust.* "Fucking mine."

Then he's kissing me savagely. Like he can't get enough. Like my taste is everything he needed.

It's only physical.

I chant in my head as I kiss him with the same animalistic need. I don't even care that the railing is digging into my back and that I can feel bruises forming.

They'll be worth it.

I love seeing the evidence of our fucking sessions, and maybe that's part of the reason why I missed him so much.

He never shied away from using me for his pleasure. In return, he gave me the most thrilling releases any woman could dream of.

We're primal. We're raw. And we're the perfect example of a compatible couple during sex.

Kirill squeezes my thigh, pulls out almost completely, then rams back in. He hits my sensitive spot over and over until my moans echo around us.

"That's it, Solnyshko," he grunts against my mouth. "Show me how much you want my cock."

I glare at him even as I jerk my hips and taste him on my tongue.

Why does it have to be him? Of all the men on this planet, why do I have to be entangled with the most monstrous of all?

Why can't he be normal?

Probably because you're not normal yourself, Sasha.

"You hate it, don't you?" He darts out his tongue and licks the tip of my nose, then my upper lip. "You hate how much you want me and that you can't stop it. You hate that your body submits to me despite your best efforts. It's why you've been pushing me away all this time, isn't it? You tried to avoid giving in to this carnal desire, but here's the thing. You can never run away from me, wife."

"S-shut up," I moan the words. Damn it.

"I've been patient, Sasha, and you know patience isn't exactly my strongest trait. I'm ready to be as patient as you want if it means you'll come back to me, but I will not be hearing that you're leaving me ever again."

His thrusts turn wilder and deeper, until my whole body is battered and pliant. Until every inch of me bleeds out right in front of him.

It's only physical., I force my mind to think as I come with a wordless scream. Then I drop my head on his shoulder and bite the space between his neck and collarbone.

I don't care that it's covered with dry blood. In fact, I bite harder, just to make sure he's here with me and not out there somewhere injured.

It's only fucking physical. It can't be any more than that.

Kirill goes faster with savage energy. My ass cheeks hit the railing with every thrust.

I continue biting him, inflicting as much pain as possible. He groans, then bites my throat, too.

And just like that, he comes deep inside me. He pulls out and releases my thigh only so he can sloppily massage my clit with his cum before he thrusts it back into my pussy.

I don't know why the fact that he always does that makes me so hot and bothered within a few seconds. It's like he doesn't want a single drop to escape and makes me take it all.

We remain like that for a few minutes. I'm catching my breath while he's sucking and nibbling on my throat. There's definitely going to be a dark hickey there tomorrow.

As I lay my head on his shoulder, the pleasure haze slowly clears, and bleak reality punches me in the face.

There's no denying it now.

I'm relapsing to old habits.

SEVENTEEN

Kirill

SASHA HAS PULLED AWAY FROM ME.

She used the pretense of needing a shower, and since I had to call Viktor, I let her go.

For now.

After washing up in the downstairs shower, I wrap a towel around my waist and dry my hair with another one.

With the phone at my ear, I walk into the living room.

"You need anything, Boss?" Viktor replies with a half-sleepy tone.

I forgot that it was early in the morning. And while Viktor needs the sleep after months of being deprived, there isn't time for it.

"We were attacked tonight."

There's silence on the other end, followed by a fumbling noise. Something knocks on his end as he says in a sobered-up voice, "I'll be there in a few."

"No."

"What the fuck do you mean by no? I told you it was a stupid idea to be on your own without any protection."

"Is this the moment where you say I told you so?"

"I'm not in the mood for joking. I should've stayed." I hear the rustle of clothes and the sound of a belt.

"Stop changing. You're not coming, and if you do, I'm going to lock you the hell up with Maksim and Anton. You hated the atmosphere there the other time, so maybe you'll change your mind if you spend a few more days in their company."

"What am I supposed to do if I don't come to protect you?"

"Look for who did this." I throw the hair towel down and stare out of the window at the pitch-black darkness outside. The cabin might appear old and unkempt, but the glass is double-glazed and bulletproof. The walls are thick enough that it's hard to hear the night animals chirping outside.

"Which is why I should go to the scene to gather evidence," Viktor says.

"I doubt there's anything left. They probably cleaned out their corpses by now."

"Is it the Ivanovs?"

"I thought that as well. It makes sense that they'd come to rescue Anton, but their weapons weren't of the variety we located at the warehouse during that mission. I doubt they changed weapons since the last operation after Sasha came back. Besides, they attacked her."

"Or she could be faking it to play along and trap you."

"That's my wife you're talking about, Viktor."

"She still belongs to the family who is out to eliminate you. I suspected it all this time, but she was the one who lured you to Russia before you got shot, wasn't she?"

"Drop it."

"No can do. You're trusting her too much when she hasn't proven to be loyal to you since she returned."

"How the fuck is she supposed to do that when she believes I hurt her family?"

"How about not thinking you're subhuman enough to orchestrate the murder of children?"

I pinch the bridge of my nose. He's annoyingly right, and I want to punch him, but since that option isn't available through the phone, I release a breath. "Have you heard from Makar lately?"

He pauses, probably caught by surprise at the change of subject. "No. Doesn't he have direct contact with you?"

"Look for him. The last location I know of is that he was in Chicago."

"Why should I locate him?"

"Because he's the traitor. Sasha thinks I tried to kill her in that cottage, because she saw Makar. I want to know who the fuck sent him there."

"On it." He pauses. "And be careful. I'm not in the mood to collect corpses."

I stare at the phone after he hangs up. The asshole is being more daring than usual lately. It's mostly due to a lack of sleep, which I should probably be apologetic for.

The thing is, I didn't ask him to be an annoying shadow. He picked that position himself, and he needs to take full responsibility for it.

"Was that Viktor?"

I slowly turn around at Sasha's voice. I fully expected her to go to sleep, or pretend to, and to have to wake her up for round two.

Good thing no waking will be happening, since it's guaranteed to make her cranky.

She stands by the stairs, wearing a woolen dress with a cut-out in the middle. It's one of the pieces of clothing I had delivered here earlier today when I devised this plan to corner her in a place where it's only the two of us.

No Karina, Rai, Anna, Kristina, or my fucking guards.

What? She chose to direct her attention toward them instead of me, and I'm not a fan of being a side character in my wife's life.

I head to the minibar and pour two glasses of vodka, then offer one to her. "Yeah. Viktor."

She takes a sip and side-eyes mine. "Since when are you a vodka person?"

"Since I'm trying to placate my wife."

She stops herself before rolling her eyes, but she smiles and hides it by taking another sip.

I mirror her, tolerating the bland vodka. Now, I'm sure my Russian ancestors would turn in their graves and curse me to the lowest pit in hell for that statement. Viktor even accused me of being a 'fake Russian' for slandering the holy messiah of his existence.

Maksim also said I should apologize to his Russian blood.

Lucky for them, my beautiful wife loves the drink, and, therefore, I'll refrain from any unnecessary shit-talking.

Sasha takes her vodka seriously. She sits on the sofa, her stance somewhat relaxed as she relishes every sip. My attention is completely stolen by the soft features of her face and the wet blonde strands that fall to her neck.

But the masterpiece is the large hickey I left on the side of her throat earlier. The belt's red marks surround it, bruising her skin as evidence of who owns her.

Spoiler alert: That would be me.

After a few moments of silence, she raises her head, and her eyes widen the slightest bit when she finds me leaning against the cabinet and staring.

She clears her throat. "You're really asking Viktor to look for Makar?"

"Someone's developed eavesdropping habits."

"I didn't mean to… I just happened to be passing by."

Just how much of the conversation did she hear? Thankfully, she couldn't have listened to Viktor's atrocious comments, since those certainly don't play in my favor.

"If you asked Viktor to search for him, that means you don't know where he is."

"Or what he's done."

"Or that," she repeats in a low, soft voice.

"Do you believe me now?"

She takes a long sip and releases a sigh. "I don't even know what to believe anymore."

"Do you think the men who attacked us tonight were sent by your family?"

She shakes her head. "At least, I hope they weren't, considering they were trying to kill me and all."

"How great is the chance of them coming after you to save Anton?"

"Seventy percent?" she says with a pained smile, and I want to kill each and every one of them who put the pain there.

This is troublesome.

If her own family won't protect her, she's under serious threat. I'm fine with them coming after me, but if they attempt to hurt her, I'll have to rip their hearts out. And she might hate me for it.

"That high?"

"I never mattered in the great scheme of things." She stares out the window at the endless darkness. "When I was a child, I was the clueless, sheltered tomboy who only cared about playing. After the massacre, I was transformed into a soldier for the family. Almost overnight, I became a weapon to be used to protect our assets and to exact revenge. I'm only a support to Anton, a tool he can use when he becomes the heir. The saddest part is that I don't think I'll have a purpose after all of this is over. Once everything ends, I'll have to find myself another role."

"Have you already started looking for that role by dressing like a woman again?"

Her lips part. "How did you know that?"

"A hunch."

"Yeah. I told them that I wouldn't walk around like a man

anymore. I'm strong enough to protect myself now. If I'm attacked, then so be it."

That's my woman.

I love how her eyes shine with determination at her decision to finally be free. Or partially free since she's still bound to her family by an unspoken code of loyalty.

"That's where you're wrong." I bring her another glass and sit beside her. "No one will be able to hurt my wife as long as I'm here."

She deposits the empty glass on the table and takes the new one. "Would you stop calling me that?"

"Well, aren't you my wife?"

"Have you ever considered that you could be hurting me the most?"

"How so? I think I've proved that none of your misconceptions about me are true. Imagine if you'd kept believing I married another woman and tried to kill you and your family."

She tenses. It's subtle, and she soon conceals it, but the image of that possibility must've passed through her mind a thousand times.

Sasha's weakness—the fact that she tends to be an over-thinker—could be her downfall.

After a moment of silence, she looks at me, her eyes a mixture of soft green and harsh brown. "You would still put your plans, ambition, and race for power before me. I can't trust that you won't do it again."

"You're being paranoid."

"Paranoid? I told you I loved you and you announced your damn engagement to the whole world a few hours later. How is that paranoid?"

I start to speak, but she lifts a hand. "Let's talk about something else. What are you going to do when you find Makar?"

"Torture him for answers. The Albanians said they colluded with a man to take you out."

"You don't think that's Makar?"

"No. He's been a servant his whole life. He wouldn't suddenly turn into a master."

"Do you think someone is behind his actions?"

"I don't think. I'm sure. Now, I need to figure out how close that someone is."

"You have suspects?"

"I always do."

"Of course." She releases a breath. "So you torture him and then what?"

"Then you do with him what you please."

"You'll entrust him to me?"

"Seems fair since he tried to kill you."

"Wow. Is the mighty Kirill giving someone else the final say about a critical matter?"

"Not someone else." I slide my arm around her waist and pull her to me so suddenly, a few droplets of vodka splash her chest. "My *wife*."

Despite her best attempts to seem unperturbed, a pink hue covers her cheeks.

I stroke those cheeks as if I can feel the blush against my skin. Sasha remains still, but her lips part as I caress her.

"Have I told you that you look hot when you allow yourself to be you?"

"Save it." She inches away. "I don't even put on makeup or anything, so there's no need for the flattery."

"What the fuck are you talking about?" I haul her back to my side again, trying not to get personally offended at the way she created distance between us. "I don't give a fuck about makeup. I'm talking about you and your stunning blonde hair."

"I knew blondes were your type," she grumbles.

I grin. "Is that why you dyed it back?"

"Nooo." She looks the other way like the most horrible liar who ever walked the earth.

"You told me you were blonde, too, when I first got engaged to Kristina."

"I don't remember that."

"You also said you could be like her. Were you *that* jealous?"

"No. Kristina who? I haven't thought about her since I left." Even as she says that, her cheeks redden and her lips purse.

I'll have to buy my new sister-in-law a thank-you card that says, 'Sorry I called you a robot' for managing to provoke out this side of my wife.

This shows that she cares, no matter how much she denies it. She can fight me all she wants as long as she stays by my side.

I will make sure she never has a way out.

Not even one.

Divorce? I don't believe in that fucking word when it comes to her.

"Why did you marry me, anyway?" she asks after a while. "You could've easily gotten yourself another bargain or partnership through marriage."

"Because you asked me for it."

She swallows thickly and her next word comes out as a whisper. "What?"

"You said, and I quote, 'If I wanted to be your wife, would you make it happen?' So I made it happen."

"Even though you don't believe in the institution?"

"I do now. And you know what? I'm still fucking enraged that you faked your death, but I'll have no other wife but you."

Her lips part, and slowly, too slowly, she lays her head on my shoulder.

Now, I'd like to point out that my cock is not amused at the prospect of having his promised round two sabotaged, but she's been through a lot today, and I can allow her to sleep.

Or that's what I think as I, myself, close my eyes. She grips my hand and places my palm on her steady heartbeat.

And just like that, I'm out.

EIGHTEEN

Sasha

PPARENTLY, KIRILL'S PLAN ALL ALONG WAS TO BRING me here.

It's been a week since we got to this cabin, and he's refusing to leave.

Honestly, I don't think I want to leave either. But unlike him, I can't completely disregard the real-life problems waiting for us out there.

Kirill should be the one who's more concerned about that, considering he's the Pakhan and all. He's new in the role, too, so he can't afford to stay away from the action while depending on Viktor, who's his only source as to what's happening out there.

That doesn't seem to deter him, though.

Not even a little.

He's more concerned about fucking me every chance he gets. I'd be lying if I said I don't enjoy being cornered by him all day long. I've been weirdly horny lately, and he indulges me whenever possible.

Kirill has always had an animalistic sex drive, but I never thought it'd get worse.

Not only does he view every opportunity as a chance to fuck my brains out, but he also doesn't finish and goes on and on until I'm spent, motionless, and on the verge of collapsing.

I think he does that so he'll have the chance to help me shower and bathe and then make me sleep cocooned in his arms.

And the greatest miracle? He's actually been sleeping. Every night. Sometimes with his head on my chest. Other times with my head on his.

He doesn't sleep the whole night, but he does get his few much-needed hours of rest.

Part of the reason why I'm willingly here, aside from the fact that he took me to see Anton again a few days ago, is the surreal change I'm witnessing in him.

It's like I'm in the company of a completely different Kirill, but not really.

He's the same enigmatic, slightly—okay, *very much*—unhinged man who's a distrustful manipulator with a beef with the world. But during the time I've spent with him in this cabin, I've discovered that he's…more.

For instance, he likes to cook and he's actually damn good at it. He says it's because when they were children, he liked to make Konstantin and Karina's favorite dishes.

Since he's Kirill, he'd never admit that deep down, he has a caretaker, protector side to him. Not everyone is entitled to that privilege, but the few who belong to that list get his unconditional support.

I was happy to see his relationship with Konstantin improve tremendously after he married Kristina. When I brought that subject up, Kirill was like, "I was only interested in the business transaction."

He's such a liar. If that were the case, he wouldn't have gone out of his way to lie for them and make sure they got married on the spot in case Igor changed his mind.

During the past few days, he's been so amicable, it's a little scary.

He's offered to teach me how to cook since I've always mentioned I wanted to learn how. He brings me flowers every morning, then places them in a vase.

No kidding. Kirill, who kills for sport, is picking flowers for me like some doting lover.

Sometimes, we talk until late into the night. Other times, we go hiking until we reach the peak and then he watches me scream at the top of my lungs with a huge grin on his face.

He's been giving me deep massages to loosen my muscles. In part, he's doing it so I'm more energized for the next fucking session, but I take it with gratefulness.

I know these things don't come naturally to him. He's putting in the effort for me. He's letting me see the side of him that I've only dreamed of.

Kirill's time all for myself?

His smiles?

His laughs?

His fooling around?

His *whole* attention?

Not in my wildest imagination would I have thought this would be possible.

But it is. And it's starting to terrify the shit out of me.

Every morning, I wake up dreading that the honeymoon phase is over. We'll have to go back to a world where he's my family's enemy.

Every time we go out, a part of me is watching our surroundings, waiting for those men to attack us again.

Just because that didn't happen today doesn't mean it won't happen at all.

And that thought process is driving me crazy.

I don't want to fall into that naïve hopeful state I was in after we got married, because I know for a fact that everything good comes to an end.

Everything.

But at the same time, I can't control the overwhelming happiness that I'm bursting with.

The need for more.

The urge to let go. Just for a while.

Unfortunately for me and no matter how much I try to fight it, Kirill is still the only person I've ever wanted to have for myself.

Not for duty. Not for family. Not for revenge.

Just someone for me.

I get a bit too excited for our morning routine, which is to basically exercise together. I've managed to punch him a few times, but those are few and far between.

He doesn't shy away from taking me down whenever he has the chance.

I come down the stairs in my workout clothes. Today, I decided to wear only a sports bra and my tight shorts that have one of those seams to define my ass.

Not that I'm trying to seduce him or anything. Okay, maybe a little.

I bought them the other day when we went shopping in the nearest town—which is an hour's walk away.

It's about two weeks until Christmas, so the entire town was buzzing with lights, decorations, and excitement. My heart hurt at the reminder of last Christmas, which I didn't get the chance to celebrate. However, I loved seeing people happy.

Kirill, on the other hand, was not impressed and kept judging the whole joyful atmosphere like a grinch.

Since we were carrying a lot of bags, we had to hitch a ride on a farmer's truck on the way back. The driver might have checked me out for a second too long and I had to stop Kirill from putting a bullet in the poor man's head.

Back to the present. Usually, he wakes me up with the flowers of the day, but today, he didn't. Though I did wake up a bit earlier than usual.

I pause when I reach the bottom of the stairs. Fresh flowers sit prettily in a vase on the dining table.

So he did come back.

I sniff them, then take a picture of them and a selfie while holding them and send it to Karina.

> **Sasha:** My flowers for the day.

She replies right away.

> **Karina:** Ugh. He's doing all the right things to keep you away from me. I'm gonna stab him to death next time I see him.

I smile as I type back my reply.

> **Sasha:** We'll come back eventually. We can't exactly stay here forever.

> **Karina:** Bet you want to, though.

If I were sure my brother would be released and wouldn't start any trouble, yes. But right now, the situation just feels like a disaster waiting to happen.

The calm before the storm.

The good thing is that there's no torture. When we visited them again a few days ago, Anton and Maksim were just glaring at each other from opposite ends of the room.

> **Sasha:** Don't be silly. Of course I want to come back.

> **Karina:** Please do. I miss you! Not Kirill, though.

I shake my head.

I swear this family can't survive without a display of tough love. They should get an award in the art.

After taking a few more pictures of the flowers, I leave them and my phone on the table and head outside.

My steps come to a halt when I find another man who's not Kirill standing in the garden.

"Viktor?"

The mountain of a man turns around, raises a brow, probably not used to me dressing this way, before he schools his expression and nods. "Mrs. Morozova."

I tap his shoulder teasingly. "What's with being polite all of a sudden? Call me Sasha, or Aleksandra since you're allergic to the diminutive form."

"You're the boss's wife. I'll call you by your official title."

I roll my eyes. "You call him Kirill when you're mad at him."

"I'll call you by your name when I'm mad at you."

Jeez. He's an unbending asshole.

And yet I've always felt that Kirill is safe as long as Viktor is there. And while I hated that he could probably protect him better than I could, I'm glad Viktor wouldn't let anything happen to him.

"Where is he?" I search around him as if a six-three muscled man is some sort of a needle in a haystack that can't be spotted right away.

"He's checking something."

"What's the something?"

He raises a brow. "I'm under no obligation to report his actions to you."

"You're really an asshole, did you know that? It wouldn't hurt anyone if you just answered the question."

"I'll be the judge of that."

I cross my arms and stand taller, which is a bit pointless since Viktor is way bigger in height and build. "You have a problem with me?"

"My," he says in a robotic, deadpan tone. "What makes you think that? The fact that you've been spying on him? Or how you nearly got him killed in Russia? Or maybe, just *maybe*, the fact that you're doing it all over again now?"

I briefly close my eyes. "The Russia incident wasn't intentional and if I'd wanted him dead, I would've killed him when I came back."

"So you just shot him in the arm?"

My lips part. "Did he tell you that?"

"No. He said that one of the soldiers got him, but I suspected that wasn't the case. He wouldn't let himself be shot that easily unless it was either someone he was close to or he allowed it. Now, I've confirmed that it was you."

"I…thought that…"

"What? He'd married someone else? Tried to kill you and your family? You were so sure without even attempting to talk to him about it."

I purse my lips, then click my tongue. "I wasn't exactly in the right state of mind."

"And you think he was? He'd just found out you were alive after burying you with his own hands. You believe he was prepared to see you back?"

My gulp gets stuck at the back of my throat and I stare at him for a few beats, not knowing what to say. On one hand, I can't fault what he pointed out, but on the other, he didn't experience the emotions I did after I had to go back to Russia.

The feelings of betrayal, rage, and utter despair. Hell, even longing was there. I missed Kirill so much, and I hated myself for it every day.

Viktor steps forward. "I'm warning you. If you attempt to hurt him again, I won't give a fuck that he forgives you. I will kill you and permanently remove you from his life, Aleksandra."

I lift my chin. "I'd like to see you try."

"Don't make me. I witnessed how he turned into a ghost of his former self after your alleged death, but I'd rather have that instead of burying him myself."

"I don't want him hurt or dead, Viktor."

"Your track record doesn't work in your favor. I'm going to need something more convincing than mere words."

"I'll prove it to you."

"Prove what?"

My spine jerks upright at Kirill's deep voice. Anyone else would've only heard the closed-off tone, but I can easily detect the rage simmering beneath the surface.

His arm wraps around the small of my back, eliciting sharp goosebumps on my naked skin.

I stare up at him and wish I hadn't. His face is sharp angles of disapproval. An unprecedented storm whirls in his eyes, darkening them to a raging blue.

And those eyes are now directed at Viktor. "What will my wife prove to you?"

The guard merely lifts a shoulder. "Why don't you ask her?"

"I'm asking you, and if you don't start giving me answers in the next breath, I'm going to confiscate all your air until you spit out your last."

"It's nothing." I place an unsteady hand on his chest.

I've been in so much bliss lately that I almost forgot just how scary he can get.

"I'll decide whether it's nothing or something once I hear the details."

"She said she doesn't want you to be hurt and I said I don't believe her, considering her spying and conspiratorial past, so she offered to prove it."

I stare at Viktor, mouth parted. The bastard just spilled it all out without sparing any detail. Not that I should be surprised, but I thought he'd at least spare me the embarrassment.

"I'm out of here," Viktor announces before he turns and leaves without waiting for a reply.

He must've driven here and left the car at the main dirt road, which is a couple minutes' walk.

Kirill's expression doesn't change, despite Viktor's secret-exposing session. If anything, the look in his eyes gets darker, his pupils nearly swallowing the irises.

I try to smile, though carefully. "Are you up for that match?"

"You look *different*."

My cheeks turn red without my permission. "Good different?"

"Bad."

"Fuck you," I whisper.

He digs his fingers into my arm. "Did you dress this way once you spotted Viktor? Didn't know he was your type."

"Maybe he is." I lift my chin.

"Is that so?" His lips curve in a smile, but it's more like a scary smirk. I don't like it when he's all calm like this. It's a sure way to know that he's plotting something nefarious.

"Yeah. I decided to keep my options open for when we divorce." I know I'm provoking him, but he did it first.

I dressed up for him and the fucking prick is making me feel bad.

One moment I'm standing there and the next, he's grabbing me by the throat, his fingers pressing on the sides so that I'm immobilized.

"You need to learn when to shut the fuck up, Sasha."

I hit his hand and kick at his leg, but he barely allows me to move.

It's always a damn struggle with this man. It's like I'm fighting a bull with no chance of winning.

"Let me go, you asshole," I strain with the little breath I have left.

"Understand this, *wife*." He speaks so close to my face, his mouth almost touches my cheek. "There are no options for you other than me. If you keep insisting there are, I will make you watch as I slaughter each and every one of them."

Something is definitely wrong with me. Otherwise, why the

hell are his savage touch and crazy words turning the temperature in my body up a notch?

Maybe I'm as screwed up as he is.

Maybe the reason I fell for him in the first place was because he speaks to the demented part of me I didn't know existed.

He pushes me back, but I fall on the grass, so it isn't much of a hit. He's been manhandling and throwing me around so much lately that I'm always expecting some sort of a thud.

"Seems like you need a reminder of who the fuck you belong to." He hovers over me like an angry god, his chest rising and falling heavily. His thin gray shirt sticks to his muscles, leaving little to the imagination.

He pulls down my shorts and I hiss in a breath as the fabric creates friction against my swollen clit.

He throws the shorts aside. "You're even wearing nothing under them."

"You told me not to."

He slaps my pussy and I jerk. Holy shit. Is that supposed to feel so good?

"Shhh. Not another fucking word, Sasha."

"Fuck you."

He slaps my pussy again and then rubs my clit. My head rolls back as my core throbs to life.

I think I'm going to come, but he suddenly removes his fingers.

"Which part of shut the fuck up do you not understand, hmm?" He hovers over me so that his knees are on either side of my head and yanks me up by a handful of my hair. Pain explodes in my scalp, but I don't have time to focus on that as he frees his cock and shoves my face against his groin. "Seems that I need to fuck that mouth to make you."

I part my lips to say something, but he uses the chance to thrust inside. His cock hits the back of my throat and he keeps it there.

I stare up at him as tears well along my lids and my gag reflex kicks in.

I can't breathe.

I can't fucking breathe.

"These are the eyes I want to look at. They look like mine."

He pulls out only to thrust in again. With his fingers digging into my skull, he uses his grip to steer my head and fuck my mouth. I don't even try to suck him. That's not what he wants right now. He needs to dominate me, use me, and the unhinged look in his eyes makes my inner thighs sticky with arousal.

"That's it, Solnyshko. Make my cock hard and wet so I can stick it up your cunt."

It should seem weird that he's using my nickname while treating me like a whore, but it's far from it.

I gag and choke on his cock and he thrusts his hips forward, making me take him as deep as I can. My own hips jerk, needing a touch, just a tiny stimulation and I'll come.

When he pulls out, saliva and tears cling to my face, but he barely allows me a breath of air before he slams back in. One of his hands fists my hair and the other nearly covers my whole face, smearing it with tears and my drool.

I reach a hand between my legs, but he releases my face and slaps my achy nipples, then wrenches my hand away. "Did being used make you hot and horny, wife?" He slides out of my mouth. "Tell me to fuck you."

I splutter and choke on my breaths. My lungs burn due to the lack of air and my vision is blurry.

"Fuck you," I whisper.

He offers me a heart-stopping smirk. "Good enough."

He settles between my legs, parts them further, then wraps both of his hands around my neck.

Not sure if it's the breath deprivation, the fact that I'm all sticky down there, or the state he put me in by fucking my mouth—or maybe it's a combination of everything. But the moment he thrusts inside, I come.

It's a sharp but strong orgasm that jerks my whole body. I want to scream, but it's impossible with his savage grip on my throat. For a moment, I think I'll die while he's fucking the living shit out of me.

"Your cunt knows exactly who she belongs to, Solnyshko. She doesn't need any other options but my cock, now does she?"

My back lifts off the ground and I grab two handfuls of grass just to stay rooted.

"You're mine." He squeezes harder and fucks me deeper, hitting my sensitive spot again and again. "Only fucking *mine*."

I think I'm going to come again, but he suddenly pulls out and releases my neck. A groan of frustration leaves my lips and he lets out a sadistic chuckle.

He flips me onto my stomach without warning and lifts me up so I'm on all fours, then pushes me down so my ass is in the air.

I feel him kneeling behind me, the warmth of his body a welcome reprieve against the chill of the outside world. While no one actually comes here, the fact remains that he's fucking me in public, and that adds a great sense of exhilaration to my arousal.

Kirill parts my ass cheeks and drags my wetness from my slit to my back hole. I tense, my heart jackhammering. "W-what are you doing?"

"Owning every inch of you. Your ass is begging to be claimed." He spits on my hole and for some reason, it's so hot, I gulp.

We've done a lot of anal play before and over the past week, but he's never fucked me there.

Now that the moment has come, I'm taken by a sense of dread. I reach out a trembling hand and clutch his wrist. "Wait…wait."

"I'm done waiting."

"But…"

"Shhh…" he says in a surprisingly soothing tone and slaps my ass cheek then spits on my throbbing back hole.

I gasp, my thighs shaking, and he uses the chance to thrust the crown inside.

Oh, God.

I'm wet, but it's still painful.

The second inch follows and I let out a sob. "Kirill, please… it hurts…"

"Shhh…you're taking my cock like a very good girl, Solnyshko."

My lips tremble and I dig my nails into the grass and dirt. He reaches a hand down and rubs my clit in pleasurable circles. "Don't push me out. Relax."

I lower my back and force myself to relax, and then he goes all the way in. The stretch is so sharp that I cry out, but the pain is soon replaced with pleasure as he keeps stimulating my clit in slow, almost soothing circles.

"You're such a good girl, wife."

"Luchik…" I don't mean to say his nickname, but now that I did, I can't take it back.

His pace picks up at that and he growls, "Say that again."

"Luchik, please."

"Please what?"

"Fuck me."

He slaps my ass and rams into it while thrusting three fingers into my pussy. "We can't have my cunt feeling left out."

The sensation of being completely filled leaves me breathless, wanting—no, *needing*—the release.

I don't think I've ever felt so needy in my whole life.

I push back against him, my ass cheeks creating a slapping sound against his thighs and groin.

He spanks my ass then sinks his fingers into the flesh. "You'll never wear these clothes for anyone but me. I'm the only one who gets to look at you like this. Fuck you like this. *Own* you like this."

"Stop being crazy…"

He grips a handful of my hair and flings me up so that my back is against his chest and turns my head to speak directly against my mouth. "You should know by now that I'm a fucking lunatic when it comes to you. Don't fucking test me."

He pumps harder into me, and this time, I scream as I come around his cock and fingers.

Kirill kisses me through it, my tongue wars with his even as he suffocates me.

He knows exactly how tight I get when he steals my breath and he never shies away from repeating the move over and over again.

But if I'd hoped he'd be done, I'm proved utterly wrong.

He throws me back down on the grass again, ass in the air, and keeps going at a maddening pace.

On.

And on.

And *on*.

Until I nearly faint.

Until I can't think of the sentence "it's only physical" anymore.

There's definitely nothing purely physical about this.

NINETEEN

Kirill

"**G**IVE UP ALREADY."

Sasha growls deep in her throat as she lunges at me. This time, I provoked her so thoroughly that she doesn't stop and think about strategy.

She's mindless, brimming with adrenaline and an unhealthy dose of rage.

Sweat trickles down her temples and throat and slips under her sports bra right between her tits. Am I annoyed at sweat for taking the place that's rightfully mine? Possibly.

I step out of the way when she tries to high -kick me, then I push her in the opposite direction. She falls on the grass, but it's not hard enough to cause permanent damage.

Or any damage, really.

She's always asked me to take her seriously and go all in, but that's impossible. I'll only hurt her, and I'd rather cut off my arms than do that.

I know she gets off on practicing and violence. She's a true product of the military life and has unknowingly turned into one of those soldiers who can't survive without physical stimuli.

And while I relate to the feeling to an extent, I don't make it my entire personality like some of my men. And Sasha.

We've been at the cabin for two and a half weeks, and whenever I'm not fucking her brains out, she demands a match. These morning duels have become a routine that she looks forward to every time. She even dresses for the occasion.

Now, I would like to point out that the tight sports bra and these tiny shorts hugging her toned legs are a huge distraction. If I didn't know better, I'd say she was doing it on purpose to scatter my attention.

"Are you done being beaten up for sport?" I cross my arms and stare down at her position on all fours and lower my voice. "We can move on to a more entertaining activity."

She glares up at me, jumps up, then holds her hands up in guard. "I'm not done."

A battle cry echoes in the air before she goes in with a punch. I engulf her fist in my palm. "Stop being stubborn. If I decide you won't get a hit in, you won't."

"Ugh." She pushes with all her strength. "I'm not giving up."

"In that case, we might have to stay here all day."

"I don't care!"

"Well, I do. I prefer other pleasurable physical activities."

"Dream on, asshole." She ducks and tries again.

I grab her by the waist while holding her hand so that her back is against my chest. Then I lower my head and whisper in her ear, "I promise you'll enjoy what I have in mind more than this. In fact, it'll help reduce that anger."

"You're making me angrier right now with your stupid nonchalance."

"I can also fix you some herbal tea to purge the strain." I nibble on the shell of her ear.

"Kirill!" she grunts, obviously on the verge of exploding.

"Yes?"

"Fight me seriously and stop playing around."

"I refuse."

"But why?" She narrows her eyes. "You think so little of me?"

"No. I'm just not a fan of the idea of hurting you."

"Really?" She elbows me and slips out of my hold. "You did that just fine when you announced your engagement to Kristina while I was standing right there."

"You're never going to forgive me for that, are you?"

"I don't know. Maybe I won't. I might consider it if you take me seriously."

"You're the one who asked for this, so don't come crying to me when you can't walk."

She grins and doesn't waste any time. Sasha comes at me with all her might. I push her to the ground, enjoying the feeling of having her trapped underneath me a bit too much.

After a few moments, she manages to escape and tries to high-kick me. I circle her ankle and yank. She loses her balance and hits the ground again.

Usually, she'd jump right back up, but she remains unmoving.

I didn't put power behind the pull, so she should be fine.

Right?

"Ow," she grunts, balling into a fetal position and holding her stomach.

"Fuck." I run to her side. "Are you okay?"

Her face is contorted, eyes half closed and sweat beading on her upper lip.

Fucking fuck.

I reach a hand toward her. "I told you not to fucking fight me! Where does it hurt? Can you move—"

In a fraction of a second, she rolls onto her back and kicks me in the face, then jumps away while wearing a shit-eating grin. "Got you!"

I touch the throbbing spot in my cheek with the back of my hand. The little fucking—

Without a word, I turn around and head toward the cabin. My tendons nearly snap with tension and my head feels like it's at the point of exploding.

Sasha soon falls in step beside me and pushes my shoulder with hers. "Don't be a sore loser. Let's continue."

I say nothing.

"Oh, come on. You throw me down all the time. You don't see me acting butthurt."

She does—all the time, whining and grumbling like a fucking baby. Sasha seems to have the memory of a goldfish about some things but has no problem recalling all the grudges she holds against me.

"Is it so wrong for me to win even once?"

No reply.

"Are you seriously pulling the silent treatment on me because I kicked you?"

I face her so suddenly, she crashes into me before stepping back.

Her throat bobs with a swallow when her eyes meet mine. "Why…why do you look so scary?"

"I thought you were seriously hurt because of me. Don't you ever, and I mean fucking *ever*, do that shit again. Do you hear me?"

Her throat works up a swallow. "I didn't think…"

"You obviously didn't. If you want to hit me so badly, I'll just stand there and take it. Don't do that fucking nonsense again."

"It's not that I want to hit you." Her voice shakes and she clears her throat. "I don't want to hurt you either, but you're a provocative asshole who never takes me seriously." She touches my hurt cheek. "Is it very painful?"

"I'll survive."

"Come on." She pulls up on the corners of my lips with her forefingers. "I won't do it again. Can you stop with the long face?"

I don't even know why I'm so fucking enraged about this.

No. Actually, I'm well aware of the magnitude of these emotions.

When I thought Sasha had died, a part of me believed it was because of me, and that only made me spiral further out of control.

I hate that wayward version of myself that couldn't stop my disintegration process.

So to be put in the same situation again—to think Sasha's in pain because of me *again*—drew out those infuriating feelings from the depths of my black soul.

I step away from her. "I'm going to town for some shopping."

She releases me, but her shoulders hunch. I was supposed to prepare her a surprise tonight, and I still am, but my mood for the occasion is nonexistent at the moment.

After I finish showering and changing clothes, I find Sasha waiting for me in front of the house, already showered and wearing her coat.

She stops kicking rocks upon seeing me. Her soft face lights up with a careful smile. "I'll come along."

I do want her to come along for my plan to work, but I didn't think she'd volunteer.

Usually, we walk to town, but about a week ago, I asked Viktor to bring me a truck in case of an emergency.

I drive in silence and Sasha fiddles with the radio stations. She loves listening to music, singing along, and trying to make me join to no avail.

Today, however, she doesn't seem to be in a singing mood. After a few minutes of changing stations, she turns off the radio and sighs.

"Are you really going to be like this?"

"Like what?"

"Like an asshole." She faces me in her seat, arms crossed. "I already said I won't do it again. What got your panties in a twist?"

"Just stay quiet."

"Fuck you." Her voice trembles before she catches herself. "I'm the one who's supposed to be mad at you for all the shit you've pulled. I won't allow you to make me feel guilty for some trivial matter."

Trivial.

Did she just call that fucking shit *trivial*?

I tighten my hold on the wheel to stop myself from reaching out and choking the fuck out of her, which defies the whole purpose of not wanting to hurt her.

"If this is one of your manipulative, reverse psychology methods, then I'm sorry to inform you that it won't work, you fucking bastard."

"If you're done, shut the fuck up. I mean it."

She huffs, opens her mouth, probably to say something more infuriating, but she thankfully closes it again.

The town is the opposite of our mood. Considering today is Christmas Eve, everyone is doing last-minute shopping. Carols sound in the distance and kids sit on a bored Santa's lap, reading their belated gift wish lists.

Colorful Christmas trees and decorations line the front of every shop and a general disgustingly joyful atmosphere lingers in the air.

I was never a fan of Christmas, or any holiday, for that matter. Those are for families, and I never really had one.

Roman was more interested in shaping me into his heir and thought the silly occasions would make me mellow. Yulia only celebrated holidays with Konstantin.

I used to wrap gifts for my siblings, but I soon quit that after my decision to put distance between us.

Now, it's just an annoying time of the year where everything is colorful and disgustingly happy.

When we first came to this town in the lead-up to Christmas, Sasha said that she wanted to love it, but couldn't.

Christmas reminds her of the day she witnessed her family die in front of her and, therefore, she prefers not to celebrate.

However, while I've turned into a grinch, she actually enjoys the town's atmosphere. Even now, her eyes brighten whenever she hears the repetitive Christmas songs or sees a family going around the shops.

She sings along with the clownish lyrics, too, sometimes.

"Just because it was traumatizing for me, I guess I like to know it's still a happy occasion for everyone else," she told me the other day.

She's always been compassionate with a pure heart—except when she holds grudges against me, of course.

And no, I won't be shutting up about that anytime in the near future.

We buy a few groceries, and I glare at anyone who gets too close to her. She notices that, smiles, then shakes her head in resignation.

When we walk the length of the main street, she snaps pictures of the decorated shops. After some time of filming the mundane things that start to blur together, she faces me. "Would you hate it if we got a last-minute Christmas tree?"

"Yes."

She purses her lips and releases a long, frustrated breath. "You're a real joy to be around today."

"Thanks."

"That wasn't a compliment. Is it so wrong to feel the spirit?"

"What spirit? Besides, we don't celebrate Christmas tomorrow. It's on January the seventh in Russia."

"Even better. We can do it twice!"

"I would rather die."

"Grinch." She pushes past me and a little girl stumbles into her.

Sasha lowers herself to the girl's height and ruffles her red beanie. "Are you okay?"

The girl smiles shyly and plays with the pompons dangling

from her hat, then shouts, "Merry Christmas!" before running off to her awaiting mother and sibling.

"Merry Christmas!" Sasha shouts back and waves with more enthusiasm than needed.

I watch her bright expression and glittery eyes intently, picturing them with our own children one day.

She'd make a wonderful mother, and most importantly, she'd look fucking hot carrying my baby.

Impregnating her is the surest way to keep her around more than the three blasphemous months she's adamant about.

The question is how.

There are no pills.

She's religious about renewing the shot. If my calculations are correct, she should be renewing it soon. In a couple of weeks, probably.

How can I tamper with that process without making her hate me?

You can just ask her.

The stupidest part of my fucking brain that's a disgrace to even exist whispers.

The answer will obviously be no. Would she agree to have damn children when she put a timeline on how long she's staying with me?

There are only seventy-one days left, by the way. I know because I'm counting every fucking one of them.

I stop beside her and jut my chin in the retreating family's direction. "One would think they're a walking Christmas tree with all the red and green."

"Stop being a grinch." She hits my shoulder with hers. "I think they look so cute."

"The children or the amateur Christmas fashion?"

She suppresses a smile. "Both. And seriously, stop it. Just because you disregard the holiday doesn't mean everyone should."

"I'm not saying that."

"You're merely judging them?"

"And the eyesore color selection they willingly wear like a badge."

"You're just jealous you won't look cool wearing a Christmas sweater and drinking some hot chocolate with marshmallows like normal people."

I stare down my nose at her. "I look cool doing anything."

"Oh yeah? Wanna bet?"

I see exactly what she's trying to do, but since I've been an asshole due to my own insecurities, I go with her subpar manipulation attempt anyway.

An hour later, we're dressed in matching Christmas sweaters that I wouldn't subjugate a homeless person with wearing. Sasha even bought the red Santa hat with the white pompon.

She offered me one and I threatened to shoot the whole store down if she put the thing on me, so she gave up.

We're now sitting on a pier overlooking the forest and sipping hot chocolate filled with more sickeningly sweet marshmallows than any human should consume. A giant Christmas tree is behind me, its annoying decorations hanging above my head. I chose this seat because Sasha wouldn't stop taking pictures of me.

She's been doing that ever since I agreed to this plan that I'm starting to regret. I don't really, though, because she's been smiling the entire time and getting as giddy as a kid with all the shopping and trying on different clothes.

"Are you going to stop taking pictures anytime soon?"

She snaps one more. "You're so photogenic."

I adjust my glasses. "I know. Comes with the superior genes."

She rolls her eyes. "Would it hurt you to be more humble?"

"No, but it wouldn't do me any good either."

She goes through her phone, probably checking her camera roll. "Would Karina feel bad if I sent her these…? What am I saying? Of course she would. She said she wanted us to celebrate Christmas together."

"What did you tell her?"

"That I couldn't. But maybe I should've. I can't not celebrate it all my life, after all."

I reach across the table and grab her chin between my fingers. Her startled eyes meet mine, brimming with green and soft yellow. "W-what?"

"Look at me when you're talking to me."

She slowly slides the phone onto the table. "You could've just said that. Why do you have to be intense about it all of a sudden?"

"How else will I be the center of your attention?" I stroke her chin before I release it. "I know I look perfect in pictures, but I'm better in real life."

"Wow. I can't take this anymore."

"That's what you said last night."

She watches the people buzzing around us and hisses while laughing. "Kirill!"

"What? Wasn't that the reference you were intending to go for?"

"No." She laughs again, her expression the happiest I've seen since our wedding day. "You're seriously impossible sometimes."

"Does that mean I'm tolerable other times?"

"I don't know. Maybe." She takes a sip of her hot chocolate but keeps watching me from over the rim. "At the risk of feeding your ego, I'll admit that you look cool even in a Christmas sweater."

"I know." I take a sip as well. "With the pure intention of feeding your ego, you look edible, even while wearing these hideous colors."

She grins like an adorable idiot. "Really?"

"Yes. In fact, I wouldn't mind you sitting on my lap to show you the evidence."

I didn't expect much from the statement, but Sasha leaves her seat and comes to sit on my lap. Her legs are on either side of my waist and she wraps her arms around my neck. "Guess it can't be helped since you're being a good sport today, I forgive you for being an asshole this morning."

"I forgive you for scaring me to death."

Her lips part. "I didn't know you were capable of those feelings."

"I am when it comes to you." I sink my fingers into her hip. "I'm traumatized from seeing your fake body."

"Is that why you asked me to apologize the other day?"

I nod.

"I'm sorry," she whispers against my mouth. "I wanted to hurt you as much as you'd hurt me."

"You went above and beyond hurting me back."

"I'm sorry," she repeats, this time peppering kisses all over my cheeks, nose, lids, and lips.

My body relaxes under her touch and I close my eyes just so I can feel her warmth colliding with mine and her heartbeat thundering against my own.

She's here.

She's actually here.

Every morning, I wake up thinking my reality is a dream and that I'll find myself in an alternative reality where she's dead.

After what seems like minutes, she pulls back and murmurs, "Now what, Kirill?"

I slowly open my eyes and stare at her expectant face. "Now?"

"After this." She throws her hands around.

"Why does there need to be an after?"

"We can't possibly live the honeymoon phase forever. You have responsibilities as the Pakhan."

My mood shifts, taking a sharp dive in the opposite direction. "Fuck that."

"Well, I have my own responsibilities."

"I don't want to hear it." I start to get up, but she palms both my cheeks.

"You can't pretend the outside world doesn't exist."

"Watch me."

"But—"

I shut her up with my lips on hers and my hand squeezing her throat. She gasps into my mouth, but she soon crashes her tongue against mine.

Sasha might pretend that she won't hesitate before leaving me, but she, too, is being held hostage by this invisible connection she and I share.

The connection that refuses to break, no matter the circumstances.

The connection that's been present for as long as we've known each other.

I'm ready to fight a million-year war as long as I find her at the end of it.

When we break apart, she's panting, her lips swollen, and her eyes glittery. "W-what was that for?"

"To shut you up." I stand and check my phone. When I find the text I've been waiting for, I grab her hand. "We're leaving."

She doesn't say anything, seemingly dazed. But she does put on some disgusting Christmas music and sings along when I'm driving away.

I find myself smiling every time she gets excited because she knows the lyrics. I might drive slower, too.

When we arrive at the cottage, she climbs out, her shoulders hunched. "We should've at least gotten a little tree."

"There's no need."

She stops short in front of the house when she sees the dozen strings of lights and two Christmas trees outside.

"You…did this?"

"I ordered it. Does that count?"

"Yes!" She hugs me, jumping up and down while doing so. Since I've become addicted to her hugs, I use every chance I get to enjoy her touch.

After a while, she notices the two cars crowding the driveway and searches my gaze. "Who did you invite?"

She doesn't wait for my reply as she dashes inside. The house is in full annoying Christmas spirit. Karina is telling Viktor that he's decorating the tree all wrong and that, apparently, the lights can't be placed like they're security wires.

Konstantin and Kristina are placing their own ornaments and smiling at each other like the protagonists of a clichéd Hallmark movie.

"Sasha!" My sister gives up on correcting Viktor's feeble attempts at decorating and runs into my wife's embrace. "What do you think? What do you think?"

"This is so beautiful." Sasha greets the others and even pats Viktor on the back, to which he grunts.

If I'm a grinch, he's a heretic.

"Is that you?" he says, judging my sweater so hard, I'm surprised he doesn't shoot laser holes through it. "Couldn't recognize you in those hideous colors."

"Very funny." I give him a forced smile and he just shakes his head, suppressing his own smile.

I go upstairs to change out of the awful thing. I'm buttoning my shirt when the door to the bedroom opens. Soon after, toned arms wrap around me from behind and Sasha buries her head in my back.

My eyes briefly close, thinking about that image of her I conjured after I thought she was dead.

No. This is real. She's back.

My wife whispers, "Thank you for planning all of this."

I turn around to face her. "You're not uncomfortable with the whole Christmas vibe?"

"Not as much as I thought I'd be. It's time I let go of that. Thank you for making me step out of my comfort zone and sharing your family with me."

"Should I tell Maksim to bring Anton over?"

She shakes her head. "He'll try to kill you or hold Karina hostage to kill you."

I'm glad she's levelheaded enough to recognize that. I only mentioned it to placate her. I'd never allow that vermin near my family. If it were up to me, I'd never allow him near her either.

"Take me to visit him later instead," she suggests. "For now, let's just live in the moment."

The moment.

I like that.

One problem, though. I'm not an in-the-moment type of person.

My mind is already full of possible plans for the future. However, all the noises quiet down when my wife gets on her tiptoes and plants a kiss on my lips. "Schastlivogo Rozhdestva, Luchik."

Merry Christmas.

I've never liked this atrocious holiday as much as I do right now.

TWENTY

Sasha

I NEVER THOUGHT I'D SAY THIS, BUT THE PAST FEW DAYS
were possibly the happiest of my life.

Nothing could've prepared me for the overwhelming
emotions I've had since Kirill's family came to celebrate the holidays with us.

Well, minus Yulia. And I'm thankful for that because she's
been glaring at me nonstop ever since I came back.

On Christmas day, I asked many of the guards I've spent years
with to join us for dinner.

Kirill definitely didn't like that turn of events and he expressed
his displeasure in the form of glares, but I made it up to him in
the shower that night.

He definitely enjoyed that, so I'd say the mission was a success.

Over the time we've been spending here, I've grown to like this
new side of Kirill. He's still the same infuriating man I first met in
the army, but he feels closer now. More real. *Touchable.*

But this sense of comfort is, as I suspected, ending soon.

I know that Uncle and Babushka will always want to kill him. Aside from wanting to gain Anton's freedom, I don't know if I share any goals with them anymore.

But then again, how can I save Anton without risking Kirill's life?

Whenever I think about it, my head hurts, which is why I choose to only focus on the now.

For as long as the *now* lasts. Be it a few days or months. I don't care as long as I'm in this dream-like state.

It'll hurt like a mother on the day when I finally wake up, but that day isn't today.

Something much more stressful is happening today.

"Maybe I'll come back another time," I murmur, even though it's only the two of us in the sterile white room.

Kristina clasps my hand in hers and smiles. "Today is as good as any."

If a month ago, someone told me that I'd be holding hands with Kristina and sitting on an OB-GYN's table, I would've called them fools.

But here we are.

It started when I got an upset stomach after lunch. Kirill was extra and said he'd take me to the emergency room, but Kristina said she'd take care of it.

She asked some weird questions about emotional reactions and body changes, then told me I could be pregnant.

Of course I laughed and completely denied it, but then I remembered that I'd missed the renewal of the shot during that time Kirill locked me up in the basement.

I only thought about it afterward since I was under a different type of stress at the time—which Kristina ironically participated in. Even unknowingly. After I went back to Russia, I thought it was pointless to renew it since I planned to be celibate indefinitely.

She said if I find myself more emotional or hornier than

normal, then it could be the pregnancy hormones. I only came here to prove her wrong. That's all.

So what if I've been abnormal lately? That doesn't mean I'm pregnant.

Yes, I came with Kristina instead of Kirill because I don't want him to catch a whiff of this whole situation until I make sense of it.

He narrowed his eyes at the idea of Kristina and me together, but he let it go when we were running an errand. Then we had to convince Konstantin to actually leave her side for once. A test could've sufficed, but I thought it's better to see a doctor straight away. Besides, I'm really starting to believe this crazy theory. At least that way, many things will have an actual explanation.

Waiting for the results of the urine test makes my limbs fidgety.

The door opens and a young short-haired doctor comes inside with a huge grin on her face.

Oh, God.

Oh, God.

Is it possible to run away now—

"Congratulations," she announces. "You're pregnant."

The doctor is saying something about regular checkups and a few other things that I should've done in the first trimester, but I'm not listening.

My heart beats so loud, I think it'll jump out of my throat.

A part of me is inexplicably happy. Overwhelmed, yes, but the thought of being a mother has always fascinated me.

However, the other part, the one that's logical and grounded, knows that this will complicate things big time.

Kirill will never let me go if he finds out.

He'll use the baby to possess me even worse than he's been doing during the past few weeks. He'll force my hand so I'll stay.

He'll suffocate me to death.

That thought makes me want to vomit, which is ironic since I've never had morning sickness, despite being pregnant for months.

Shit.

The reality dawns on me with creepy speed and I listen to the doctor's words. Apparently, not all women have bumps this early, which explains why my stomach is somewhat flat. I thought I was gaining some weight, but apparently that's the result of the pregnancy.

He's such a little fighter, this baby. Not only did he survive that bombing, but also the shit ton of physical activities I've put my body through. Not to mention the stress, the traveling, and the crushing heartache.

The doctor asks me if I want to do an ultrasound and possibly find out the gender of the baby. After I agree, a technician comes along. The moment I see the moving bundle of black and white on the screen, all my thoughts quiet down.

My lips part as I watch the fetus moving and hear the booming heartbeat.

"You're fifteen weeks pregnant," the doctor says with a smile. "He looks healthy,"

"H-he?" I look at her. "How do you know?"

She points at a dark spot in the middle. "That's why he's a he."

"Aww." Kristina smiles. "Congrats, Sasha. I can't wait to find out the gender of my baby."

I keep watching the screen, moisture gathering in my eyes. I think I might be getting emotional or something.

Because I really want to hold this baby in my arms. I thought I had no purpose after revenge, but maybe this is fate telling me that I most definitely do.

After looking at the ultrasound image for an eternity, I slip it in the back of my jeans and ask Kristina to hide the prenatal vitamins the doctor gave me in her bag.

Before we leave, I clutch her arm. "Don't tell Kirill or Konstantin, or even Karina. Actually, don't tell anyone."

Her brow furrows. "Why?"

"It's complicated. I need to sort a few things out before I tell Kirill."

"Okay."

"Really?"

"Sure. It's your good news to share anyway."

"Thanks, Kristina."

"You're welcome. I'm happy to have someone to share a pregnancy with." Her expression falls. "I tried being close to Yulia, but I don't think she likes me."

"She doesn't like anyone but Konstantin."

"I know, which is why I tried to do my duty as the daughter-in-law, but she's never approved of me."

"Ignore her like I do. She's not worth your effort."

"Thanks. We can go to these pregnancy classes together…if you don't hate me, of course."

"Why would I hate you?"

"Because of the engagement?"

"Oh. That. Don't worry about it. That whole thing is all in the past."

"Thank you for saying that. If it's any consolation, Kirill never even liked me. You're the only woman he looks at as if he's terrified of breathing without her."

I laugh. "You're exaggerating."

"You weren't there when he thought you'd died. He visited your supposed grave every day and got drunk until he passed out. He barely functioned without you and only came back to life after you returned."

I gulp, my heart hammering fast as if it was never stomped upon and torn to shreds. This better be just the hormones.

It has to be.

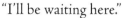

"I'll be waiting here."

I stare back at Viktor, who accompanied me to visit my brother today.

New Year's came and went, and Kirill was under the obligation to go back to his duties. So we all returned to New York.

Since he has an important meeting with the other leaders, he assigned Viktor to drive me here. Let's just say the ride with him wasn't as bad as I expected. We simply ignored each other.

When we arrived at the annexed room, he opened it with his thumbprint and told me to go inside.

He probably wants to stay outside in case I try something and help Anton escape.

I carefully take the few steps down. I stopped training and have only been doing pregnancy-approved sports. Kirill kept asking why we're not having our morning duels anymore, but he stopped after I told him that I don't want to hurt him either.

He said that I'm not fighting anyone but him and I agreed, which he narrowed his eyes at. I know he's suspicious, but I'm not sure about what exactly.

However, that's a thought for another day.

My priority right now is the little boy I'm carrying. I wasn't able to take care of him in the first trimester, so I'll do it properly now.

My stomach is starting to show a bump, and he'll definitely notice it soon, considering all the fucking he treats like a religion.

Problem is, I'm not sure how the hell to approach him about this.

I can't tell him until I figure out what to do about this entire situation, namely my family.

My feet come to a halt at the bottom of the few stairs.

What the…?

I have to blink to make sure the scene in front of me is real and not a hallucination.

In the corner of the room where Anton usually meditates on the bed, something entirely different is happening.

My brother and my friend are sleeping, arms wrapped around each other's waists and foreheads connected.

And they're naked.

Or at least, their upper halves and their legs are. I'm glad there's a sheet thrown over their intimate parts.

I must make some sort of a noise, because Maks jumps up in one swift movement. Anton follows right after and I turn my head in time to not see them entirely naked.

"Fuck" and "Shit" echo behind me, followed by groans and fumbling of clothes. I slam my eyes shut, even though I'm turned away. I don't want to risk accidentally witnessing their nudity and traumatizing myself for life.

"What are you doing here?" Maks asks with a note of frustration. "Boss didn't tell me you were coming."

Is that what Kirill used to do? Inform him of our visits?

"Maybe he forgot. Also, Viktor is the one who brought me here."

A hand touches my arm and I slowly open my eyes. "You guys decent?"

"Yes," both say at the same time, Anton sounding more frustrated than Maks.

The latter is the one who touched my arm. He rubs the back of his head, looking flustered for the first time ever. For a moment, he appears lost for words before he points at the entrance with his thumb. "I'm just going to talk to Viktor."

He casts a fleeting glance at Anton, who looks back momentarily before my friend leaves, and I hear the door closing behind him.

My brother is sitting on the bed, his head lowered and his shoulders tense. I slowly approach him, then sit beside him. "Is there something I need to know?"

"If I say no, would you leave it alone?"

"Probably not."

He groans and runs his fingers through his hair. His face looked so peaceful earlier, but now, a war rages in the depths of his soul and spills outside his body in droves.

"Tosha…" I touch his arm. "What's going on?"

"Nothing."

"That didn't look like nothing just now."

"I don't know what the hell it is. I know nothing at this point. Everything is fucking complicated."

I squeeze his shoulder. "I've never related to you in my life like I do right now."

His eyes meet mine, slowly calming down. "On which part?"

"The fact that everything is complicated and that nothing makes sense anymore."

Silence stretches between us for several moments before we sigh at the same time.

I chuckle at that and Anton offers a hesitant smile back.

"What the fuck are we even doing?" he asks in a whisper, more to himself than anyone else.

"I have no clue," I reply anyway.

"We can't go on like this. We have the deaths of our family members strapped to our shoulders."

I have no clue if he's trying to convince me or himself at this point.

"I know," I say.

"Have you figured out a way to get me out of here, or are you now comfortable staying as Kirill's wife?"

"Even if I were comfortable, I don't like the fact that you're locked up."

"But?"

"I don't want you to hurt Kirill."

"Fuck, Sasha. You're falling into the same trap all over again."

"No, I'm not. Kirill never planned to marry another woman or kill me. Besides, I don't believe he's involved with our family's death."

"So you trust him now?"

"On that front, yes." *I just don't trust that he might use me as a pawn in his upcoming manipulation games.*

"You were always loyal to a fault." He sighs. "Whether to the family, the men you served with and especially Kirill. Now I get why Papa wanted to preserve your sickeningly naïve nature and why Mama babied and fawned all over you. They didn't want you exposed to the real world."

"I'm thankful, but I don't think it did me any good afterwards."

"Believe me, it did. At least you didn't turn into a monster."

"You're not a monster either, Tosha."

He grumbles a reply then exhales deeply. "You're at a crossroad now."

"Well, aren't you, too?"

"That's…different."

"Yeah, right. I'm not even sure if you're lying to me or yourself at this point. There's no black or white in this world. It's just impossible to keep to the extremes."

"What are you suggesting then?"

"Can't…can't we rectify this situation and also have something for ourselves? Just once?"

"I'm not sure if that's possible."

"But why?" My voice breaks and my lips tremble.

It's Anton who squeezes my shoulder this time. "People like us don't deserve happiness, Sasha. The concept was ripped from us that day, never to return."

I shake my head.

I refuse to believe that we have no life after this.

Anton might have already chosen the path he'll go down, but I haven't.

I still have time to figure out what to do and how to end this ill fate once and for all.

For the sake of my child.

For *my* sake.

TWENTY-ONE

Kirill

SOMETHING IS WRONG.

I know it, feel it, and can smell it in the fucking air.

Things haven't been the same since we returned from the cabin three weeks ago.

Sasha has been subtly keeping her distance. It's not as blatant as when she came back and chose to spend her time with anyone but me. This time, it's more in the little details.

Like how she stopped the morning training, no longer waits up for me, doesn't have drinks with me, and she prefers to go visit her brother in Viktor's company instead of mine.

I can't really do anything about the last one since I'm overwhelmed by all the shit in the Bratva, namely, keeping Damien's killing spree in check.

While the above changes are noticeable, they could be viewed as fleeting compared to everything else.

For one, she's not talking about leaving me in a few weeks anymore.

She's not using every chance she gets to remind me that she's my wife only temporarily.

And, most importantly, she holds the same level of fucked-up desire for me as I do for her. I've been trying to wake her up with my mouth on her cunt, but lately, she's been reversing the roles, so I'm the one who wakes up in heaven with her lips around my cock.

The biggest red flag, though, is that she's been spending more time with the ex-robot Kristina, much to my and my brother's dismay.

I snatch a champagne glass from a passing waiter and stand beside said brother. We're holding a gathering at the house to celebrate the brotherhood's alliance with the Yakuza. The brotherhood leaders and the heads of other factions have shown up, too.

The reason for the strengthening of this relationship—Damien—has fucked off to God knows where. I haven't seen his fiancée, either, since her father introduced her earlier.

The downside of being Pakhan is the obligation to conduct private meetings and indulge in stupid small talk, but that's the last thing on my mind.

I haven't been able to find an explanation for the feeling that's been plaguing my insides these last couple of days.

The simple definition would be unease and dread of the unknown where Sasha's concerned. The first reaction my brain came up with was to suffocate her further, lock her the fuck up if need be, so there won't be a way out no matter how much she tries.

But that would mean completely eradicating whatever semblance of peace we've been having.

She'd hate it and me.

Besides, it's not that she's trying to leave.

Or maybe that's what she's doing, but discreetly so I won't be able to thwart her plans.

"They're surprisingly close," my brother says from beside me, his attention on the two women.

They're standing with the annoying Rai and Adrian's wife, Lia, as if this is some sort of a sorority.

Sasha is wearing a loose black dress that stops right above her knees. Her shiny blonde hair is loose, now reaching the middle of her back. She hasn't cut it once since she went back to being a woman.

Although her heels aren't as high as the others', she's still the tallest of the bunch. The most beautiful, too. Just saying.

"More like, your wife is surprisingly clingy." I direct my malicious glare at my brother. "Keep her away from my wife."

He raises a brow. "Not sure that's how it works."

"Find a solution that works, then."

He smiles, and it's surprisingly mischievous. "Is it so bad that she's making women friends? At least they're not the guards you strongly oppose of."

"I don't like anyone who's prone to steal her time from me."

"You need help."

"Yes. Yours. In the form of stopping Kristina from taking away my wife to fuck knows where."

Even Karina has been getting annoyed at not being able to spend as much time as possible with Sasha. My sister is hiding in her room as we speak. She may have started to leave the house at times, but crowds still freak her out.

"Ever thought she might actually need a social circle outside of yourself?" Konstantin asks like an idiot.

"No."

"I would say I'm surprised, but that would be a lie..." he trails off when our mother—correction, *his* mother—appears at the bottom of the stairs with her brother, Yakov.

He's on the board of the family bank and has always disregarded me, unlike the rest of her siblings, who have supported me since day one. Including my eldest uncle, who's the head of the family and the bank.

Yulia has always gotten along with Yakov. He's the only sibling she's visited over the years, but he rarely came here in the past because he and Roman hated each other with passion.

He only started showing his face in our family home after his death.

My attention slides back to Konstantin, who's gripping his flute so tight, I'm surprised it doesn't break into pieces.

It's no secret that he and Yulia have a strained relationship since he indirectly picked Kristina over her and married a woman his mother doesn't approve of.

But it'd take a miracle for Yulia to hate her golden child. I thought Konstantin was using this chance to put some form of distance between him and his toxic mother, but maybe that's not the whole story.

I narrow my eyes on Yulia and Yakov, then direct my gaze at my brother. "Is there something I need to know?"

He purses his lips but says nothing.

"Konstantin." I adopt my most diplomatic tone as I face him. "I know we haven't been model siblings, but you're still my brother. If Yakov is giving you shit of any sort, I'll hang him by his balls before he can blink. You don't need to worry about the repercussions. I have enough power to squash him—"

"It's Yulia."

"You want me to hang Yulia by her imaginary balls?"

He snickers, but it's fleeting. "Be serious."

"What's the problem?"

"Something happened this morning, and I…I want to believe I'm wrong."

"Let's hear it."

"She…I've heard her whisper something to her maid a couple of times before. Something about giving Kris herbs that improve immunity and fuck knows what. I didn't think much of it in the beginning, but out of precaution, I offered to give Kristina whatever herbs my mother had prepared, then I dumped them down the drain. I asked Kris to never drink or eat in her company and to only consume what Anna gives her." His Adam's apple bobs with a swallow. "Tell me I'm being paranoid."

"Have you tested said herbs?"

"I got the results today."

"Let me guess. They're toxic."

The clenching of his jaw is all the answer I need. "Maybe she didn't know…"

"Wake the fuck up. That woman never does anything without a purpose. She wants your baby dead."

"But it's her grandchild."

"And Kara and I are her fucking children. Do you think she took that into consideration when she tried to kill us? You've seen her throw herself down the fucking stairs when she was pregnant with our sister. You were old enough to remember." I pause and soften my tone. "She's always been obsessed with your safety and well-being, but she can't stand Kristina. She's the woman because of whom you went against her. Your mother isn't the type who takes no for an answer. She probably thinks if she gets rid of Kristina's child, you'll have no reason to stay with her and will divorce her."

"That won't happen."

"Then she won't stop until it does."

His chest rises and falls in an intense rhythm. "What am I supposed to do now? I don't think Kris is safe around her anymore."

"I can kick Yulia out."

He pauses, touches his neck, then sighs, "She'd ask me to come along."

"Then say no, motherfucker. Unless you're in the mood to witness a tragedy?"

"Of course not."

"Then I will make it happen first thing in the morning." I clink my glass against his.

He drinks, though he still seems hesitant. Konstantin's problem is that he always tries to see some of Yulia's good side. It makes sense, considering all the love she poured out on him. At some point, she ended up asphyxiating him, and he always hated her attitude toward us, even if he pretended he didn't.

"You might want to look further into Yakov," Konstantin says.

"What for?"

"He's her right hand in everything I refuse to take part in."

Hmm.

Interesting.

This could be the clue I've been missing at the basis of my theory. I shoot Viktor a text.

Check Yakov's whereabouts around the time of the cottage's bombing and any possible communications with Makar.

Soon after, we're joined by Adrian, who's also not a fan of being separated from his wife. We don't have to enjoy each other's company, though, because thankfully, our evening is all set.

I have a few meetings with the Yakuza and the Luciano leaders, but my mind is occupied with other, more pressing issues.

When I go back to the main hall, I catch a glimpse of Kristina with Konstantin, and Rai is talking to Kyle. Lia is with her husband's guards, but there's no trace of Sasha.

A potent sense of paralyzing terror grabs hold of me, and I have to force myself to breathe properly as I call her. Her phone is turned off.

Fuck. Fuck. Fuck!

I ask Kristina about my wife's whereabouts, and she says Sasha left a while earlier.

Does that mean she left for good? Have I been blindsided?

I head to our room two steps at a time while twisting my wedding ring until I nearly break my finger the fuck off.

When I open the door and go inside, my breathing slowly returns to normal. Sasha is lying on the sofa, eyes closed and arms wrapped around her middle.

Fuck.

Fucking fuck.

If I keep going like this, I might have a heart attack the moment she disappears on me again.

I need that tracker on her. *Now*.

Yes, I still have her at the moment, but who knows what will happen in a few days or even a few hours.

My alarm has reached levels I can't control anymore. It's gotten to the point where I've become apprehensive about leaving the house and, therefore, her.

I've just finished texting Viktor to make the arrangements, when Sasha stirs. She props herself up on her elbows, eyes sleepy and voice husky. "Who is it?"

"It's me." I slip my phone back into my pocket.

She sits up, recognition slowly returning to her eyes. "Have I been gone for too long? I just needed a little nap."

"Since when do you need naps?"

She swallows but soon smiles. "You haven't been letting me get enough sleep lately, in case you didn't notice."

"Hmm."

"And you probably won't hold back tonight either, will you?" She starts to stand up, but I shake my head.

Sasha's confused eyes meet mine, and I watch her closely for a few seconds. "What's going on, wife?"

"What…do you mean?"

"You know exactly what I mean. You've changed, and I need to figure out the reason why. I'm offering you the chance to tell me yourself amicably. If you refuse, I might have to use methods you don't approve of."

"Nothing's changed."

"Bullshit. One more chance."

"Kirill…"

"Is it your family? Are they sucking you in again? Is it

because of any of the meetings with Anton? Is he turning you against me? Are you choosing to believe their propaganda?"

"That's not—"

"Then give me something!" I cut her off, my voice losing all its cool before I release a breath and attempt to grasp onto my nonexistent calm. "Last chance."

"It's really nothing."

"Very well." I adjust my glasses. "Come here."

She walks carefully, her eyes shining when she notices the animalistic lust that must be visible on my face.

Sasha is the perfect mirror of my primitive tendencies. The fact that she gets excited whenever I'm close to the edge is a clear indication of how compatible we are.

"Stop," I order, and she comes to a halt. "On your knees."

Sasha gets into the position slowly, as if she's never been there before.

"Now, crawl to me. Show me how much you want my cock."

Her lips part, and I swear she's about to say something, but instead, she gets on all fours and slowly crawls to me. The slope of her pale tits tease from beneath the décolletage, creating a contrast against the black fabric.

A gentle sway lifts her hips, and a pink blush covers her cheeks and throat. My Sasha takes her time in the seduction game, not hurrying nor slowing down, as if she knows exactly the type of effect she's having on my starved cock.

My erection thickens and strains against my boxer briefs, demanding her heat.

I manage to stay in place, though, patiently waiting for her to get her ass over here.

My expression must be unwelcoming, though, because Sasha pauses when she finally reaches me. Her inquisitive eyes plunge into mine as if she's trying to get a read on the situation.

"Get my cock out," I order in a closed-off tone.

Her soft hands unbuckle my pants, and she fumbles with my zipper and boxer briefs before she frees my cock.

It's been semi-hard during the whole show, but it gets painfully hard in her hold. She has to take it in both hands, stroking gently as she peeks up at me.

My palm covers her cheek, and she leans into my touch, eyes closing briefly.

"Don't just caress it, Solnyshko. Choke on my cock."

A shiver goes through her, but she slides me in as far and as gently as she can without triggering her gag reflex. Then she pulls it out and licks and sucks on the crown before sliding it back in again. The friction of her wet little mouth has me hard as fuck.

But that's not the only emotion going through me. Lust is prevalent, but it's mixed with a tinge of rage. A wave of anger so steep and hollow, I don't know how far I'll go if I act on it.

Which is why I'm not.

I'm giving her the liberty to do it herself, because if I fuck her mouth, I'm going to hurt her. No doubt about it.

Her noises of pleasure echo in the air as she deep-throats my dick, probably because she knows I like that. And because she's learned my tendencies so well, she doesn't stop there and uses her tongue to give me more friction.

I might know all her buttons to push, but she's also learned mine by heart. And maybe that's why it's pissing me the fuck off.

"I'm not hearing you choke, Sasha." My voice teeters between lust and control.

Her eyes, now green with a smidge of yellow, fill with determination as they meet mine. She ups her pace, takes me down her throat, and even strokes my balls.

Sasha continues in that rhythm, sucking my cock like it's a Popsicle until her noises echo in the air. I have to force myself not to thrust down her throat.

If I do that, I won't stop.

If I do that—

She slides me out of her mouth, her eyes glittery and her lips glistening with precum and her saliva. "Kirill…"

"Yes?"

"What are you doing?"

"What am *I* doing? You're the one who's supposed to be giving me a sloppy blowjob."

"Yeah, but ordinarily, you would've taken control by now."

A smirk lifts my lips. "You want that?"

Her head bobs up and down with an eager nod.

"What else do you want, Solnyshko?"

She lies back on the carpet, opens her legs, and lifts her dress enough to reveal her soaking- wet white panties. I always love how she gets horny, even by sucking me off.

"Fuck me," she says in a throaty voice that nearly makes me come.

"What if I'm not in the mood?" I say as I kneel between her legs and remove my belt.

"Oh, please. You're always in the mood."

"Maybe I'm in a bad mood today, Sasha." I wrap the belt around my hand and slap her panty-covered pussy.

She gasps, her nails digging into the carpet, but her eyes fill with lust. So I remove her panties and groan at the *Luchik's* tattooed on her skin forever.

"You shouldn't have asked me to fuck you when I'm in this mood, because I won't stop." *Slap.* "I'll have to wear you down and *own* you, wife." *Slap.* "I'll have to make you mine again and again so that you can't think about leaving anymore."

My name leaves her mouth in a moan as she jerks off the ground, her inner thighs shaking and her eyes rolling back.

"No, don't come." I stop spanking her pussy and wrap the leather around her throat.

She releases a groan, jerking her hips so that my cock is at her opening. "Please, please, don't do the stupid orgasm denial. I hate it."

"And you think I don't hate it when you lie to me?"

"Kirill…" She tries to push herself against my cock, but I tighten the leather belt around her throat, stopping her from moving.

She reaches a hand out and strokes my cheek, my nose, and my lips. "Please…please…"

The desperation in her voice does me in. I can't really deny her when she looks at me with those glittery eyes.

I would do any-fucking-thing for those eyes.

Her moan echoes in the air as I thrust inside her, but it's cut off when I hold each end of the belt on the carpet, pulling in opposite directions.

My Sasha comes at that because she's made for me. I get off on stealing her air,; she gets off on having her oxygen taken. I get off on fucking hard; she gets off on being handled roughly.

I pound into her through her orgasm, hitting her sensitive spot over and over. Her lips form in a wordless scream, and her back arches off the carpet.

She doesn't try to ease the belt from around her throat. There isn't even that natural instinct to save herself.

That's because she trusts me not to kill her.

Not to hurt her.

Not to…violate her trust.

I release the belt when her face becomes too red and then lift her up with my hand around her back. Now that she's sitting on my lap, the angle is deeper, and I thrust faster from beneath.

"You're taking my cock like such a good girl." I'm about to remove her dress, but Sasha wraps her arms around my neck and crashes her lips to mine.

She kisses me like a madwoman while matching my rhythm. Her ass slaps on my groin again and again.

Well, fuck.

It doesn't take me long to shoot my load inside her. My wife doesn't stop kissing me while rotating her hips, going up and down in a slow, seductive rhythm.

I pull away from her. "Are you massaging your cunt with my cum, Solnyshko?"

Her bright eyes meet mine. "Don't you do that all the time?"

Yes, I do. But I didn't know she enjoyed it this much. I slowly slide out and reposition her, so she's sitting on my parted thighs. My cum and her arousal drip onto the carpet.

"So messy." I gather my cum from her pussy lips and thrust it back inside her.

Sasha shudders, an erotic smile parting her mouth as she lifts herself up and down on my fingers.

She's still chasing the remnants of her orgasm, judging by her trembling legs and clenching cunt.

I indulge her, loving the feel of her in my arms a bit too much. I fucked Sasha for four hundred twenty times, and the spark still remains the same.

What? Of course, I'm still counting.

I release her after a while, and she sags against me, her head hidden in my neck and her legs wrapped around my waist.

We spend a few moments like that before I say, "Are you not going to tell me what's going on?"

She shudders against me, her heartbeat picking up against my chest. "How do you know something is going on?"

"Because you're not acting normal, and I notice everything about you."

She pulls away, but keeps her fingers threaded at my nape. "Can you give me time?"

"How long is time? A day? Two?"

"A bit longer than that. I…need to meet my family first and—"

"No."

"I can't just avoid them forever. Just like you can't lock up Anton for life."

"Both are doable."

"Kirill," she says with a note of frustration. "Be reasonable."

"I perfectly am. The last two times you went to see your fucking family, I got shot twice, and you made me believe you were dead."

"We'll never be at peace this way."

"Let me worry about that."

"This is our lives. Yours and *mine*. You're not the only one who gets to worry about it. I have a say in it, too. You keep calling me your wife, but you'll never be my husband unless you make me your partner in everything."

"You already are."

"Not if you don't talk to me about the decisions you make concerning the two of us."

"Did you talk to me when you faked your fucking death, Sasha?" My voice raises, and she goes still, her breath catching. "How would you feel if I did that, hmm?"

"I already said I'm sorry," she murmurs, her fingers stroking my nape. "We both made mistakes, but we're in new territory now. You have to give me time, please."

Every cell in me revolts at the idea, but I know this is exactly what I need to do so we can have our new beginning.

"Fine, but you're not meeting them without me."

She rolls her eyes, but a smile paints her lips as she lays her head on my shoulder again. "Thank you."

"Don't thank me until we get this over with."

She releases an affirmative sound. "Do we have to go back to the party?"

"Yes."

"Ugh. But people will know that you fucked me."

"I don't give a fuck. In fact, it's good they know you're mine and off-limits."

"Caveman."

"*Your* caveman."

"Mmm. I like that." Her voice trails off, sounding sleepy. "Give me ten."

I'm stroking her hair as she falls back against my chest when my phone vibrates.

The name on the screen makes me pause.

Boss. This is Makar. I'm sorry for disappearing, but I have to tell you that you're in danger. Can we meet?

TWENTY-TWO

Sasha

"WHAT ARE WE DOING HERE?" MY GAZE FOLLOWS the patterns of the carpet in the waiting area of the in-house clinic.

Kirill brought me here first thing this morning after he kicked out Yulia. He told me about her posing a danger to Kristina's pregnancy and that even Konstantin agreed to this.

It was so much drama. She refused to leave, and when Kirill ordered Viktor to remove her by force, she went ballistic. Since she couldn't possibly hurt Kirill, she turned her malicious energy to Karina and tried to slap her.

Before anyone could stop her, I stood in front of a trembling Karina and pushed the woman away.

She's now packing her things after Konstantin talked her out of whatever toxic plans she had.

I'm still uncomfortable with the exchange that took place this morning. I can almost see her venomous eyes glaring me down as if she wants me dead.

Today, I'd planned to spend time reading pregnancy books with Kristina—only from an e-reader, though, since I can't be so obvious.

The most pressing question is—how long can I fool Kirill? Even though we've been fucking all the time, I try not to get completely naked. I'm scared he'll notice how slightly bigger my breasts are or the bump in my stomach. It's actually not as noticeable as Kristina's and can be chalked up to gaining weight, but it'll probably grow bigger.

And while I try to distract him so he doesn't focus on my body for too long, that can't last forever.

Kirill isn't an idiot. He already senses that something is wrong. If I don't tell him, he'll eventually figure it out himself.

A part of me wants to say it. I even stopped myself from blurting it all out last night.

But the other part realizes that if I take this step, there's no going back.

I'll just be trapped in Kirill's web with no way out and I'm not sure that's where I want to be.

Especially since I've been trying to contact my uncle and haven't been able to get through. The situation is muddied at best, and I'm at a crossroads where nothing makes sense.

Nothing but the baby.

I've been surprisingly elated since I found out about him. He's the only thing I want with everything in me. The rest is blurry.

Okay, that's a lie. I want Kirill, too. I want him to the point of madness, and I don't only mean physically. I want his heart. I want to be so far inside him, he won't be able to replace me.

But the wound is so raw; I don't think I can ever throw caution to the wind this time.

Even when I was secretly happy when he introduced me to everyone as his wife.

And I don't only mean his family, members of his staff, and the leaders of the brotherhood, but also his entire social circle.

He took me around the room with his hand on my lower back, saying, "Have you met my beautiful wife? She's Russian."

Yes, all the small talk was tiresome and I'm pretty sure he did it so everyone would know that I'm his and, therefore, off-limits, but I enjoyed every second of it.

Probably because I never dreamed that I'd be on his arm as a woman.

No, not on his arm.

His wife.

The only wife he'll ever have.

"Kirill?" I step in front of him, so he stops walking.

He's been ignoring my questions since we left the house. His expression is closed off, his eyes are more intense than those of an arctic wolf, and his jaw is set.

I touch the lapel of his jacket, taking in the hint of tattoos peeking through the top open buttons of his shirt.

Although I woke up with his cock sliding inside me, and he fucked me senseless just this morning, I can't seem to get enough of him.

My sex drive matches his—if not more. I could blame the hormones, but then again, there has never been a day when I didn't want Kirill Morozov.

Even during the time I planned to kill him.

"What's going on?" I ask in a careful tone.

I hate it when he deliberately closes himself off from me.

"You'll find out soon enough." He takes my hand in his and basically drags me into one of the rooms.

The nurse and doctor are waiting while carrying a tray with some equipment on it.

"You can get started," he tells them and applies pressure on my shoulder so that I sit down on the bed.

"Get started on…what?"

Shit.

Don't tell me he already found out I'm pregnant? And if he did, what is he getting started on?

Kirill looms over me, his shoulders appearing wider and more frightening. "The doctor will now put a tracker in your arm. It shouldn't take long."

My lips part. "W-what?"

"You heard me just fine, Sasha."

"Yes, I did, but I'm trying to figure out if you're joking."

"I never joke."

"You already track my damn phone. Why would you need this as well?"

"Because your phone isn't reliable when it's turned off or when you lose it intentionally or unintentionally."

"So you're putting a tracker in me? Just like that?"

"It's the only option to ensure your safety."

I stand up and jam a finger in his chest. "More like, the only option for you to monitor me. I'm *not* doing this."

I start to move past him, but he grabs my arms and sits me back down so fast, dizziness assaults me.

He lowers himself so that his cold eyes are level with mine. "Don't be difficult."

"Difficult? So I'm the one who's being *difficult* in this?"

"You have a tendency to disappear, so this is the best solution to make sure you're safe."

"Don't do this," I whisper gently. "This isn't how you make me your partner, Kirill."

"I can't make you my fucking partner when you're thinking about running off." He looks back at the doctor and nurse, who have been watching the show silently. "Do it."

I start to fight, kicking and clawing at his arm, but he pins me down on the bed with brute strength. His knees are on either side of my thighs, keeping them in place, and he imprisons my wrists above my head on the bed.

I have to loosen my muscles so he doesn't crush my belly or something.

He hovers above me and releases a hand, but he keeps my shoulder flat and immobile on the bed.

The nurse disinfects my upper arm. The coldness of the alcohol isn't even uncomfortable, but moisture gathers in my eyes.

I stare at him through my blurry vision, then whisper, "I hate you."

"You can hate me all you like as long as you're safe."

"The one person I need to be safe from is you, asshole."

"Get it all off your chest," he says in a nearly sarcastic voice.

"I'm going to remove this the moment we're divorced in a few weeks."

He doesn't like that. In fact, he dislikes it so much that I feel the weight of his negative emotions squashing my chest.

Good. I said it to hurt him as much as he's hurting me.

I expect him to say that won't happen or that I'm dreaming, but he says nothing and leaves me at the mercy of his darkness.

The prick of whatever the doctor is doing doesn't hurt. The fact that Kirill is subjugating me to this does.

I glare up at him. "How would you feel if the roles were reversed and I forced you to do this?"

"I'd do it."

"You're just saying that."

"If you want a tracker on me, I'll get one this instant, Sasha."

"Then do it. Let's see how you feel when I monitor your every move."

A second passes.

Two.

On the third, he lifts himself off me and sits on the foot of the bed. Then, he announces, "Put another tracker in me."

The nurse is finishing with my arm, but I can't focus on her as the doctor heads to the closet and then returns with another tray.

Kirill removes his jacket and unbuttons his shirt with meticulous, calm movements before he bares his left arm.

Once the nurse is done, I slowly sit up and settle beside him. "You're really doing this?"

"If it makes you feel better that we're on the same page, I don't mind."

I prefer that neither of us gets a tracker, but since that's not possible, this puts some form of a balm on the wound.

There's still the tiny fact that he's doing it willingly, and I don't have to hold him down for it.

If I weren't scared about the baby's safety, I would wrestle the asshole and pin him down.

The doctor finishes with him in record time and then says Viktor should be able to have it activated.

I leave the clinic first, my shoulders drooped and my steps forced.

Kirill catches up to me and wraps an arm around my waist. I try to push it away. "Don't touch me."

"Why wouldn't I touch my wife?"

"I don't know, maybe due to the fact that I want to claw your eyes out right now?"

"How will I look at you if you do that?"

I roll my eyes and focus on the horizon. "This is the last time you force me into anything. Do something like this again, and I'll disappear to where you'll never find me, even if I have to cut my damn arm off for it."

His fingers sink into my hip, bruising me. "I wouldn't have to do this if you didn't think about nonsense like that."

"Maybe I'm thinking about it because of your actions." I shoot him a glare. "I won't tolerate it if you don't see me as an equal or value my opinion. I mean it, Kirill. I stomped on my feelings for you when I left for Russia, and I can do it again in a heartbeat."

A slow smirk tilts his lips. "So you have feelings for me."

"Seriously? That's all you took from what I said?"

234 | RINA KENT

"Isn't that the highlight?"

"You know what? Forget it. We're just going down a closed path."

"So feelings are a closed path now?"

"When I'm mad at you, yes, they are."

We pause in front of the house, where a dozen suitcases are being loaded into the back of a van. Kirill only stopped because I did. He's so distant from the situation that he doesn't spare the car or the staff any attention.

I wonder if he always wanted to do this but kept Yulia around for his brother's sake. Now that Konstantin is wary of her, Kirill probably figured it was time for her to go.

He probably let her live in the house in a 'keep your enemies closer' way, but he's the Pakhan with stakes in the bank her family owns now, so he doesn't need to do that anymore.

When we go into the house, a palpable tension lingers in the air. Karina stands by the stairs, hugging one of the railings for dear life.

Kristina grabs her by the shoulder, fingers stroking it with comfort. Yulia gets into Konstantin's space, and while she looks as elegant as usual in her knee-length dress and with her styled hair, a destructive energy emanates from her.

"You, of all people, can't do this to me, Kosta. If I'm leaving, you're coming with me."

"He's a grown married man, Yulia." Kirill strolls inside with me in tow. "Get the fuck over it already."

She swings around, her venom instantly directed at him. "I should've known you were the one who planted this nonsense in his head, you damn devil."

"What can I say?" He grins, even though his expression is closed off. "I'm a better influence than you."

"It's not like that, Mother." Konstantin tries to salvage the situation, but I think it's too late.

"Let her believe whatever the fuck she wants." Kirill stares down at her. "Konstantin isn't your flashy toy or a pet you tell what to do or want. Let him go, or I'll make you. Believe me when I say you won't like the second option."

"If you think you can take my son from me—"

"I'm not taking anyone. He's choosing to stay here of his own accord because I actually respect him as an individual. Something you've never done—"

She raises her hand to him, but I'm already capturing and twisting it, then throwing it back. "I told you not to do that again."

Yulia snarls at me, then at Kirill, "I should've killed you and your demon sister when I had the chance. I should've ended your miserable lives before you were born."

A hiccup comes from the other side of the room, and Karina shakes in Kristina's hold. She was always the emotionally weak one out of the three of them and seems to have never gotten used to her mother's treatment.

"Mother, stop." Konstantin hauls her back with surprising force, his voice rising on her for the first time. "Stop. Just stop it already!"

Her lips part. "Kosta, what are you—"

"I'm done trying to find excuses for you, done being hated by my own brother and sister because they think I abandoned them all those years ago." He stares at Kirill and Karina. "Mother said she'd send boats for you, too, if I went out of there first. Whenever I tried to explain that afterward, she'd threaten that she'd plot against Kirill's next training mission or she'd have Kara sent to boarding school. The only way for me to keep you safe was to pretend I couldn't care less about you anymore. Like you did when you tried to protect us from Papa, Kirill."

My husband's lips purse, and his whole wrath zooms in on Yulia.

But it's Konstantin who goes on, "I never liked your suffocating care, Mother. I always felt like I had to walk on eggshells around you and had to meet your grandiose expectations. I started hating you when I realized you hated my siblings and didn't hesitate to hurt them. I hated you more when you tried to make me loathe them as well. But do you know what the tipping point was? It was you trying to hurt my wife and child. That's something I'll never forgive you for."

Yulia's chin trembles, but she holds her head high. "I only want the best for you."

"We're your children, too," Karina says in a small, brittle voice. "Why can't you want the best for us?"

"Because your fucking father raped me!" she screams and turns to Kirill. "You're the reason behind everything, you fucking devil. Roman wanted me and couldn't have me, so he raped me over and over and fucking over again until I was pregnant with *you*. He made me marry him and tied me down because of *you*. He forced me to have you, even though I hated you and him more than anything in my life. Whenever I look at your fucking face, I remember how you were conceived, and I want to kill you with my bare hands. I want to stab you to death and watch you flounder in your own blood. You and your fucking sister were both conceived by rape, do you hear me? Every instance of sexual intercourse with your father was nonconsensual and painful, but you two came out of it like little demons. Konstantin is my son with the only man I ever loved, so, of course, I would love him and not *you*."

Deafening silence falls on the living area as Yulia's words slowly register.

Konstantin and Kristina are pale. Karina looks like she's going to be sick, and even Yulia, who's usually as emotionless as Kirill, is shaking.

On the one hand, all her deep hatred toward Karina and especially Kirill makes complete sense.

On the other hand, it's still not right.

Out of everyone present, Kirill is the only one whose expression doesn't change. But then again, he's always eerily calm during extreme situations. It's why he was the perfect captain in the military and is now highly fit to be Pakhan.

But just because he's calm doesn't mean he's unaffected. He does such a wonderful job at erasing his emotions that he forgets they exist sometimes.

"Since Roman was adamantly against Konstantin having any form of power or inheritance, I suspected he might have a different father," he says with baffling nonchalance. "Who is he?"

The others are still recovering from the weight of the news she just announced, but the woman herself glares at Kirill.

"Is that all that you care about?"

"What were you expecting? That I'd be a doting son when you were never a mother to me? News flash, Yulia, it's not my or Karina's fault that my scum of a father raped you. We didn't ask to be fucking born to you or him. We had no choice in our existence, but you had all the choice to like or hate us, and you chose not to be our mother. I'm choosing not to be your son."

"You killed him." Karina leaves Kristina and slowly walks to her mother. "You killed Papa…right? All that time you were preparing his daily coffee…you…you're the reason he got worse very quickly."

Yulia lifts her head in the air. "It took years more than I would've preferred, but at least the idiot wasn't suspicious."

"You bitch!" Karina lunges at her, but Konstantin grabs her by the waist before she can hit her.

"What?" Yulia yells. "*What*? Are you all sad for that fool now? I'm the one wronged in this."

"I'm the one wronged!" Karina screams back. "At least he loved me. He screwed my life up, but he loved me afterward. He kissed me good night and asked how I was doing. He might have been a horrible person, but he tried to be my father. You were never my mother!"

Yulia clicks her tongue as if she can't stand the sight of her own daughter. "It's pointless to communicate with you people. Let's go, Kosta."

Her son doesn't move as Karina cries against him, her whole body trembling. He watches his mother with a dead expression. "Who's my father, Mother?"

"We'll talk about it once we're out of this snake's den."

"I'm not going anywhere with you. Who's my father? Is he still alive, or did you also get rid of him?"

"Konstantin!" Yulia clutches her pearls and then slowly releases them. "We'll talk when you're calmer and you realize no one cares about you as much as I do. Least of all this devil."

She glares at Kirill on her way out. Her head is held high, and her steps are measured.

I admire that woman's strength, but I still despise the role she played in her children's lives.

Karina is sobbing as Konstantin pats her back. He exchanges a look with Kirill. I'm not sure if it's comradery or understanding.

For some reason, it feels as if I'm intruding on the siblings' relationship. Maybe they gave each other this look when they were growing up.

After a moment, Kirill goes up the stairs. I pat Karina's and Konstantin's shoulders, then follow after.

Even though I'm supposed to be mad at him, I can't possibly leave him alone after that. He's the type who hides his emotions to the point it backfires against him.

I find him in the closet. His jacket has been discarded on the floor, and he's removing his shirt.

"Are you okay?" I slowly approach him.

Kirill throws his shirt down, revealing tense muscles. "Why wouldn't I be?"

I stand in front of him so that I'm between his body and the closet door. My fingers find his scruff, and I stroke his cheek. "It's okay not to be okay."

"I'm perfectly fine. It's actually good to know why she never liked me and never will. I have her assaulter's genes, which isn't something she'd ever approve of."

"I feel sorry for what she's been through, but she had no right to treat you and Karina as if it was your fault."

He says nothing, but he leans into my touch, slowly closing his eyes.

I wrap my arms around his waist and bury my face in his naked chest. Turns out, this is the type of consoling he needs, because Kirill circles my waist with his arms and engulfs me in his embrace.

His low whisper nearly stops my heart. "Thank you for being here, Solnyshko."

TWENTY-THREE

Kirill

I'M ANNOYED.

No, that's an understatement. I'm teetering on the edge of rage and loss of control.

It's taken inhuman strength to keep a cool head about the situation I've found myself in. Namely, the distance Sasha has slowly but surely continued to implement between us.

It's been getting worse since I put that tracker in her about a week ago. But then again, it's not like she wasn't doing it before. The only difference is that she's taking it further.

She's been trying to spend as much time with anyone but me. And while she has a surprisingly heightened sex drive lately, she pulls away almost immediately after, throwing out all sorts of excuses.

I have to meet Kristina.

I promised Karina I'd go on a walk.

Rai and Lia invited me for lunch.

Viktor is taking me to see my brother.

Every day, there's some sort of reason why she can't spend time with me. It doesn't help that I've been caught up in some new shit Damien stirred, and I've had no time to corner her.

Maybe I should take her to that cabin again so that it's only the two of us and no one will dare to interrupt us.

Otherwise, she'll keep getting further away until we reach the fucking deadline she imposed on this relationship.

"I have a bad feeling about this. It smells like a trap," Viktor says while watching our surroundings with a gun in hand.

We're near a shipping dock on the outskirts of the city. It's one of the sites where we complete our transactions with the cartels. I haven't been here in ages, though. Especially not since I became Pakhan.

All these petty operations can be taken care of by others.

It's late at night, so the only sound is Viktor's harsh breathing and the occasional crash of the water against the pier.

"We already have backup stationed all around the dock." I adjust my glasses. "So even if Makar planned to ambush me, we have enough manpower to eliminate him and whoever he brings along."

"What if he colluded with the Pakhan of the Chicago branch and brings more men than we have?"

"One, that's paranoia. Two, you're overestimating Makar's influence."

"Or maybe you're underestimating it..." he trails off and tenses, and I sense a third presence near us.

Sure enough, Makar carefully slips out from between the containers. He carefully studies the area as he approaches us.

His steps turn heavier after he notices Viktor by my side. He asked to meet alone, but he should know by now that Viktor vehemently refuses to stop being my shadow.

Makar is a bald man with an average build, a pointy nose, and thin lips. He also always wears suits that look a size too small.

"I thought we were meeting alone?" he asks when he's in front of us and motions at Viktor with his chin.

"You have no place to set down rules, motherfucker," my senior guard says in his usual blunt way.

"You know how he thinks we were born attached at the hip." My tone is welcoming and less intense than Viktor's.

Makar manages to relax a little, even though his gaze keeps shifting sideways.

"Care to tell me where you've been?" I ask in the same friendly tone.

"Around." He releases a breath. "I was never supposed to come in contact with you again."

"What made you change your mind?"

"I found out that the person I worked with is planning to take you out, and that was never part of the plan. I couldn't just sit back and watch. Your father told me to help you get to the top, not get rid of you."

Viktor steps forward. "You have the goddamn audacity to stand there and admit that you colluded with someone else against your own boss?"

"I didn't have a choice! My family was threatened."

"You could've come to me for that, and I would've made sure they were safe." I grab Viktor by the shoulder and pull him back. "But there was another reason, wasn't there?"

Makar scratches the side of his bald head. "I thought Sasha was taking away your concentration from what's important. Besides, she's the daughter of your father's enemies."

"So you decided the best way to take care of that was to kill her." My affirmation is calm, so calm that he swallows.

"I was only asked for assistance."

"By whom?"

"Konstantin."

My body goes rigid, and a ringing sounds in my ear. Even Viktor's brow furrows as if he can't believe what he's hearing.

Have I been too mellow and too negligent with my brother? How can I possibly ignore that he could've participated in this mission?

It makes sense from what the Albanian guy said about meeting secretly and how his ally wanted to hurt me as much as possible.

Was everything he's done in the past few months excellent acting? Or have I slept on the fact that he could be a better manipulator than me?

He said the right words. Displayed the right emotions. He stood by my side like when we were kids and looked up to me as a brother.

"Proof," I say with enough tension to make Makar stand upright.

He shows me texts he exchanged with my brother about the plan and some photos of them together.

Logically, that shouldn't be enough evidence since they can be faked, but my mind is veering in the exact opposite direction.

This is the detail that I've been missing during my search for Sasha's killer—or the one who attempted the blasphemy.

Ever since my wife told me she'd left a fake behind, and I realized the DNA results had been manipulated, I knew the perpetrator was close.

I just didn't know *how* close.

I was willing to suspect my guards, but I never really suspected Konstantin. Especially since I'd started to see glimpses of the old him after his wedding.

Maybe all of that was a façade, too.

He must've enjoyed seeing me crumble and lose control during the two months I thought Sasha was dead.

He must've been laughing on the inside while offering his support.

"You said he was planning to take me out." I glare at Makar. "How?"

"I don't know, but he thinks you're not fit to be Pakhan and that he should be the one to take your position instead. You have to believe me, Boss. I would never help him with that. Your father didn't want him to ever become the leader of the family and I agree."

"Did Roman already know that Konstantin wasn't his son?"

Makar's lips part, but he nods. "He put all his effort into finding the man Yulia cheated with. He became friends with him, too, since the bastard didn't even know he was her husband. When the time came, he eliminated him."

The pieces of the puzzle start to fall together. "Was he perhaps part of the Belsky Organization?"

Makar nods again.

"Which one?"

"Anatoly Ivanov."

Sasha's uncle. Thank fuck it wasn't her father, or else the situation would get too complicated too fast.

She's still cousins with my fucker of a brother, though.

"How did Roman find out?"

"Yulia goes to Russia's countryside every summer. The first time she went was a year after you were born. But then she started going religiously. In the beginning, we all assumed it was a holiday. But Roman found out that she used that time to meet with a certain man. Apparently, they had an affair that lasted for years, but they only met during the summer in some nameless Russian town, away from everyone they knew. After that time was over, she'd come back to New York and he'd go back to his family."

"So Roman decided to annihilate him and his entire family."

"He only thought about toying with him and then killing him in front of her, but then he was approached by the Russian government to infiltrate and eliminate the threat that the Belsky Organization posed, so he immediately agreed. In their last days, Yulia could've found out about Roman's involvement and might have tried to warn Anatoly, but it was probably too late."

"Did my father keep any records of that operation?"

"Only a few notes hidden in the pages of his favorite book."

"Crime and Punishment." I was wondering why the fuck he put that book in the safe, but now I've got my answer.

"You need to be careful, Boss. Eliminate Konstantin before he manages to eliminate you."

"I will." I pull out my gun and point it at his forehead.

His face blanches. "What…you promised my safety."

"Only for the duration of your confession. You made a terrible fucking mistake by attempting to kill my wife, Makar, and that sin is punishable by death."

I shoot him between the eyes, the echo of the gunshot filling the air as he falls to the ground with a thud.

Ah. Fuck.

I promised Sasha that I'd let her decide his fate, but I went ahead and lost control. Again.

My face is too tight, I'm surprised no tendons snap.

Viktor observes the scene and then focuses on me. "Now what?"

"Now, I punish the other motherfucker who thought he could kill my wife."

No one gets to hurt Sasha and live.

Not even my fucking brother.

⌒

When we go back, I find my family—or what I thought was my family—having dinner.

Konstantin is laughing at something Karina said while Sasha and Kristina pass dishes to each other.

This mood has been prevalent ever since Yulia left. Konstantin hasn't gone to visit her, not even once, and has preferred to remain here with his wife and the rest of his family.

Or, more like, he wanted to keep his eyes on the prize—aka my position.

The moment I step into the dining room accompanied by Viktor and a few of my other men, their attention turns to me.

"Kirill," Konstantin says, still smiling. "You should hear the nonsense Kara's been talking about."

"Wanting a dozen nephews and nieces isn't nonsense. You and Kristina can have half, and Kirill and Sasha can have the other half."

Sasha peers up at me, a blush covering her cheeks, but the moment she sees my face, her movements freeze.

If there's anyone in the world who can figure out when something's wrong, it's that woman right there.

I don't have to say anything, and she's already sensed the black aura that's been surrounding me ever since I heard Makar's confession.

"How about you, then, Kara?" Konstantin waggles his brows. "Are you not planning on children?"

"Nuh-uh. I only want to be the cool aunt." My sister glares at me. "You better hurry up and worship Sasha so she agrees to have your children."

Sasha forces a smile, but her attention immediately slides back to me as she mouths, "What's wrong?"

"Come and join us, Kirill," Kristina says. "Viktor and the others, too, if you like."

Karina grins. "Yes, join us!"

I give Viktor the signal. "Take him."

Silence falls on the dining table as two of my men head to Konstantin. His eyes widen when he realizes the reality of the situation.

He has the audacity to look at me with a betrayed look, as if I'm the one stabbing him in the back and not the other way around.

"Kirill...?" he asks in a choked voice.

Karina latches onto his arm and glares at me, shrieking, "What are you doing? Tell them to let him go."

Sasha swings up from her chair, but her tone is gentle as she asks, "What's wrong?"

"He attempted to kill you and is vying for my position, among other things that I'll fully investigate."

Konstantin struggles against my men. "What the fuck are you talking about? I've never done that!"

"I wouldn't expect you to admit it easily, but we'll get to that point. Take him to the basement."

"No, please." Kristina's voice and body shake as she gets to her feet.

She's been watching the whole show with a pale face and bulging eyes as if she can't believe the turn of events.

"There must be an explanation for all of this," Sasha says, her attention on Kristina and Karina, who are trying to claw at the guards fruitlessly.

"I already know the explanation, which is why I'm taking him for his punishment."

"Kirill, please…" Kristina's eyes fill with tears. "He's your brother."

"It's because he's my brother that I have zero fucking tolerance for his betrayal. Viktor, take him to the basement. *Now*."

He and the other guards comply. Konstantin is dragged away, despite fighting and cursing and asking me to talk this out.

Karina starts kicking and screaming and hitting me in one of her extremely dramatic episodes, but I have no time for her nonsense, so I push her away.

The most drastic of the bunch is Kristina. The more she sees her husband being taken while fighting, the paler she gets. Tears stream down her cheeks, but when she tries to go after him, she loses her balance.

Sasha catches her and sits her back down, then gives her a glass of water.

Konstantin goes crazier at that, and he nearly manages to escape the men's clutches, but he has no chance when Viktor takes over.

Once he's out of sight, I go upstairs without another word.

I choose not to hear Karina's screams and wails, Kristina's brittle pleas, or even Sasha calling my name.

The traitor will pay, no matter what those women say.

I go to my office, open the safe, and retrieve the old Russian copy of *Crime and Punishment* by Fyodor Dostoevsky.

Although I found nothing weird when I first looked into this, I still kept it in the safe. Maybe because I already knew Roman wasn't the type who did things arbitrarily. He wouldn't have just put a book in the safe, even if it was his favorite.

The door to my office barges open as I'm laying the book on my desk. Sasha storms in, looking as fierce as a warrior, even though she's wearing a loose navy blue dress. I think those are her style now, even though they're staggeringly unflattering.

She stops in front of my desk, her eyes blazing with fire. "What are you doing, Kirill?"

"I told you. Punishing a traitor."

"I don't believe anything you're accusing him of. You don't have any proof."

"Makar does. He showed me his exchange with my dear brother."

"You…met with Makar?"

"And killed him, but not before he revealed the identity of who put him up to plotting your murder."

She shakes her head a few times as if she's not hearing me. "I refuse to believe that Konstantin would ever do that."

"Then you'd be as naïve as he made sure you'd be."

"There's more to it. You must feel it, too. This is Konstantin! He always respected you as a brother, even when he had to pretend he hated you."

"Maybe the hate part is real, and this whole thing was a pretense."

She releases a long breath, her shoulders drooping. "You're not going to change your mind, are you? You'll always be this man who's doubtful about everyone, your family included. Maybe one day you'll lock me up and torture me at the thought of betrayal."

"Don't be ridiculous."

"How is that ridiculous? If your own flesh and blood doesn't get any benefit of the doubt, how would I? The moment I do anything you don't approve of, you'll suspect me."

"And why would you do anything that I don't approve of, Sasha? Hmm? Why the fuck have you been creating distance between us lately?"

"Because you're a fucking idiot, that's why!" She breathes harshly. "Are you going to release Konstantin?"

"No."

"In that case, I'll be staying with Kristina until you let her husband go."

And then she turns and leaves, slamming the door shut behind her.

I'm tempted to follow after and yank her back by the hair, but that would just complicate matters.

So I take a few moments and release a deep breath before I focus on the book again.

Sure enough, two pages are glued together. I carefully peel them apart and find a small memory card and letter inside. I open the piece of paper and stare at the words scribbled in my father's messy handwriting.

To Kirill,

If you're reading this, then it means I'm dead, and you've become my heir.

There are a few things you need to know…

The more I read, the clearer the picture gets. On and on, it feels as if I'm in Roman's head when he wrote this.

Once I finish, I know exactly what to do to punish the traitor.

TWENTY-FOUR

Sasha

"I'M SO CLOSE TO GIVING UP AT THIS POINT. SO DAMN close!"

I'm ranting now, but I'm lucky to have someone who listens to me without complaining.

Or more like two people.

Anton and Maks sit on either side of me. My friend has a hand on my shoulder while Anton nods silently. He's the least talkative, but he's an excellent listener.

It's been three days since Kirill imprisoned Konstantin as if he were a criminal. None of us have been allowed access to the basement, so we don't know what the hell he's even been doing to him down there.

And the lack of knowledge is worse because it encourages thoughts of bad scenarios.

I've tried to comfort Kristina and Karina, but it's impossible when none of us knows Kirill's plans. He could kill him at any second, and then what?

Has he thought about what will happen to Kristina and her child? Her family doesn't really like her since she went against their wishes and married Konstantin.

Then there's Karina. Has he thought about how her state would decline if her brother killed her other brother?

But then again, Kirill has never given two fucks about other people's emotions. He only has his plans and manipulations and gives everyone else the middle finger.

Me included.

The bastard hasn't tried to talk to me. He took what I said that day in his office literally and has ignored my existence. It doesn't help that he's often outside the house until late. Or that I glare at him every time I see him.

His expression doesn't change as he stares back and then locks himself in his office with damn Viktor.

"You know, it's funny how he said I was creating a distance between us when he's the one who's digging a hole right in the middle of us." I breathe harshly. "And what's with staying with Viktor all the time?"

Maks smiles, and I narrow my eyes at him. I had Viktor bring me here because I needed a breather from the tension in the house.

I was glad to actually find Anton and Maks joking and teasingly hitting each other. When I came the last time, Anton said that Maks lets him out all the time as long as he promises not to run away.

Not sure how long my brother can forget about his duties and keep that promise, but it's going well so far. He doesn't appear strained or stressed. In fact, I don't think he's ever looked as peaceful as he has these past few weeks.

"What are you smiling at?" I ask Maks.

He does a shitty job of trying to hide his amusement. "Is it just me, or do you sound jealous of Viktor?"

"That's not true."

"It is, actually," Anton supplies needlessly.

"Now that I think about it, you were always jealous of him in some way," Maks continues.

"Right. She was personally offended whenever Kirill had a one-on-one meeting with him."

"Tosha!" I nudge him with an elbow. "What's with you two ganging up on me? I didn't come here for this."

"It's true, though." Maks strokes my shoulder. "You need to get used to the fact that Viktor is there to stay. He'll only leave Kirill when he dies."

Anton subtly pushes Maks's hand from my shoulder.

I smile at him with unconcealed gloating. "Who's the jealous one now?"

Anton side-eyes me. "I don't like anyone touching my sister."

"Liar. You didn't like Maks touching anyone in the past, not just me."

"He's too clingy. It's revolting."

My friend grins, completely ignoring Anton's comments. "Oh? What's that about, Sasha?"

"Don't," my brother mouths, but I'm already turning toward Maks.

"Remember when he twisted your arm and got suddenly violent occasionally?"

"Oh, right. He had moments where he acted out of character."

"More like, he lost control because he didn't like how you were so touchy with everyone. Especially me since he thought you liked me."

"Someone was jealous, huh?" Maks's expression lights up as he looks over my shoulder at Anton, who's wearing an unamused expression.

"Are you done?" He glares at both of us.

"No. I actually like this." Maks leans closer to me. "How was he when he was a child?"

"An adult." I smile. "I don't remember Anton ever being a child, except when you dragged him into all those games during the past few years."

Maks forms an *L* at his chin. "So that means I'm a good influence?"

"The best."

"Stop inflating his dick-shaped ego," Anton grumbles. "He already thinks he's God's gift to humans."

"I sure as fuck am. Right, Sasha?"

"Yeah." I laugh. "You're too extra. I love it."

"Hear that, Antosha?" Maks nudges my brother's foot with his. "You need to take appreciation lessons from your sister. She's more emotionally mature than you."

"If she were, she wouldn't have fallen in love with a literal sociopath."

My humor dampens, and my shoulders hunch. "Ouch."

This time, Maks hits Anton's foot. "Read the room, dick."

"What? It's true."

"She didn't come here to be reminded of that, now, did she?"

"Oh, I'm sorry. Is it better to bury her head in the sand and pretend all of this is okay and that our family isn't coming for us or something?"

Both Maks and I tense.

"And you can't wait for that, right?" my friend asks in a tight tone.

"Of course. You think it's my dream to be locked up in here?"

Maks's face hardens, and his muscles tighten to the point I think he'll punch something—or, more accurately, someone.

Instead, he stands in one swift movement. "I'm going to see if Viktor has anything for me."

"Maks…" I say, not sure how to dilute the tension.

"You're a fucking asshole," he tells Anton, then storms out of the room.

My brother watches him the whole time, his brow furrowed.

When Maks is out, Anton rubs the back of his head and curses under his breath.

"You shouldn't have said that, Tosha."

"I'm not you or him. I can't just forget about the looming battle that'll take place sooner or later." He rubs his hair again, harder this time. "None of us can stop it."

"*You* can. If you talk to Uncle and Babushka, they'll listen. You're their hope for the future, and if you tell them you've given up on whatever crazy coup they're thinking of carrying out—"

"That's not how it works. Picking up where Papa left off is my duty."

"What's more important to you? Maks or your duty?"

His Adam's apple moves with a swallow, but he says nothing.

"If you go down this path, you'll lose him. So if you're fine with that, by all means." I touch his hand and soften my tone. "I can see that he's the best thing that's ever happened to you, Tosha. You need someone like him by your side so you'll stop thinking about duty and wars. You've never lived your life or had dreams of your own. This is your chance to."

"It's not as utopian as you're thinking. Reality is much more nefarious than dreams."

"How would you know if you never fight for that dream?"

"What about you? Are you going to fight for Kirill again?"

"I don't know, but I'll definitely fight for this." I take his hand and place it on my stomach.

Anton's brow furrows, but then his lips part with recognition. "Are you by any chance…?"

"Pregnant. Yes."

"Wow. That didn't take long."

I hit his shoulder jokingly. "It happened before I left. I'm in my second trimester now."

"Kirill must be ecstatic that he has a reason to keep you by his side."

"I haven't told him exactly because of that." I release his hand

and intertwine my fingers on my lap. "I don't want him to force me to stay because of the baby, but at the same time, I don't know how long I can hide this from him. I just want him to…I don't know…"

"Love you like a normal human being?"

"Yeah, I guess."

"No one in that family is normal. Least of all, Kirill."

"And you are?"

"I could be."

"As if. You went all defensive mode on Maks just now because you're scared of the unknown."

"That's different. Maks has a soft core, but Kirill doesn't. He's more interested in the success of his plans than anyone or anything else."

I wanted to believe otherwise, but after he imprisoned his own brother, I'm not sure what to believe anymore. Maybe Anton and everyone else who described him as emotionless is right.

After all these years, I have to admit that I was wrong to believe there's another side to him that he keeps under wraps.

A side dedicated to only me.

Maybe I was the delusional one in this equation.

"What do you plan to do now?" he asks when I say nothing. "You and I both know we can't keep the status quo forever."

"I've been trying to contact Uncle Albert to no avail."

"Try using my code of emergency. He'll come for me."

"But not for me?"

"Probably not."

"Ouch."

Anton offers me a sympathetic look. "They never trusted you after you saved Kirill when they were close to killing him. They think you'd do it again, and they're probably not wrong."

"Do you expect me to let them kill the father of my son?"

"You wouldn't let them kill him even if there was no child involved."

Well, that's true.

A part of me will always be protective of Kirill, no matter what he does. I might hate him, want to slap and kick and punch him, but I'd never allow anyone to hurt him.

Which is the definition of a toxic relationship.

"At any rate, get me out of here already," Anton says.

"Only if you promise to help me."

"Help you kill our family?"

"No, just make them see reason for once." I squeeze his shoulder. "Do it for Maks and, most importantly, for yourself, Tosha. You need a fresh start."

He grumbles but doesn't say anything.

On my way out, I cross paths with Maks at the door.

"You going, Sasha?"

"Yeah. I can't leave Kristina and Karina alone for too long when they're miserable."

He clutches me by the shoulders. "Don't listen to the nonsense your asshole brother says. I've never seen Kirill care about anyone as much as he cares about you. According to the men, he was at the point of self-destruction when he thought you were dead. He's not the best at expressing his emotions, but I know for a fact that you mean the world to him."

"Aww, thanks, Maks." I touch his hand that's on top of my shoulder. "And if it's any consolation, my *asshole* brother goes on the defensive when he thinks he's cornered, so don't listen to his bullshit. You said you've always wanted someone who looks at you the way I look at Kirill, right? Well, that someone is Anton."

His lips part, but he soon clears his throat. "Don't be ridiculous."

"Don't be blind. You didn't see the look on his face when you left." I kiss his cheek. "Take care of each other, okay?"

He releases an affirmative noise, and I leave with a smile on my face.

But it soon disappears when I find a grumpy Viktor waiting

HEART OF MY MONSTER | 257

by the car. He definitely hates driving me here instead of being glued to his boss's side.

I could probably ask Kirill to let me come on my own since he has the damn tracker on me now.

Viktor starts to open the back door for me, but I settle in the front passenger seat.

"You can just ride in the back," he says after taking his place behind the wheel.

"I don't like the idea of you being my driver."

He grumbles in his signature displeased voice as he drives down the dirt road. When we're on the highway, I ask, "Are you really okay with the way Kirill is torturing his own brother?"

"My opinion, or the lack thereof, has no importance whatsoever."

"Well, it should."

"We'll agree to disagree."

"Viktor, come on. This isn't some member of another gang that he's teaching a lesson to. It's his *brother*. If he hurts him, he won't only lose Konstantin, but also Karina and Kristina and his niece in her belly."

"You're saying that as if he didn't think about the consequences before deciding to do this."

"That's way worse! Does that mean he doesn't care, even if he causes irreparable damage to his family?"

"Why are you asking me? Ask him. Besides, are you sure you're his wife?"

"What is that supposed to mean?"

"I don't know. You tell me."

"Is there something I'm supposed to know?"

"Possibly."

"Like…"

"I'm not at liberty to tell."

Ugh. He's as infuriating as Kirill sometimes. No wonder they get along so well.

"Stop the riddles, Viktor—"

My words are cut off when a bang sounds, and the car swerves to the right. I hold on to the seatbelt as Viktor tries to keep it on the road.

"We're hit in the rear tires. Stay down!" Viktor grabs my head and shoves me forward. I fumble for my gun and then the extra ammunition I know we always have in the glove compartment.

I push at Viktor's hand, and he has to release me, or he'll lose concentration on the road.

His blazing eyes fly to me. "What are you doing?"

"Taking a shot while you drive."

"Don't even think about it. If you get hurt, Boss will kill me."

"I don't give a fuck about your boss when both of us are in danger right now."

I slide the window down and take a few shots at the two vans that are following us. But they hit us with more since they have damn rifles.

Shit.

"Just stay the fuck down!" Viktor's harsh words echo in the air.

He struggles with driving a faulty car while trying to evade the shower of bullets directed at us.

We can't hold on forever.

My ammunition is running low, and my adrenaline level is being affected by damn fear.

I wouldn't be this scared under different circumstances, but now that I'm carrying a child, I can't go all out or else he'll be hurt.

My aim isn't as great as I want it to be, and my heart is thundering harder in my chest.

Finally, we swerve to the side of the road, but thankfully, Viktor manages to stop the car right before we tumble off a steep cliff. It teeters on the edge, threatening to take us down the abyss.

We exchange looks and rush out at the same time. The moment we're out, the car falls to the ground below.

Before we can release a breath, however, the two vans stop not far from us.

"Run," Viktor says as he holds his gun with both hands. "I'll take care of this somehow."

"No way in hell. You'll just get killed."

"Don't be an idiot. If you stay here, you'll also be killed."

"I'll be killed even if I run away now."

"At least try." He glares at me. "Kirill won't forgive me if you die."

"He has nothing to forgive when you're also dead, genius."

"Aleksandra…" he warns.

"What?"

"You're the Pakhan's wife. Act like it, for fuck's sake."

"And you're his senior guard. You think he can function without you?"

He releases a long breath, but there are no more words exchanged as several men step out of the vehicle.

I'm so sorry, baby. I'm sorry you were conceived to stupid parents who live on adrenaline and can't protect you.

Tears cling to my eyes at the thought of not meeting my son. Not holding him in my arms. Or kissing his cheeks.

On the bright side, we're going together.

The last thought that comes to mind is Kirill. I hate that I won't see him one last time, or that the last time I saw him, I glared at him, or that—

My thoughts scatter when an elegant Mercedes stops behind the vans.

The person who comes out of it causes my lips to part.

Babushka…?

TWENTY-FIVE

Kirill

LET'S SAY EVERYTHING IS GOING ACCORDING TO PLAN. Well, not *every* single thing, per se, considering Sasha hates me and is probably counting the days until she can leave me.

The leaving part won't be happening—just saying.

She can be mad at me all she wants. She can criticize my methods and forbid me from touching her for three whole blasphemous days.

She can delude herself into thinking that she can leave me if she chooses to, but in reality, however, none of that nonsense will take place.

The more she insists on that, the faster I'll come up with solutions to make her stay.

If she hates me for it, then so be it.

I'd rather be hated than be forced into a life without her.

I've been there, done that, and the mere thought of those two months from hell still terrorizes me.

Sasha has always been important to me in one way or another, but it wasn't until I thought I'd lost her that I realized she's more important than the air I breathe.

But that's a thought for another day.

Today, I'm staring at my phone while listening to Damien blabber about his adrenaline dose and what-the-fuck-ever.

The downside of being a Pakhan is conducting business from home. It's not something I particularly care for, and is definitely something I could do without it.

Especially since my house is a war zone at the moment. Karina is literally out to get me, and Kristina looks like broken china and bursts into tears whenever she sees me.

Add the fact that my wife glares at me anytime our eyes meet, and it's safe to say I'm not a fan of the house right now.

So I imposed myself on Adrian under the pretense that we need to discuss a recent plan that he proposed. The execution of said plan coincidently involves Damien. I might have sent him a text to meet me here if he wanted.

What?

I'm bored while waiting for the result of my efforts, and Damien is the most entertaining clown I have immediate access to.

But even his over-the-top suggestions aren't doing it for me today.

Perhaps it's the thought that once this storm ends, I'll either have everything or nothing.

Adrian, who's sitting beside me on the sofa in his office, nudges me. "If you're done using my house as an entertainment parlor…"

I lift my head that I was resting against my fist and stare at him. "Are you kicking your Pakhan out?"

"Some of us have work to do."

"And you think I don't?" I motion ahead. "We're here for a very important issue…what was it again, Damien?"

He wipes the remnants of a brownie off his lips. The guy has the worst sweet tooth on the planet and is personally offended when people don't offer him cakes, brownies, or cookies.

One day, he'll get poisoned by his second obsession. That is, if his first obsession—violence—doesn't take him out first.

"Listen up, Pakhan. This is the last time I'll repeat it." He takes a swig of his second glass of vodka, although it's early afternoon. "You know those all-out wars we have whenever someone offends you personally?"

"By *all-out*"—Adrian narrows his eyes—"what do you mean, exactly?"

"Come on, Adrian. Don't be an idiot."

I snort out a chuckle and Adrian side-eyes me.

"What?" I feign innocence. "I find it amusing that Damien is calling *you* an idiot."

"Well, he is." Damien slams his glass of vodka on the table. "An all-out war includes bloodbaths, killing anyone who moves, and I'm the only one who gets to lead the action, including those from the others' territories. They can worry about profit, and I'll take care of counting the bodies."

I nod thoughtfully. "Which faction did you have in mind?"

"Why the fuck are you indulging him?" Adrian whispers under his breath. "He'll just go crazier."

I lift a shoulder. "It's fun."

Damien snaps his fingers in my direction. "I'm glad you asked! I prefer any of the Italian families. They're more hardcore than the other losers. Even better, some Russians from Chicago or Boston."

"Hmm. Something to consider."

Adrian tilts his head in my direction. "Seriously?"

"What do you mean, *seriously*?" Damien gives him a death glare. "I'm telling you, motherfucker, don't even try to ruin my fun with your annoying gibberish."

"Your craziness is costing the organization more than we can afford."

"Blah, blah, and more fucking blah. The Pakhan doesn't mind. What's got your panties in a twist, nerd?"

This time, I laugh out loud.

"What the fuck did you just say?" Adrian asks in a grim voice.

"You're always behind your computer and hacking and what-the-fuck-ever. Definition of a nerd, if you ask me."

"He's not wrong," I say after my laughter subsides.

"I'm going to erase you from existence while you sleep, Orlov. Let's see if you can handle this nerd then."

"Doesn't count, because a real fight doesn't happen while I'm asleep." He slides his attention to me. "Anyway, back to the real talk. When are you going to make that war happen, Pakhan?"

"Me?"

"Have you been listening? You need to get offended so this whole thing can start."

"Right. How does one get himself offended?"

"You're smart. Figure it out yourself. I can't be doing all the work for you."

"I see," I say in a feigned thoughtful tone. "I'll keep you posted on any progress I make."

"Is that going to happen anytime soon?"

"No."

"Why the fuck not?"

"Because you have a very important role to play."

"What?" His eyes light up. "Another war?"

"Marriage."

"How can that substitute for fucking war, Pakhan?"

"It does. In case you didn't know, marriage can be a war at times. Isn't that right, Adrian?"

He grumbles an affirmative sound. "The worst you'll ever have, Orlov."

"Word," I agree. "Your wife will try to win at every turn, and you have to lose. Willingly."

"Fuck no. I'm losing no war."

"There's no winning in marriage," Adrian says. "Your wife is the only one you'll relinquish power to, or you have to be prepared to lose her."

I nod. "Sometimes, you have to pretend you lost her just to get her back."

His brow furrows the more we talk. "This is so fucking confusing. I'm gonna win. End of story."

"Too new," I tell Adrian.

"Too inexperienced," he replies.

"He's going to learn the hard way."

"And we're going to enjoy watching every second of it."

"Hey!" He stares between us. "What the fuck is that supposed to mean?"

I'm about to reply, when my phone vibrates in my hand. I look at the screen and pause.

Sure enough, it's a text from an anonymous number. I expected them to get in touch sooner rather than later to ask for a meeting, but what I didn't expect was this message.

We have your wife. Be here in an hour alone, or she dies.

My hand tightens around the phone and my jaw clenches so hard, I'm surprised a tendon doesn't snap.

The fucking—

They must've kidnapped her on the way back from visiting Anton. I call Viktor, but I gothe call goes straight to his voicemail.

I briefly close my eyes, trying to purge the worst-case scenario. If they'd kidnapped her, Viktor would've told me right away.

Unless they killed him and took her.

I scroll to the tracker and pause. The location is about forty-five minutes away.

"What's wrong?" Adrian asks, seeming to have caught on to the sudden change in my demeanor.

"I'm going to need you to do something for me."

"What?"

"Infiltrate a security system if there's one."

"Which one?"

"I'll text you the details while I'm on the way." I stand up and stare at Damien. "I just got offended, so you have the green light to kill everyone at the location I'm sending you to. Everyone but my wife and Viktor."

On my way out, I call Maksim. He answers after two rings. "Maks speaking."

"It's time."

His voice hardens. "Yes, Boss."

I knew they'd do this, but they made a terrible mistake: getting Sasha involved.

It's not the first, but it'll certainly be the last mistake they make.

TWENTY-SIX

Sasha

DRIP.
Drip.
Drip!

I slowly open my eyes, bracing myself for the image of my family members' dead bodies and their blood splashing on my face.

A groan sounds from my right, followed by a low curse and a "Come on!"

I look up, but instead of the bodies hanging above my head, there's a dark green roof full of spots of black mud at the corners. Cracks spread across the walls like sporadic spiderwebs.

A repugnant stench of humidity makes it hard to inhale properly. My lungs suffocate with every breath, nearly triggering a claustrophobic reaction I never knew I had.

There's no window, and the only exit is a rusty metal door. Couple that with flickering fluorescent lights, and it's like a scene from the army's interrogation room.

The dripping sound comes from a wobbly faucet that's spilling into a yellowish sink in the corner.

The source of the groaning, however, is Viktor, who's sitting on a metal chair beside me. Both of us are bound with thick plastic straps that create uncomfortable friction.

I release a breath after I've made sure he's alive and well, despite the dry blood that trickles down his temple.

If something happened to Viktor, Kirill wouldn't be able to cope, so I'm beyond relieved that he made it.

I rack my brain to think of the reason we're here.

The last thing I remember was seeing Babushka before someone knocked me out. I assume they did the same to Viktor, but he probably struggled more, which explains the wound he has.

I remember nothing after that except for waking up here.

Judging by the way Viktor is struggling in the chair, it doesn't look like he can undo the bindings. I test them myself, but they're strapped too tight all over my arms, chest, and my legs.

"Any luck?" I sound a bit groggy, and I have to clear my throat.

Viktor directs his attention at me and shakes his head. "I've been trying to no avail."

If he can't make an escape, it'll be hard for me to come up with an alternative.

Just when I'm thinking of the logistics of trying to flip one of us over or sitting back to back to help one another, the door creaks open.

Both of us freeze as our kidnappers walk inside.

I already saw Babushka earlier with her closed-off expression and terrorizing cane, but the other two who accompany her are a surprise.

My jaw nearly hits the floor as the three of them stop a safe distance away from us.

Babushka stands in the middle and slams her cane on the ground in a clear demand of attention, but I couldn't look at her even if I wanted to.

My focus is stolen by the other two.

One is Uncle Albert, and while that's predictable, the third presence isn't.

Even Viktor narrows his eyes on her, despite still struggling in his chair.

The person who's staring down at us with her holier-than-thou expression is none other than Yulia.

She looks as elegant as ever in a dark red dress and black designer heels. Her golden hair is pulled into a French twist, and her arms are crossed over her chest.

"What…" I trail off, lost for words. What should I ask in a situation like this?

"I'm disappointed in you, Sasha." Uncle's voice carries in the air and slaps me across the face. "I really wanted to give you another chance, but you went ahead and chose to stay with the man who killed your family."

My lips tremble. "I…don't believe he did it, and I haven't seen any evidence that convinces me otherwise."

Babushka approaches, swings her cane, and hits me with it across my middle. That sense of terror I experienced while we were chased returns with a vengeance.

My baby.

"Insolent! Your father must be rolling in his grave for having a daughter like you."

"My father wouldn't have been as heartless as you." I glare at her and then at Uncle. "What is Yulia doing here?"

"I'm an ally," the woman herself replies, her nose nearly reaching for the sky. "Since we share the same enemy, it only makes sense that we join forces."

"If you think Kirill will fall for your tricks—"

"He's already on his way," Uncle cuts me off. "Seems that we had his weakness all along. *You.*"

My spine jerks upright, and the possible subsequent events come to mind.

They kidnapped us to make Kirill come alone, and when he does, they'll kill him.

I have hope that he knows it's a trap and won't come. Or at least, he'll bring backup.

Surely he'll realize that he'd be walking straight to his death.

…Right?

"Once that devil is dead," Yulia says. "Kosta will be the new Pakhan."

"And Anton will be released and return to his rightful place as the leader of the family," Babushka says. Her voice is fainter, and upon closer inspection, she looks so much older, as if the winds of time have been blowing in her face.

My mind keeps going back to the fact that they plan to kill Kirill, and if they do that…

No.

I refuse to think of that possibility. No one will be able to take Kirill's life.

No one.

I meet my grandmother's malicious gaze with my own. "Ever thought that Anton isn't interested in leading the family's shady business? Maybe he's thinking of another life outside of duty and needless drama and wars."

"Nonsense. Anton knows his role, and he will take it proudly, unlike a certain traitor in our midst."

"Traitor? I'm the *traitor* now?" I ask incredulously. "For the past six years, I lived as a man just to be a puppet for the family that never appreciated me or made me feel like I belonged. I sacrificed myself and my identity to protect *you*, but you still never made me feel like I was a member of this damn family. You know who did? Kirill! He unconditionally made me his family just because I asked, and if you think I'll let you kill him based on no proof, then you're delusional."

"You're the only delusional one here," my uncle says. "You can't stop us anymore, Sasha. That's why you're tied to that chair."

"We'll make sure you see him getting killed right in front of your eyes," Yulia adds.

"He's your son!"

"I never considered that devil my son. He's just an eyesore reminder of his fucking father. Once I get rid of him, I'll finally stop seeing Roman in his damn face."

"Stop saying that! He has nothing to do with what his father did, and neither does Karina."

"I'll get rid of them both one at a time."

It hits me then, and I slide my attention to Uncle Albert. "When you said you had a source who told you about who executed the massacre and who said Kirill was the mastermind, did you by any chance mean Yulia?"

He nods. "We've been exchanging information for a few years."

"You can't be serious. You just heard her. All she ever wanted was to get rid of Roman and Kirill. She poisoned her husband for years so his health would deteriorate, and he eventually died. She's lying so that she'll be able to throw Kirill under the bus."

"She heard Roman and Kirill talk about the plan right before he enlisted in the army."

"She's lying!" I can't believe I almost fell for the idea that he could be the one behind the plot of my family's annihilation.

I should've held on to the truth I knew deep in my heart—the fact that Kirill isn't the type who targets unarmed civilians or children.

And yet I fell for their plans so stupidly, I want to kick myself.

I have not a shadow of a doubt that all of this is part of Yulia's elaborate plan to snatch power for Konstantin. All these years, she was struggling to even have her family's support, but she never gave up and never looked like a loser.

Probably because she knew that her alliance with Babushka and Uncle would eventually give her the desired results.

"You're delusional." Yulia approaches me and leans forward so that her face is level with mine. "You think he's all that, but he's nothing more than a monster. I was right behind the door when Roman asked him what he should do with a certain family that was obstructing his way. Kirill gave him a full report on how to effectively get rid of each and every one of them. You should be thankful, really. I'm delivering you the revenge you couldn't get yourself."

I spit on her malicious face. "You're a narcissistic liar and a bitch. If you think I'll believe a word out of your mouth, *you're* the delusional one."

Her eyes close, and she wipes her cheeks with the back of her hand, then she slaps me so hard, I reel in my chair.

Her handprint burns on my cheek, and my eyes sting. Viktor tightens his muscles against his bindings and curses. "Don't touch her!"

"Or else what?" She glares at him. "You're as useless as she is."

He growls, and it sounds animalistic in the silence. I exchange a look with him to communicate that he can't let her rattle him. She's cut from the same cloth as Kirill, and their type really enjoys playing with other people's intense emotions.

"You're right," Viktor tells me. "She's a liar. Boss never gave his father any of the plan she's talking about. In fact, ever since he was shot in Russia, he's been trying to find out why the Belsky Organization targeted him."

The answer is as clear as day: it's because Yulia fed them this information.

"You should've stayed dead after that explosion." Yulia glares down at me. "I even went through all the trouble of falsifying the DNA test to make that devil believe you died."

My lips part. "You planned that?"

"And I enjoyed every second of watching Kirill suffer. If you didn't come back, he would've gotten himself killed, but no, you had to be uncooperative."

"You...you..." I'm lost for words. A part of me can't believe a mother would willingly hurt her son this deeply, but the other part knows that she can go further than this.

Not only did she never consider Kirill her son, but she also thinks of him as an enemy.

Uncle Albert checks his phone and then smiles. "He's finally here."

My heartbeat picks up, and I swallow the saliva flooding my mouth.

Please tell me he brought backup. Please—

My hopes dwindle when the door opens again, and two burly mercenaries lead Kirill inside.

He's alone.

Fuck.

Damn it!

What the hell was he thinking?

They must've taken away his weapons before they led him here, so he's well and truly defenseless.

All focus turns to him, but his light eyes land on me, and he studies me from toe to head. When he reaches my face, a muscle clenches in his jaw, probably at seeing the red mark on my cheek.

I look back with what must appear to be terrorized fear, my mind reeling with endless questions. *Are you here to get killed? How could you fall for this?*

But the calm expression on his face manages to ease the agitation, even partially.

The men push him to his knees in front of the three. I wince when he hits the ground with a thud. His back is to me, but I can almost see his nonchalant expression as he looks up at them.

"Lower your damn head, devil." Yulia slaps him across the face so hard, his head flies to the right.

He looks up at her again, probably with a more provocative expression, because her eyes blaze, and she slaps him harder. "I said lower your head."

"Stop it!" I struggle against my bindings, wanting to claw her eyes out for daring to hit him after everything she's made him go through.

"Don't mind her, Sasha. Mother seems to have an overwhelming hatred toward me, so I'm letting her get the dissatisfaction off her chest."

"You can be sarcastic all you want, you bastard, but today is the last day you breathe. I was willing to let you get higher and enjoy your married life a little more before I destroyed you, but you made a fatal mistake by locking up and torturing my son."

Oh. So this is why she's extra venomous today. I was wondering what she'd do if she heard about what Kirill did to his brother, but I didn't think she'd already had this plan prepared.

Uncle Albert retrieves a gun and points it at Kirill's head. "Any last wishes?"

"No…" My voice is brittle as I swing back and forth in my chair. Viktor does the same, his face too tight and red.

"Don't do it, Uncle," I plead. "He's not the one behind the massacre. Please, Uncle, if I ever meant anything to you, don't do this."

"Shut up, you insolent child." Babushka taps her cane on the ground. "Do your thing, Albert."

"One second," Kirill says with so much nonchalance, it's baffling, considering the situation. "I assume your proof that I plotted the demise of your family is that Yulia told you so, no?"

Uncle Albert raises a brow. "Are you also going to say that she's a liar like Sasha did?"

Kirill looks back at me, and a proud, heart-stopping smile lifts the corners of his lips. I return the smile even as tears burn my lids.

I believe in you, I say with my eyes. *I'm sorry I wasn't sure until now.*

He stares back at my uncle. "I'm curious. Did you know that my dear mother had an affair with your brother?"

Babushka's face pales. "What is this nonsense?"

"Shoot him already," Yulia says.

Uncle Albert's face doesn't change as he starts to do just that. I scream, "No," but before he can do it, Babushka hits my uncle's hand, sending the gun flying against the opposite wall. "I want to hear what he has to say."

Yulia's expression remains cold, but her whole body becomes eerily still.

"Much appreciated. I knew you were the voice of reason," Kirill says in the same detached tone. "So, the thing is, Yulia had an affair with your son Anatoly for years. As a result, he's my brother's biological father. I thought the story ended there, but I found out through a recent letter left by my father that your son ended the affair after his wife got pregnant with their youngest child. Of course, Yulia, who always gets what she wants, didn't like that. She's a bit too possessive, my mother. Correction, a *lot*. If she couldn't have Anatoly, no one else could. So what did she do? She deliberately let Roman know about the affair. She thought he wasn't aware of her manipulations, but she missed the fact that he always employed private investigators to make sure any allegations were true. That's how he knew Anatoly broke up with her exactly a year before the massacre. He still didn't like the idea of another man having his possession, so when the government approached him with a request to annihilate you, he agreed. But here's the most important piece of the puzzle, Mrs. Ivanova. Yulia is the one who gave him that plan. But that's not the end of it. My father left me a memory card that has pictures of Yulia and Anatoly together as well as videos of Anatoly kicking Yulia out of his club when she went to Russia. I invite you to listen to this little recording that will explain my next point better."

Kirill retrieves his phone, and both Uncle Albert and Yulia lunge at it. Babushka surprisingly hits them both with her cane, keeping them away as Kirill hits Play.

"You mean to tell me I'll have an opening?" Roman says in Russian.

There's a sound of skin against skin like someone is peppering kisses all over his face, before Yulia's voice follows. "Yes, dear. I have an insider in that house who'll make sure there's little to no resistance."

"Are you positive? I will kill your lover."

"I'm proving that he's not my lover. You're the only man I've ever loved."

"*Really?*"

"Really, dear."

Gag. Even I can hear the fakery in her tone. Judging by the way he asked, Roman most likely knew, too. However, he probably decided to go with the flow because he wanted to use her anyway.

"Who's your insider?" he asks.

"Albert. He never liked being under the dictatorial leadership of his mother and brother. Never liked his wife or even his children. They're good to go, too, as long as he and the old lady stay alive since she's the one who'll be able to put him as the head of the family—"

Yulia's voice comes to an end when Uncle Albert shoots the phone right out of Kirill's hand.

Babushka's pale face must mirror mine.

The load of information I just heard makes my head spin, and my heart shrivels in my chest.

Uncle Albert and Yulia were the ones who planned the massacre.

My uncle.

My *own* uncle killed everyone I ever cared about.

My father's brother plotted the inhumane butchering of his own family—children included.

"What…" Babushka is lost for words. Her thin, wrinkly lips open and close in a scene I've never witnessed before. When she speaks, her voice is barely audible. "What is the meaning of this, Albert?"

"Ahhh." He laughs almost mockingly. "Fuck. It actually feels good that I can finally drop the annoying mask."

"Albert!"

"What, Mother, *what?*" he screams in her face. "You always worshiped Akim and adored Anatoly, but I was the one missing from your list. You never thought I was capable of anything and pushed me back in favor of those other two fuckers all the damn time. You made me marry the least influential woman just to stop me from ever climbing to the top."

"So you *murdered* your family?"

He raises a shoulder. "I never considered them my family. They were just a hurdle on my way to success. I would've preferred it if Sasha and Tosha hadn't survived, so I wouldn't have had anyone blocking my path, but oh well, I will just kill them now."

"And Mike," I snarl. "What about him?"

"I needed an heir." He rolls his eyes. "His mother was alive with him in the closet, and she was so happy that I came to their rescue. I shot that bitch in the head and took him from her arms."

"Albert…" Tears stream down Babushka's cheeks for the first time ever. "What have you done?"

"Shut up, Mother. For once in your life, just shut up. I put up with your presence all these years for the power you hold over all the other families. I put up with Tosha and Sasha because they were my eyes in enemy camps. But all of you are unnecessary now."

My vision is blurred with a waterfall of tears. It's like I'm staring at a stranger. All these years, I thought we were fighting for the same cause, even if we had different methods, but he's been the villain all along.

He didn't only fool me, Anton, Babushka, and Mike, but he's also been pretending that we're a family.

My lips tremble. "You…did all of this for power?"

"And to get rid of the annoying people who didn't allow me to reach my potential. Especially your goddamn father. You and Tosha are so much like him, I want to stab you in the eyes every time I see you. Fuck! It was hard to pretend I liked you when all I wanted to do was kill you. It's why I sent those mercenaries to attack you on that Spetsnaz mission. Too bad both of you only suffered injuries and refused to die already. And again, you refused to be killed when I sent people trailing after you in the forest after you came back here."

Oh. My. God.

No wonder that sniper was so focused on me. If Kirill hadn't been there—in Russia and in the forest—I would've died for sure. Same for Anton—if Maksim and Viktor hadn't been there, he wouldn't have been able to escape with a mere hand injury.

"So it was you."

Everyone's attention turns to the newcomers, Anton—the one who spoke just now—Maksim, and…Konstantin.

He's standing there without a single bruise on his face. Their grim expressions indicate that they heard the entire thing.

Only Babushka is still gaping at her second-born as if he's a ghost.

Or perhaps a demon in human form.

The guards glance at my uncle, probably waiting for an order, but if he tells them to go after the three who just arrived, that means they'll have to let go of Kirill.

Given that, shouldn't they have more guards around here?

"That's also why you didn't come to my rescue all this time," Anton continues. "You hoped Kirill would kill me while you convinced Babushka that you were working on the logistics. An excuse you always use whenever you need more time."

"Aren't you the bright one?" my uncle says with a note of mockery. "You should've died with your parents, but you refused to, even after they put three bullets in your body."

"You…" Babushka's voice sounds raw, haunted, as she chokes on her tears and raises her cane in his direction. "You murdered my children…and my grandchildren… I will tear you limb from limb, you ungrateful bastard—"

Her cane hits the floor first as a bullet lodges in her forehead. I scream as she drops to the floor, her lifeless eyes staring at nothing.

"I told you to shut the fuck up." My uncle sighs and shakes his head. "Now you'll be silent forever."

Anton runs to Babushka, followed closely by Maksim. "Babushka…"

"You're next." My uncle points the gun at him. "And then Sasha and her bothersome husband. That way, no one will be in my way to get to the throne."

Anton glares up at him and brings out his own gun. "Put down your fucking weapon. This place is surrounded."

"Nonsense," Yulia says. "Didn't your men make sure Kirill came alone, Albert?"

The man in question, Kirill, looks at the guys holding him. "Are we going to do this nicely or not so nicely?"

They exchange a look but hesitantly remain in place.

"Not so nicely, then."

He effortlessly removes his shoulder from one guy's hold and starts to kick the other away, but Yulia steals a gun from one of the guards and points it at Kirill.

"Not another move. I won't allow you to keep living."

"Mother, stop!" Konstantin rushes to her side.

"Don't even try to change my mind, Kosta! He locked you up and tortured you."

"He didn't. He just wanted to prove something."

"Prove something?" she echoes.

"The fact that you used Makar to try and kill my wife," Kirill says with harshness that chills me to the bone. "You made him tell me it was Konstantin and even forged evidence for it. You provoked me to hurt him so that you could save him and prove that I don't care about him. You wanted him to come crawling back to you because you're the only one who loves him. But what to do, Mother? I'm one step ahead of you. I pretended to fall for your trick and made everyone in the house believe it so your spy would give you the right information. I forced you to reveal your true colors to Konstantin."

"You can't possibly believe this devil, Kosta," she says with calm determination. "Everything I did, I did for you."

"Then stop it, Mother," he pleads. "Just stop it already. I never wanted anything you gave me. Never asked for it, either, so stop forcing it on me."

"How…how can you say that?" She glares back at Kirill. "It's all because of you! I knew you'd be a damn nightmare from day one, you fucking devil spawn. Just die!"

"Nooo!" I scream as she takes the shot.

Everything happens too fast.

Uncle shoots at the same time, and then a few more shots follow.

Blood spills.

And more blood.

And it splatters on me.

No, it's coming from inside me.

My head gets dizzy as I look down and find my thighs soaked with blood.

Someone calls my name, but my head rolls back, and everything goes black.

TWENTY-SEVEN

Sasha

A NIGHTMARE STARTLES ME AWAKE.

I don't know what it's about. All I remember is floundering, gasping, and choking in a pool of blood.

"Sasha?"

I blink the moisture from my lids, and my breathing returns to normal as I meet Karina's bloodshot eyes. Anna stands beside her, a compassionate look covering her usually stern features.

Alarms blaze in my head, and I start to sit up. The IV tube digs into my arm, and Anna helps me straighten.

I stare down at the hospital gown and recall the blood between my legs.

Memories attack me all at once. Being strapped to the chair helplessly as Kirill got—

"Where's Kirill?" I blurt.

"With Kosta," Karina replies. "He said Yulia tried to kill him, so Kosta pushed her away, and Kirill shot her. She's in the ICU."

Oh. A sense of relief grips hold of me and I release a long breath. I was so certain he'd definitely been shot this time.

The door opens and Kristina walks inside. She smiles upon seeing me, even though her face is pale and tired.

"Sasha, you're awake. Thank God."

"Is…" I study all their faces. "Is my baby okay?"

"Yes, yes." Kristina clutches my hand. "You had a little complication, but you protected him. The doctor said you need a lot of rest, though."

My chest deflates and tears fill my eyes as I place a palm on my stomach. When I saw the blood earlier, I thought that I'd lost him for sure.

Both of them. My husband and our son.

"Does…Kirill know?"

"About the pregnancy?" Karina asks. "Of course. He was the one who brought you here and threatened to kill everyone in the hospital if they didn't save you."

"How did he take the news of the pregnancy?" I feel awful that I didn't get to tell him myself. Worse, I wasn't even there to see how he reacted.

All my reasons for hiding it from him have vanished now. So what if he uses this to keep me by his side? That's exactly what I want.

"It wasn't clear," Anna says in a motherly tone. "He seemed more concerned about your safety."

"Oh."

Doubt starts to niggle at my insides. Maybe I've miscalculated this. What makes me think Kirill wants a child? Knowing his parents, he could abhor the family institution.

We've never spoken about children before, and he didn't seem interested when Karina mentioned it the day he locked up his brother.

"Are you okay?" I clutch Karina's hand. "About Yulia."

She lifts a shoulder. "I don't give a fuck about that woman. I'm just glad you, Viktor, and my brothers are safe."

Me, too.

I hope Konstantin thinks the same and doesn't hold a grudge against Kirill.

My husband might pretend that he's a lone wolf, but he needs the level of support only Konstantin can provide him.

My stomach churns at the idea of seeing him and talking to him about the pregnancy. What am I supposed to say? *Should* I say anything?

Everything is muddy right now, and I can't seem to concentrate on one thought for too long.

At the same time, I can't stop thinking about Kirill. Am I a bit disappointed that he's not by my side? Yes. But I also know why he needs to be with Konstantin after he shot his mother.

At any rate, I need to find him. But before I can do that, the doctor comes to check on me and tells me that both the baby and I are safe. However, I need to rest for a few weeks to avoid putting any more strain on my condition.

No physical activities aside from walking. No rough sex—that bit got me frustrated. No journeys that extend over an hour. No flying either.

After she leaves, I stand up and put on a fuzzy robe that Karina brought for me. As Anna helps me tie the belt, I ask, "Oh, by the way, did any of you see my brother?"

Karina's face pales.

My heart nearly drops to my feet. I think I remember Uncle Albert shooting, but Anton also had a gun. He couldn't have hurt him, right?

"What is it?" My voice shakes. "Is he okay?"

"Yes, don't worry." Kristina pats my shoulder. "He's safe."

"Why do I sense there's a but there?"

"Maks saved him and got shot instead. He's also in the ICU," Karina blurts, tears brimming her lids.

Oh, God.

No.

I don't know how I get the energy, but I'm already wheeling the IV drip and storming out of the room.

I don't listen to them calling my name or asking me to be careful.

My whole body feels like it's on fire as I take the elevator to the ICU. Then all my chaotic emotions come to a halt when I arrive near the waiting area.

A bulky mass of muscles sits on one of the chairs, blood soaking his neck, hands, and shirt as he holds his head in his palms.

I slowly approach my brother, my heart thundering so loud, I'm scared it'll bust out. Once I'm in front of him, I carefully touch his shoulder.

Anton lifts his head, and for the first time in our lives, I see tears clinging to his eyes.

"Malyshka…" he whispers in a low tone, and I just hug him to my chest.

His arms wrap around my middle, and his whole body shakes against me.

"I'm so sorry, Tosha."

"I could've killed Uncle Albert in that moment, but I hesitated and only killed him when it was too late. I'm the reason Maks threw himself in front of me. He didn't hesitate, Sasha…he just offered his life for mine without even thinking."

"That's because he loves you, Tosha. And I know you love him, too."

"What if…what if I lose him, Sasha…? What am I supposed to do then?" I can feel the anguish and pain emanating from my brother in waves.

I have to stop myself from giving in to the dooming thoughts, but I can't control it as we both shake.

"You won't." I pull back and stroke his hair. "Maks is a fighter and won't die just like that."

"He…lost a lot of blood."

"That still won't kill him. He's Maks, remember?"

"He's Maks," he repeats in a less assured tone.

I hug him again, and we remain like that for what seems like an hour before the doctor comes along.

My brother staggers to his feet and nearly hits the wall when the doctor says that Maks is stable.

I squeeze his arm, smiling through my unshed tears. "I told you."

He smiles in return, his expression easing before it sobers. "Remember when you said I needed to have something for myself?"

I nod.

"I will."

"Yeah?"

"Yeah. You were right, Sasha. Maks is more important than duty."

I grin like an idiot. What? I'm their number one supporter.

"What do you plan to do?"

"Once he's okay, I'm leaving this life and starting anew. Now that Babushka and Uncle Albert are gone, I'll raise Mike and clear up the mess our family made in Russia."

"Do you know where they left Mike?"

"Back in Saint Petersburg with a nanny. I told her to fly him here for now, so they're on their way."

"I can raise him, Tosha. I love Mishka to death, and you were never good with children."

"No, I will. Mike and I need each other. Besides, you have your own son to worry about."

"Mishka is not a burden. We can share his custody until I think you can take care of him properly." I pause. "How did you and Maks end up there anyway?"

"Kirill let me go. He came earlier that day and said that he had evidence he wanted me to see personally."

Right.

Everything is part of an elaborate plan for Kirill. He made Anton and me see our uncle's true colors and did the same with Konstantin and Yulia.

Although I doubt he calculated all the shoot-outs that happened. At least, I hope he didn't.

"Do you...know where he is?" I ask my brother.

"Probably the next ward."

"I'll come back, okay?"

"No need to. I'm going to go clean up and visit Maks."

"I will come back," I repeat, then give him a quick hug.

After I make sure he can stand straight, I wheel the IV drip to the other section of the ICU.

Sure enough, Kirill is sitting opposite the vending machine. Legs apart, his jacket thrown over the back of the seat, and his face closed off.

It looks cold under the bright lights, and I don't know why that makes me hide around the corner.

He adjusts his glasses with his middle finger as Konstantin grabs two cups of instant coffee and then joins him.

The brothers sit shoulder to shoulder, silently sipping their coffee.

"This stuff tastes like recycled urine," Kirill grumbles as he takes another sip.

"I have too many questions, but the most important are: one, how do you know what recycled urine tastes like? Two, is urine even recyclable?"

"A hunch for the first. Yes, for the second." Kirill clutches the cup with both hands and steals a glance at his brother. "Are we not going to talk about the elephant in the room?"

"You drinking instant coffee?"

"Yulia being in a coma because of me."

Konstantin exhales deeply, but he doesn't say anything.

"I won't apologize for putting her right where she belongs, but I know your feelings toward her are different from mine."

His brother pauses, and I hold my breath until he releases a sigh.

"You know, I've thought long and hard about this, but I always come to the same conclusion. If you didn't shoot her, she would've shot you." He stares at Kirill. "I prefer this outcome much more than the alternative. I'm glad you're the one sitting beside me right now."

Konstantin probably didn't notice it, but Kirill's chest expanded with relief just now. Even if his face still looks like the same unperturbed cold entity.

In a fraction of a second, that emotionless gaze zeroes in on me. Although I'm half hiding behind the wall, he sees me immediately.

I don't know why I feel the need to run.

My legs, however, don't move.

Kirill stands and squeezes Konstantin's shoulder. "I'll be back."

He abandons the cup of coffee in the nearest trash can and strides toward me.

Once he stops in front of me, it's like he's gained a few inches of height. The dark tattoos peeking out from the collar of his shirt appear monstrous when coupled with his closed-off expression.

"What are you doing here?" His voice is harsh and authoritarian, like in our army days. "You should be resting."

"I'm…fine. The doctor said I can move around."

"The doctor also said not to put a strain on your health."

I swallow. "Is this because I'm pregnant? Are you concerned about your son's life?"

"I'm concerned about *your* life, damn it." His eyes blaze with flames. "Why the fuck didn't you tell me you were pregnant? Why did you choose to act suspicious and pull away from me instead?"

Emotions clog my throat, and I hate the feeling of being so vulnerable. So…damn inferior.

"I…didn't want you to force me to stay because of the baby. I wanted to come to terms with us first."

"There's no us anymore since we're divorcing in a few weeks."

I jerk as if someone punched me in the gut. My body trembles, and my eyes sting. "You…will divorce me?"

"Isn't that what you wanted when you came back? You clearly demanded a divorce after three months."

But that was before I knew everything. Divorce is the last thing I want right now.

Also, I genuinely thought he'd never grant me that, considering how often he reminded me that he wouldn't let me leave him.

"I…" I trail off, not knowing what to say. "We can…extend that until after I give birth. You know, so he's not illegitimate."

"No."

I reel again. What the hell is with him punching metaphorically today?

"I also don't want you to stay with me just because of the baby," he says.

Oh.

"But…you want me to stay?"

"Only if you love me." He takes my hands in his. "If you don't, I will pursue you again and for as long as it takes until you fall head over heels for me."

"Then, the divorce…"

"I was testing you. The word divorce doesn't exist in my dictionary with you. The day I married you, I promised to be your husband till death do us part, and I intend to keep that promise. I already lost you once, I'll be damned if I lose you again."

My throat closes. "Does that mean you love me?"

He caresses my hair in gentle strokes. "I don't only love you. I'm nothing without you. I don't know when it started or when it grew into this fiery explosion, but I know for a fact that you've become an undivided part of me. You're the solace I need every night and the light I look forward to every morning. I might have strived for power and prestige, but it took losing you to realize that my universe revolves around you."

A whole-body shudder grips hold of me, and I'm barely preventing myself from bawling my eyes out.

I've always wanted Kirill to tell me I'm special to him. He's shown it in action plenty of times, and I thought I was okay with that, but deep inside me, I wanted to hear it, too.

The words he just said are more than I ever imagined.

More than I ever wished for.

I place an unsteady palm on his chest. "Does that mean if I ask you to stop being Pakhan, you'll give up the position for me?"

He catches hold of my hand and kisses my palm. "Today if you want."

"Really?"

"Whatever my beautiful wife wants."

"But you worked so hard for it."

"That position means nothing without you."

"Oh, Kirill." I throw myself in his arms. "Of course I won't ask you to give up your hard-earned power. I'll stand by your side every step of the way."

"Does that mean you still love me?"

I pull back and stroke his cheek. "I never stopped, idiot. It's hard to live without you and impossible to forget you, but I had no choice in loving you."

"Good. Because I don't intend to ever let you go."

"Even if I hate you sometimes?"

"Especially then."

"Even if I'm difficult?"

"I'm difficult, too."

"Even if you get tired of me?"

"I'd get tired of the world, but never you, wife."

"You better not." I wrap my arms around his neck. "Because I will also never let you go, husband."

I'm his.

He's mine.

And neither of us has a say in it.

EPILOGUE 1

Sasha

Five months later

DESPITE ALL THE CRAZINESS, LIFE HAS GONE ON.
It feels like forever since that day many bodies dropped and crucial decisions were made. Probably because a lot of things have happened since.

Yulia died about two weeks after she fell into a coma. While Konstantin looked sad and Karina had a conflicted expression, Kirill stood at her funeral like a cold statue.

For him, she was already dead, probably had been since he was young. I'm glad he at least got closure when she told him why she hated him with passion. That's when he learned for sure that she'd never love him or even tolerate him.

Kirill represented everything she abhorred—Roman's temperament and a constant reminder of the abuse she suffered. But what made it worse was that he also got her intelligence and knack for manipulation.

I still hate that woman with everything in me. She ruined all her children's lives—Konstantin's included. Not only did she fig-uratively choked him with her love, but she also had a hand in his biological father's death.

If Kirill had a different mother, he wouldn't have been emo-tionally or physically abused. At least I'm glad he had Anna in his teens since he considers her the only mother figure in his life.

Kirill also killed Yakov—his maternal uncle. Apparently, he's the one who helped Yulia with the Makar angle. My husband eliminated him before he could plot revenge or pose a threat to our family.

On the other hand, Maksim took his sweet time recovering. Anton and I were there for him—mostly my brother, though. I stopped being as involved.

One, because Kirill found out that Maks had some sort of a crush on me when I was pretending to be a man and threatened to kill him.

And yes, it was Anton who told him that piece of information because he's also still inexplicably jealous of it.

Two, turns out Maksim was enjoying being the center of Anton's attention so much that he might have prolonged his re-covery process on purpose.

After he got back into shape, he resigned from Kirill's team, which my husband welcomed because he's an asshole who doesn't even like the idea of a harmless crush.

Now, my brother and my friend are in Russia with Mike. In the beginning, I kept Mike with me, and while he loved it here, he was confused with all the English. Besides, after we went to Russia and saw how carefree he is in my brother's company.

My cousin adores Maks to death—something Anton was

annoyed with since everyone seems to love Maks since the first meeting.

I'm glad Mishka spent the first period with me because Anton faced difficulties as soon as he got back to Russia. He had to relinquish the family's illegal arms to the government and strike a deal with the higher ups. It's better now, but he's still cleaning up the mess Uncle Albert made and trying to veer the family's resources in a safer, more profitable direction.

I was heartbroken when we had to separate, but it wasn't a goodbye. I FaceTime with them every day, mostly with Maks and Mishka because Anton is still allergic to showing emotions and only joins when he's forced to.

Besides, I'm sure the three of them will be just fine. They're starting to look and feel more like a family every time I see them.

Which is so wholesome, considering what every one of them went through. It's beautiful when the most damaged souls can find solace in one another.

I guess that also applies to Kirill and me.

I stare at him from across the room as he talks with the other organizations' leaders. The party that's held to celebrate another win Kirill brought is in full bloom around me, but all I can concentrate on is my husband.

He has a hand in his pocket, and the other cradles a glass of champagne.

Authority looks sexy on him. He was always meant to be at the top, no matter what methods he used. It's not only about the position with Kirill. He really has a knack for managing people and getting the best out of them.

Besides, he's never fully satisfied with the lengths he reaches and keeps striking more alliances and ending wars—to Damien's dismay.

I can't help being sucked in by my husband's presence, even from a distance. The tailored tuxedo stretches over his shoulders and puts his impressive agile physique on display.

The nonchalant, seemingly relaxed aura he exudes is only a façade. That man can turn into a lethal weapon in a fraction of a second.

And I don't know why I find that kind of exhilarating.

It's probably the hormones. They haven't gone down, not in the second trimester or this final one.

I'm due to give birth to our boy in about a week, but my bump has never really grown. Kristina, whose husband is feeding her an assortment of buffets, looks well and truly pregnant with a huge belly and a curved posture.

Me? I look like I'm no further along than my fifth or sixth month.

The bump is there, but since I'm wearing a somewhat loose dress, it doesn't show as much.

The doctor said the difference between Kristina and me could be because everyone carries differently. The good news is that both our babies are healthy and will hopefully grow up as best friends.

They'll also be heirs to their fathers' fortunes since Konstantin has been appointed to Kirill's previous role in the brotherhood. My husband left that position empty after he became Pakhan, but I think he always wanted his brother there. The only reason he didn't do it before was because he didn't want Yulia to try and influence Konstantin or get her hands on internal information.

We're now growing into a big family. I felt it that day when I celebrated Christmas again after nearly seven years of shunning it, but now I'm happy to have this new family.

It's better than anything I could've wished for.

I have two sisters who are not related to me by blood. The quirky Karina, who's arguing with Viktor in the corner while he ignores her. She's been in therapy since Yulia died and has been making a lot of progress.

The other unexpected sister is Kristina. We've been doing this pregnancy thing together. She's helped me tremendously, and I wouldn't have been able to do this without her.

There's also Anna's support, Konstantin's compassion, and even Viktor's grumpy existence. Not to mention the rest of the guards, who bring me all sorts of exotic fruits and delicious desserts in case I'm craving something.

Those men were and always will be my comrades, despite Kirill's narrowed eyes and silent threats to eliminate them.

But the most important member of my family is my husband. Sometimes, it scares me how much I love him.

How frightened I am about his well-being and protection.

If he's ever in danger, I have no doubt that I'll pull a Maksim and use my body as his human shield. And the best part? I know he'd do the same without hesitation, too.

We spent so much time either suspecting or being wary of one another, so this phase of mutual understanding and trust has been heaven-like.

"Excuse me," I tell Lia and Rai, then swiftly leave the small circle.

I don't even blame it on the hormones anymore, I just want my husband.

He says he was traumatized by the two months of thinking I was dead, but I also longed for him to the point of madness—including when I thought I hated him.

Kirill lifts his head, sensing me approaching him even when I'm still far away. His eyes blaze a bright blue color, and he leaves the people he's with in an instant. After abandoning his glass of champagne on a table, he meets me halfway and wraps an arm around my middle.

My whole body comes alive when I'm in his embrace, and I place a hand on his shoulder, needing to feel his warmth against me.

"You should be resting, Sasha." He strokes my hair behind my ear. It's reaching the small of my back now, and while it's a hassle to wash and style, I'm fine with that as long as he always touches it, whether like this or when he tugs me by it during sex.

We sway to the music while hugging one another. "I'm tired of resting."

"Your feet were more swollen than usual this morning."

"That's normal. I can take it."

"Well, I can't. I don't like it when you're in pain."

"I'm not, really."

He raises a brow. "Yesterday, you were crying because you wanted a glass of water."

"Yeah, well, it happens."

"The day before yesterday, you were crying because, and I quote, 'You aren't fucking me properly, you fucking bastard.'"

"You were too gentle."

I really hate how he's become freaked out about hurting our son or me lately. A few weeks after that incident, the doctor said sex is okay, including rough, but he always takes it easy on me.

Am I wrong for wanting the version from before he found out I was pregnant?

"Looks like I've created a monster." He chuckles. "In all seriousness, I really don't want you in pain or even strained, Solnyshko."

"I'm not. Really. The doctor also said it's okay." I get on my tiptoes and kiss his stubbled jaw. "You know I love it when you don't hold back."

He groans when I rub my belly on his growing erection. "Sasha…"

"What?" I ask innocently.

"Stop that unless you're in the mood to get fucked."

"You know I am."

He curses under his breath and barely lasts a few seconds before he grabs me by the wrist and drags me to a spare room on the first floor.

It's more like a sitting room with a few sofas, a coffee table, and a fireplace.

As soon as he closes the door, he pins me against it, and his mouth clashes with mine. Kirill always kisses me with heat and boundless desire, but right now, it's more animalistic and raw yet also tender.

Ever since I was in the hospital, he's been kissing me as if he loves me. As if he's grateful to have me.

Someone like Kirill will always be an authoritarian monster with skewed views of the world, but he makes me feel like I'm the center of his world.

The one person he looks for every morning and hugs to sleep every night.

The one person he tells everything to, whether it's brotherhood business or his family business.

He didn't only make me his wife and partner with words but also with his actions.

He also offered me the official position of his counselor if that's what I want.

Without leaving my lips, he drags me to the sofa and lays me on top, his large hands groping me everywhere. I'm so hypersensitive that I moan from each touch. He pulls back and I'm slammed by the passionate, animalistic look in his eyes.

"I've been trying." He unbuckles his belt and releases his hard cock. "I've been *really* trying to take it easy on you, but you're making it impossible, Solnyshko."

I inch up my dress and slide down my panties, then kick them away and part my legs as far as possible. My pussy is throbbing wet as I palm his cheek. "I never asked you to take it easy on me."

"Is that so?"

I bite his lower lip and then release it with a pop. "Fuck me, Luchik."

That's all the invitation he needs as he thrusts all the way inside in one go. I'm tight, and the friction feels so good.

"You want it like this, wife?" he asks against my throat, then bites down. "You want me to fuck you like an animal?"

"Yes, yes…" I hold on to him and jerk my hips.

"You're driving me fucking insane." He wraps his hand around my throat and goes deeper, harder, giving me the stimulation I've been begging for.

Yes, he gives me orgasms, but mostly by eating me out or stimulating me. He usually doesn't want to go to these lengths.

If I'd known all I had to do was provoke him, I would've done this ages ago.

My legs tense, and I bite onto his neck as I come with a muffled scream. Kirill goes on, pounding into me with delicious intensity until he finds his own peak.

"I love you, Luchik," I whisper against his neck as we bask in the afterglow.

He runs his finger over the tattoo with his name on it, then kisses my belly. "I love you more, Solnyshko."

"No way in hell."

He pulls out, tucks himself back in, and changes positions so that I'm sitting on his lap. He doesn't care that I'm messing up his pants with the evidence of our pleasure that's dripping from between my thighs.

"I got your name tattooed on me," I say.

"Why do you think I have too many suns tattooed on my skin? Besides…" He unbuttons his shirt and traces his fingers over the tattoos he got on top of his gunshot wound.

I lean closer, and my eyes widen. All this time, I thought it was a sun and a skull intertwined with lines, but in the middle of it, I read it loud and clear in Russian.

Solnyshko's.

Like our rings.

"I also got your name tattooed on me."

"How…" I swallow. "Why didn't you tell me?"

"I thought you would've noticed it by now."

"I didn't know it was a word."

"You do now."

I lean over and kiss the tattoo, but more the scar from the bullet. "No one will be able to hurt you anymore. I promise."

"I should be the one who says that, wife."

"Well, I'm capable of protecting you, too, husband."

"For now, worry about protecting yourself." He sits me down on the sofa, then lifts my feet and removes my flats. "See? I told you the swelling had gotten worse."

Like every day, he places my feet on his lap and rubs them with slow, soothing circles.

I release a contented sigh and lean my head back to enjoy the sensation.

"How many times do I have to tell you that whenever you feel them getting more swollen, let me know, Sasha? If I don't check regularly, you become like this."

"It's okay. They don't hurt that much."

He shakes his head and continues with his task for more than fifteen minutes. Once he's done, he helps me stand up, and I freeze as I feel something wet splashing down my thighs and then onto Kirill's shoes.

We share a look.

It seems like our little boy is looking forward to seeing us as much as we're looking forward to seeing him.

We smile as the realization hits us.

We're officially going to be parents today.

EPILOGUE 2

Kirill

Eighteen months later

I'M ANNOYED, AND IT HAS EVERYTHING TO DO WITH ALL the people crowding my house.

Remember when I said I hate Christmas?

Now, I'm willing to take the Grinch's position and turn into the number one plotter of sabotage.

Last year, we spent it at Anton and Maksim's new mansion in Russia, but this year, they came over, accompanied by this little shit Mike, who won't leave Sasha's side.

Am I jealous of a nine-year-old? Possibly.

Turns out, he's the one she was talking to on the phone years ago and telling him that she missed him. And here I thought he was a lover who I've been planning to assassinate for years.

That idea is still plausible if he keeps stealing my wife's time as if he's entitled to it. Not only do I have to put up with his presence twice a year, but he also calls her daily.

She gets worried when she doesn't receive a call from him or Maksim.

Another asshole who's at the top of my shit list. How dare he have a crush on her when she was dressing as a man?

And no, the fact that he's gay is irrelevant. He still looked at what's mine, and I'm not a fan.

Thankfully, Anton isn't a fan either, and we share the same level of pettiness.

It's the one thing that's allowed us to get close over time.

That, and the fact that our respective partners are still best friends, despite our best efforts.

I share a look with him from across the room, and we shake our heads at the scene in front of us. Sasha and Maksim helping Mike assemble some new toy she got him for Christmas.

My brother and his wife are reading the instructions, a bit too focused on the mundane task.

Karina, however, is chasing her nephew and niece as they squeal and break into a fit of giggles.

My son, Vaughn, is obviously the smartest one, because he leads his aunt in circles and then breaks her rhythm. Lidya, however, is just a little ray of sunshine and stupidity, because she gets caught easily.

Although she does have her moments of toddler intelligence, because whenever she gets frustrated, she hides behind Vaughn for protection and even makes faces at Kara.

My son and my niece look nothing alike. While he has dark hair and his mother's chameleon eyes, she's a platinum blonde with her mother's features. The only thing she got from Kosta is her eyes.

Lidya was born exactly two weeks after Vaughn, but unlike him, she likes to behave like a child.

Sasha always reminds me that they *are* children and that I

can't roll my eyes just because they act like an irrational drama king and queen.

The two people who are in love with these children the most are Anna, who's the ambassador of their healthy diets and habits, and Karina. She's spoiling them rotten as expected, but what wasn't expected is how much they've helped her regain control of her life.

She's no longer scared of the outside world, and the blasphemous little shit even asked me to give her Viktor now.

No kidding. My sister actually stood there and said, with a straight face, I might add, "Hey, Kirya. I want Viktor, so give him to me."

For the past couple of years, she's been openly flirting with him while he's been trying to pretend she doesn't exist.

I did tell him that he'll lose his dick the moment he touches her, to which Sasha laughed and said that wouldn't be happening.

She's encouraging bad habits that I won't be standing for. Of course, no one will know that I'd rather Karina be with him instead of an outsider. He's the only one I can call a friend. He's never doubted me, never shied away from calling me on my shit, and he's responsible. Sometimes, too much so.

The problem in this equation is really Viktor. He thinks Karina is too spoiled and high maintenance, not to mention the fact that she's *my* sister, so he refuses to touch her, even with a ten-foot pole.

Now, he's helping Anna with opening presents and not giving Karina one sliver of his attention. Which is wise, considering I'm around.

Vaughn gets bored with his aunt's antics and runs in my direction. I crouch to catch him, and he wraps his tiny arms around my neck.

"Papa!"

"Hi, little one. Who won?"

"Me!" He points a thumb at himself and sighs. "Kara too slow."

"I'm not slow, you little demon!" She tries to catch Lidya, who squeals and runs to her mother.

"She is slow," I whisper to him, and he grins.

"I heard that!" Kara glares but continues on her mission with her niece.

"Mama, Mama." He opens and closes his palms in her direction.

"Seems your mama doesn't have time for us today," I grumble loud enough for her to hear.

She lifts her head, and I'm trapped by how beautiful she looks. Her long blonde hair falls freely down her back, and she's sexy as fuck, even while wearing hideous Christmas pajamas. Everyone but Anton, Viktor, and me are wearing those ugly things.

Kosta is included in the happy go lucky crowd. He was so easy to convince when his wife got him a matching set.

Sasha gives Anton the piece of the game she was holding and walks toward us.

"Did you need me?" she asks in a soft voice.

I adjust my glasses. "No, we're mad at you."

"Mad at you," my son repeats like a good sidekick and even crosses his arms.

"You say he's a drama king, but I wonder who taught him?" She nudges me with her shoulder. "I'm certainly not petty and I don't keep glaring at everyone so they'll leave."

"I'm ready for this whole week to be over so I can have you to myself."

"You always do. Isn't that right, baby?" She tickles Vaughn, and he giggles, completely forgetting about the battle.

I take it back. He's not that good of a sidekick.

She places her hand on my chest and adjusts the collar of

my shirt. "Instead of being a grinch for sport, how about you help us out?"

"I'm going to have to pass."

"If you do this, I might have a special present for you later."

I raise a brow. "What type of present?"

She does the motion of zipping her mouth, locking it, and throwing away the key. "I promise you'll love it, though."

"Love it, huh?"

"Uh-huh."

"You know I can't say no to that."

"Yes!" She smiles and then kisses me on the lips before taking Vaughn from my arms.

He holds on to her with all his might and grins up at me like a little angel.

I lived my whole life not believing in family. I never imagined I'd have one of my own, but these two people have made me proud to be both a father and a husband.

For a long time, I was looking for a purpose, and I thought it was the grandiose things, the prestigious position, and the endless money.

Turns out, it was as simple as having a woman who challenges me every step of the way but loves me unconditionally anyway. And a son who looks at me as if I'm his role model.

I grab her by the waist and kiss her forehead. "Thank you."

She looks up at me with a beautiful smile. "For what?"

"For being my family, Solnyshko."

"I should be the one to thank you for that." She faces me. "Thank you for giving me this happiness that I thought I'd lost for good, Luchik."

I lift her chin and kiss her as our son claps like the best cheerleader.

We met as broken beings, but now we're putting each other together again.

One piece at a time.

We were separate entities, but now, we're one.
I'm hers.
She's fucking *mine*.
Until death do us part.

THE END

You can check out the books of the characters that appeared in this book:

Adrian Volkov: *Deception Trilogy*.
Rai Sokolov: *Throne Duet*.

WHAT'S NEXT?

Thank you so much for reading Heart of My Monster! If you liked it, please leave a review.
Your support means the world to me.

If you're thirsty for more discussions with other readers of the series, you can join the Facebook group, Rina Kent's Spoilers Room.

Next up is the complete Standalone in Legacy of Gods series, *God of Ruin*.

ALSO BY RINA KENT

For more books by the author and a reading order, please visit:
www.rinakent.com/books

ABOUT THE AUTHOR

Rina Kent is a *USA Today*, international, and #1 Amazon bestselling author of everything enemies to lovers romance.

She's known to write unapologetic anti-heroes and villains because she often fell in love with men no one roots for. Her books are sprinkled with a touch of darkness, a pinch of angst, and an unhealthy dose of intensity.

She spends her private days in London laughing like an evil mastermind about adding mayhem to her expanding universe. When she's not writing, Rina travels, hikes, and spoils cats in a pure Cat Lady fashion.

Find Rina Below:

Website: www.rinakent.com

Newsletter: www.subscribepage.com/rinakent

BookBub: www.bookbub.com/profile/rina-kent

Amazon: www.amazon.com/Rina-Kent/e/B07MM54G22

Goodreads: www.goodreads.com/author/show/18697906.Rina_Kent

Instagram: www.instagram.com/author_rina

Facebook: www.facebook.com/rinaakent

Reader Group: www.facebook.com/groups/rinakent.club

Pinterest: www.pinterest.co.uk/AuthorRina/boards

Tiktok: www.tiktok.com/@rina.kent

Twitter: twitter.com/AuthorRina